THE TRELAYNE INHERITANCE

"Fans of vampire romances and gothic tales will delight in Colleen Shannon's *The Trelayne Inheritance*...a twist or two on the classic gothic/vampire romance [adds up to] a delicious treat."

—*The Midwest Book Review*

THE WOLF OF HASKELL HALL

"A provocative tale...emotionally intense [and] will prey upon your senses and shatter your illusions."

—*Romantic Times* (Top Pick)

"A classic gothic romance...fast-paced and exciting."
—*The Midwest Book Review*

HEAVEN'S ROGUE

"*Heaven's Rogue* is a magical tale of epic proportions. Author Colleen Shannon has a special way of bringing together a wonderful blend of supernatural elements that makes this story a 'finely chiseled' tale readers will love."

—*New-Age Bookshelf*

IN THE THROES...

In her dream, as the light was extinguished, Arielle froze, her heartbeat making her thin night rail flutter on her full bosom. She was half eager, half afraid, for she knew the other came, bringing darkness with him. He was not so kind, but fascinating, withal.

Sharp claws raked through her night rail into her flesh, not enough to wound, just enough to hold her and drag her back into the darkness. At first she struggled and tried to escape, but as a teasing claw trailed over her, goose bumps appeared on her skin. The pain was pleasure, the scratch a mark of honor.

For this she was born.

To be strong, and immortal, and one with the lion god, warrior king and protector of the realm. Arielle reached out to him in the utter darkness, wondering if he were the one after all, rather than the being of bright bold beauty.

As she debated, feeling torn between the anguished growl coming from a distance and the pleased purr of the being holding her, her hands were teasingly caught by great extended claws, still half sheathed.

See, he didn't hurt her. Not even when he lifted her hands to her mouth. "Taste," rasped a deep, magnetic voice as he forced her to lick her own wounds.

She tasted, wondering how her own blood could be so sweet.

"Drink. Taste the essence that belongs to me, blood of my blood."

Catspell

COLLEEN SHANNON

LOVE SPELL NEW YORK CITY

LOVE SPELL®

January 2006

Published by

Dorchester Publishing Co., Inc.
200 Madison Avenue
New York, NY 10016

ISBN 0-505-52611-5

Printed in the United States of America.

Visit us on the web at www.dorchesterpub.com.

Flowers in the Garden

...Thou makest the heart equable.
I do unto thee that which it desireth,
when I am in thine arms.

· · · · · · · · · · · · · · · · · · ·

How pleasant is mine hour! Might an hour only
become for me eternity, when I sleep with thee.
Though didst lift up mine heart when it was night.

· ·

The beautiful place where I walk about,
when thine hand resteth on mine,
and mine heart is satisfied with joy,
because we walk together.

—From the Papyrus in Turin.
First brought to notice by Maspero in 1886.
Ancient Egyptian Poetry and Prose, *Adolf Erman.*
Translated by Aylward M. Blackman, Dover Press, 1995
(Original German version)

Chapter One

"Arielle," purred the rasping, sensual voice. "Come to me . . ."

Like one possessed, Arielle Blaylock tossed and turned in her massive four-poster bed carved with lion's feet. In Arielle's vision, she wasn't trapped; she was fleet-footed, her twisted leg strong and nimble. She had perfect night vision, the stygian darkness like day to her luminous gaze. Here brambles might slither after her, snakelike, to trap her, but nothing frightened her. She was invincible . . .

. . . and truly happy only in this strange netherworld, caught between two mystical beings, both ever out of reach. Both tempted her to a strength of limb and will beyond her in the real world people always told her to face. Why should she? She detested cold reality as much as she despised her weak earthly form.

Only in dreams could she be free.

1

Only in dreams could she find *him,* the one the gods decreed would be her consort. But which of them was destined to be her lover? The one of the night? Or the one of the light?

There, at the end of a tunnel, bathed in a luminescent glow, she saw the one of brightness. He was always turned away, his broad back naked, his loins covered in an Egyptian-style sarong. He wore a headdress carved like a flowing lion's mane, his burnished skin golden, as if inside and outside he were richly endowed with the royal metal of the Egyptian pharaohs and the warrior gods they worshiped.

"Look at me," she pleaded in her vision. "Let me see your face."

As he began to turn, she sensed the power in him, yet the gentleness, too. She reached out her arms, longing for that first glimpse of his face, but now the light was so bright she couldn't distinguish his features in the glare. She felt his utter stillness, however, and his repressed wild need. As if it were not her he distrusted, but himself. Arielle ran faster to bridge the gap, but now her feet seemed to move in molasses, stuck in place.

Why could she never reach him? Or distinguish his face?

Standing over the bed, watching Arielle's bad leg moving as easily as the good one were two people. The man had a bearing that came naturally only to the titled and the wealthy, yet he wore every father's grimace of despair for his only child. He tried to soothe Arielle's brow with a damp cloth, encouraging her to return to him with a hummed lullaby, as if hoping some part of her tormented mind would follow the childhood beacon back to him.

Instead she tore the cloth away, arms outstretched, but not to either her father or the woman he'd brought to cure her. Arielle's deep blue eyes were open now, yet glowing amber in the half-light, unseeing and unaware of anything but her inner journey.

Beside the Earl of Darby stood world-famous investigator of psychic phenomena Shelly Holmes, detective nonpareil. In contrast to the earl's overwrought emotional state, she appraised the situation dispassionately. She made no conclusions and formed no judgment, moral or otherwise.

Shelly Holmes merely observed, seeing things other people missed.

Her keen gray eyes moved from the girl to the windows barred from the outside and covered with wooden panels bolted shut on the inside. Even the gas fireplace had been blocked with a giant metal screen it would take Atlas himself to move. This luxurious room was more secure than any of the fortress keeps Shelly had seen, but by all accounts the precautions were futile. Even as she watched, tiny scratch marks began to appear on Arielle's shapely arms one by one, as if drawn by a talon both playful and cruel.

A talon of neither form nor substance, yet leaving a very tangible mark.

Could it be the same talon that had slashed throats and ripped open the chests of three women in various parts of London? The motive, so far, was mysterious even to Scotland Yard's renowned detectives. There seemed to be no link whatever between the victims: a baker's daughter, a countess, and a preacher's wife.

And now a frail, virginal girl bore the same marks, though this assault seemed to be just beginning.

The earl grasped his daughter's shoulders, shaking her slightly in an effort to bring her back to him, but he withdrew his hands with a gasp of horror. Deeper scratches had appeared under his hands while he held her, dotted now with spots of blood.

He stared at his own reddened palms and then whirled on Shelly. "What sorcery is this? Do something, woman! I'm paying you a fortune to bring her back to me whole."

Shelly gave him a cool glance. "I'd remind you, my dear sir, that I agreed to review your case. I have not yet agreed to the stipend."

She looked back at the girl, knowing, despite her disclaimer, that she'd already decided to take the case. Arielle's strange behavior was the most persuasive evidence Shelly had ever beheld of astral projection, the ancient art of wizards and gods that allowed the spirit to travel where it willed even while the body remained imprisoned. A skill Merlin himself was rumored to possess, though by all accounts, the practice began long before Merlin—on the desert plains of ancient Egypt.

Even as Shelly watched more scratches appear on Arielle's delicate shoulder, she felt a twinge of envy amid her concern. She had supernatural powers aplenty of her own, but astral projection . . . what a skill to have. Even if it manifested itself as a curse. Shelly knew something of the blessings curses could sometimes offer, and she suspected, even without yet exchanging a word with Arielle, that the girl's experience was similar.

Despite her wounds, Arielle seemed more enraptured than tortured.

Shelly tested Arielle's temperature with the back of her hand. She'd expected the skin to be burning hot. Instead Arielle was cool, as if the torment that marked her body and racked her mind did not overstress her fragile constitution. It almost seemed as though this horrific seizure that suspended her spirit between the real and twilight worlds were somehow normal.

As if it were her destiny and her birthright.

Balderdash, Shelly groused to herself.

Shelly had never believed in the concept of destiny, for if one were merely a puppet on a string dancing at the behest of some larger force, then the mores guiding Shelly's life were pointless. From the time she'd reached her precocious teens, Shelly had pursued two goals: betterment of self and betterment of society. These worthy ends were attained not by the maudlin sentimentality of do-gooders, or even by the guilt of the repentant. No, the unerring pursuit of truth and justice, and the fair society they promised, could be accomplished only by that great leveling power that bridged the gap between kings and peasants: logic.

Its application had shaped not only Shelly Holmes, but those she touched and saved by her use of it.

Never, so it seemed, had she needed that impartiality more than now. She, too, was moved by the increasing mutilation she seemed powerless to stop. Seizing for inspiration, Shelly looked around. There must be something in the surroundings that fed the girl's ailment.

One thing was immediately apparent: Arielle seemed obsessed with cats.

Figurines of every type of feline imaginable lined the shelves on the wall. A cat drawing done by a juvenile hand was framed and displayed opposite the bed. And even the pillow on the plush Turkish divan next to the fireplace was a needlepoint of a lioness with her head trustingly resting on the neck of an enormous male lion with a flowing black mane. The bed also bore a family crest in the headboard: a lioness rampant with a dove perched on her outstretched claw.

"The crest . . . is that your own?" Shelly queried of the earl.

"What? Oh, the bed. No, it's one her mother's grandfather had made up. It's not in the Domesday Book, I can tell you that. Miss Holmes . . ."

When the earl's shoulders began to shake as the dotted scratches deepened, and his voice broke, Shelly took pity on him. "I accept. Now answer my questions quickly. First, who named the child?"

He gave her a strange look. "What possible bearing . . . Oh, very well, don't scowl at me. Her mother. It was a family name she was fond of."

6

"Do you have her picture?"

He went to the mantel above the fireplace and brought back the daguerreotype of a lovely woman who had Arielle's luminescent beauty and black hair. She wore the same strange amulet now around the girl's neck. Shelly looked between the picture and Arielle's necklace to be sure, but the amulet looked the same, though its golden luster had faded a bit over the years. Shelly knew that the central embossed image of Bast, the cat goddess, was of Egyptian origin. It was obviously a precious family heirloom, also obviously passed down from mother to daughter. And since Arielle meant "lioness of God" and the child had a fixation on cats, it seemed likely that Arielle's ailment had been handed down from her own mother.

Shelly handed the picture back. "How did the countess die?"

He turned the picture face-forward into the wall and said through his teeth, "Suicide."

"Was she of English birth?"

"Her mother was Egyptian. Her father was English."

"Her given name?"

"Isis." His voice had grown increasingly curt, as if he wondered how such stupid parlor-room politesse could save his daughter from being marked for life. He hurried back to Arielle's bedside, watching a deeper scratch form, this time on the back of her hand, before running his hands though his thick hair as if he actually wanted to tear it out rather than stand here helpless.

Arielle was unaware of his anguish or Shelly's keen observation. In her dream, as the light was extinguished, she froze, her heartbeat making her thin night rail flutter on her full bosom. She was half-eager, half-afraid, for she knew the other came, bringing darkness with him. He was not so kind, but fascinating withal.

Sharp claws raked through her night rail into her flesh, not enough to wound, just enough to hold her and drag her back into the darkness. At first she struggled and tried to escape, but as a teasing claw trailed over her, goose bumps appeared on her skin. The pain was pleasure, the scratch a mark of honor.

For this she was born.

To be strong, and immortal, and one with the lion god, warrior king and protector of the realm. Arielle reached out to him in the utter darkness, wondering if he were the one after all, rather than the being of bright bold beauty.

Perhaps in this world, too, as was her fate in the earthly vale, she was meant to remain in shadows. As she debated, feeling torn between the anguished growl coming from a distance and the pleased purr of the being holding her, her hands were teasingly caught by great extended claws, still half-sheathed.

See, he didn't hurt her. Not even when he lifted her hands to her mouth. "Taste," rasped a deep, magnetic voice as he forced her to lick her own wounds.

She tasted, wondering how her own blood could be so sweet.

"Drink. Taste the essence that belongs to me, blood of my blood."

Arielle felt the heat of him, the indomitable strength of him. The sharp scent of his arousal twisted her face into a grimace of response. Her memory of the other, even his anguished growl growing ever farther away, faded as she lapped her own blood.

As she watched the girl, a dozen more questions formed on Shelly's tongue. When she saw Arielle's face twist into a mask of sensuality, Shelly shivered. Then Arielle, her eyes still glazed and unseeing, lifted her own hand and licked the blood away with a daintily curled tongue, like a cat. Her nipples hardened under the thin night rail.

And she purred.

The earl turned a ghastly puce and backed away a step, but Shelly followed her instincts and did the only logical thing—she jerked the amulet off the girl's neck, strode to the door, flung it wide, and tossed the amulet over the stair railing. Then she slammed the door shut again.

Immediately Arielle went very still. Her feet stopped moving. One more barely visible scratch appeared as they watched, this one on her flawless bosom, but then it stopped. That faint sense of menace in the room receded, and the gas lamps sputtered and flared more brightly.

They both waited, breath held, but they shared a sigh of mutual relief as slowly Arielle returned to herself, her eyes blinking back to awareness. Shelly noted that the eerie amber glow was also gone, leaving her eyes wounded pools of bottomless blue despair.

Bewildered, Arielle looked between her father and the tall, rather ugly woman with the strong jaw and unrelenting gray eyes. "Papa, what is wrong . . . ?" She gasped as she saw the marks on her arms and hands. "Oh, no, not again!"

The earl took his daughter into his arms. Above her head his eyes met Shelly's. "Thank you," he said softly. "I'll have it destroyed immediately."

But to his apparent confusion, Shelly shook her head emphatically. "I must have it to investigate, but I'll keep it under lock and key. Now if you'll excuse me, I'm weary from my journey." Nodding at father and daughter, Shelly quit the room.

"Who is that woman?" she heard Arielle ask as she closed the door.

Downstairs, she picked up the amulet and turned it from side to side. There were hieroglyphs on the back, but of the five languages she spoke fluently, none included ancient Egyptian. She'd have to have help. She was also not terribly pleased with the earl, for she suspected there was much he wasn't telling her.

Including the fact that he must have seen similar behavior before—from his own wife, before she killed herself. There had been . . . recognition in his horrified gaze as he backed away from Arielle's bed when she licked her own blood.

When the butler approached to show her to her room, Shelly pocketed the amulet and carried her own baggage despite his horrified protests.

* * *

The next morning, after breakfast, Shelly had a private meeting with the earl in his study to discuss Arielle's affliction. At first the earl was resistant to the idea that his daughter had some mystical ailment that made her exhibit catlike tendencies, but when Shelly stated, "She has the strongest case of astral projection I've ever witnessed," the earl sagged back in his chair and bowed his head.

"How would you propose to combat it and bring her back to me?"

"How often does she socialize with others her age?"

"Almost never. I believe she attended a friend's tea party some . . ." He calculated mentally and then added with horror, "By Jove, it's near two years ago now."

"The best way to make her cling to her humanity is by exercising it. Are there any balls or teas she can attend where some of her friends might be present?"

"I fear since these incidents began occurring, she's let all her friendships lapse."

"Well." Shelly rose decisively. "She's not changing that by sitting alone in her room, prey to nightmares. I'd strongly suggest that you speak with her and wheedle her into socializing, preferably some type of outing in which she can enjoy herself and be around others her age."

The earl nodded his agreement.

So it was that a few nights later, Arielle descended from their best carriage on her father's arm.

Wheedling was not a word she would have used to describe Rupert Blaylock's tactics in getting her here, standing before one of the grandest mansions in London on one of the grandest streets, dressed in the new gown he'd insisted on purchasing for her. He'd said she'd want to look her best at this, her first ball since her own coming-out some years back.

She swallowed as she looked up at the brightly lit facade and saw the posh guests entering the colonnaded exterior in a constant stream. "Father, I feel ill," she whispered, trying to turn back to the carriage, but it had already been driven to the back by the efficient lackeys in uniform who were organizing traffic.

"Nonsense. You're just nervous. Come, Arielle. This will be fun if you let it be, or torture if you agonize over every step."

"But how can I dance with my limp?"

"No one will notice it but you. Now quit complaining and have fun."

She had to smile at his scowl. "You're ordering me to have fun?"

He laughed and squeezed her arm affectionately. "Only if you don't cooperate."

The beautiful ballroom was packed with beautiful people, but even when a few smiled and nodded, she was too tongue-tied to do more than nod uncomfortably. The slight unevenness in her gait felt like a mortal sin to her, akin to a scarlet A painted on her chest, so different did she feel from these other simpering misses.

For the first hour she did try—truly she did—to

enjoy herself and mingle as she partook of the watery punch and tiny sandwiches, but she felt so small and insignificant beneath the grand ballroom ceiling. It was gilded and mirrored, and gaslights blazed everywhere. Most of the other young people seemed equally awestruck and as tongue-tied, so she finally gave up idle conversation.

When the orchestra struck up a country dance, she walked with as much dignity as she could, limp notwithstanding, to the sidelines, where she vowed she'd take up residence until her father returned from the cigar room. Then she'd insist they leave.

She'd let him coerce her into forsaking her comfortable solitude, but not only was she not enjoying herself, she was getting irritated that he'd subjected her to this farce "for her own good." What was the good in feeling worse even than a wallflower? In this company she was more a weed buried in prickly thorns! She'd never had the proper temperament for the marriage mart. Indeed, against her father's wishes she'd insisted on wearing blue this evening, when virginal white was the norm, and every word out of her mouth seemed as awkward as her gait.

She could only twist her kerchief between her gloved fingers and scowl at the parquet floor, wondering what was taking her father so long. He was deliberately lingering, hoping she'd mingle and make new friends. *Right-o.*

Shiny, large evening slippers appeared in her field of vision. She followed them up long, lithe legs to a superfine cutaway coat and white vest. Higher still to a chiseled jaw and . . . Her heart flip-flopped. His features were disguised by the bright lights behind his head, his countenance illuminated by a nimbus of light that added to, rather than detracted from, the glory of his spun-gold hair.

Just like in her dream, here was a man she could see in gorgeous detail but for his face. Except in this case he was properly clothed, though it was so easy to picture his perfect form in nothing but a sarong, fit for a god on an Egyptian relief.

The dream-come-true spoke.

"Why are you scowling? Should I fear for my life or offer to save yours?" His voice was equally pleasant, mellifluous, with an intriguing undercurrent of an accent she could not place.

She blushed and would have risen to her feet if she hadn't been certain he'd still tower above her. From a place she didn't know she had came a pert retort: "Most gentlemen on first acquaintance introduce themselves before they take it upon themselves to be guardian of my person."

"Pity, that. It's such an enticing person. But if you insist." He bowed deeply. "Luke Simball, your most abject servant." He leaned close so only she could hear. "But only until I can work my way up to white knight. How am I doing so far?"

Based on the goggling stares of the other wallflowers around her, he was doing quite well indeed. Since some of these girls had blatantly snubbed her at her own coming-out ball, she would not have been human if she hadn't enjoyed the brief glow of feeling so desirable. But when his gaze fell upon the dance card dangling from her wrist, she put her hand behind her so he couldn't see that she had not a single entry.

"Arielle Blaylock," he read from the top of the card before she whisked it away. "Arielle. Lioness of God. Charming name. May I have this dance, Miss Blaylock?"

She hesitated. "I do not dance. Normally." She rose and unconsciously rubbed her wounded leg.

"Then it's a good thing neither of us is normal this evening. It is far too fine a night for such restrictions, anyway." He offered a regal hand to her.

She could finally see his face, and this time, when her heart flip-flopped, it did so not from recollection of a dream but from tangible reality. His eyes were the exact sun-dappled green of her favorite isolated pond on her father's estate, and his skin was burnished almost golden. On second glance he resembled a gilded god even more than on the first. In short, he was gorgeous. And he was flirting with *her*.

Accepting his invitation, she put her hand in his and let him lead her to the middle of the floor. They were in position between staring couples before she realized the graceful music now beginning was a waltz. She froze, one hand on his broad shoulder, the other in his warm clasp.

The golden face smiled down at her, reckless, daring, and so handsome she knew most of the stares were directed at him. "Afraid?"

She lifted her chin. "Merely wondering how well you lead."

His gaze dropped suggestively to her well-covered but rather agitated bosom. His smile deepened as he said, "Shall we find out?"

His appreciative laugh purred above her flushed cheeks, and then he swept her away into the dance. At first she was self-conscious about her leg, but he was quickly attuned to her rhythm and disguised the slight halt of her limp in the way he dipped her slightly backward when their movements put weight on her damaged leg. Indeed, the next time she glanced at the couples around them, she realized they now stared at each of them equally.

She even heard a muttered, "What a handsome couple they make. Night and day. Bright and dark."

Emboldened, she forgot about her infirmity, forgot even that she detested socializing. For the first time since her accident, she knew only the joy of losing all her troubles to gaiety and the warm touch of a handsome man.

Some ten minutes later, her father found his sullen, unsocial daughter dancing so well with a golden-haired stranger that most of the other couples had slowed to watch them. He stood stunned, a cup of punch halfway to his mouth, as Arielle was not only dancing; she was dancing a *waltz* with a total stranger. The gentleman held her far too close for a father's comfort.

He was about to weave forward through the dancers when a vaguely familiar voice said at his elbow, "Would you like me to cut in?"

The Earl of Darby had to look up at the man, and that alone was a rare experience for him, as he was rather tall himself. But this vaguely familiar

16

young man in a somber black suit was much taller, lean and lithe. When he moved, his feet made no sound on the hard parquet floor. The earl looked down, thinking the music merely covered the sound of his hard-soled shoes, but no, when the young man moved to face him fully during a lull, the earl still heard no scrape of heel.

Somewhat disconcerted, and wondering why he looked familiar, the earl answered, "Do you know my daughter, sir?"

"No. Not personally. But I have heard you speak of her." He inclined his shining black head, his strange golden-brown eyes as somber as his dress. "We attend the same club."

"Ah, yes!" They moved in totally different circles, but at least that explained why the chap was so familiar. Name started with an S . . . something biblical.

"Seth Taub at your service." Seth bowed slightly. "I shall be more than happy to intercede and lead your daughter in a much more proper dance."

"Would you? I wanted her to have fun. But not quite that much fun." The earl turned to glare back at the floor, where the blond man was whirling his daughter around so fast that her hair was coming loose from its pins.

He watched Seth wend his way through the dancers, apparently startling them also with his soundless stride, for in several cases he had to dodge aside to miss a collision. As the waltz ended with a gay crescendo, he was standing beside the couple who made, even the earl had to admit, a pleasing duo. His daughter was small and dark, and the man who held her was tall and golden. It almost seemed as if—and the earl was not fanciful—they completed each other, night and day, bright and dark, each needing the other to rule the sway of time. . . .

The earl cleared his throat, wondering if he was dizzy from cigar smoke. He was sounding like his deceased wife, poor insane woman that she'd been. And no matter what it took, how much money it cost paying Miss Holmes or others like her—well, other investigators, for there was no one like her—he'd see his daughter safe.

The golden-haired man had relinquished his intimate hold on Arielle, but he looked straight into Seth's eyes and said something obviously cutting.

Seth retorted. The set-down must have been excellent, judging from the shocked expressions of the couples within earshot. The golden-haired man took a slight, aggressive step toward Seth, stopping only when Arielle clasped his arm and murmured something. He looked down at her, his body stiff with anger, but finally he nodded shortly and stalked through the dancers, who made way for him.

When another tune began, this one a lively country dance, Arielle started to move away, but Seth blocked her, bowing deeply. She glanced around at the staring dancers. Short of giving him the cut direct, she had no other option but to accept his invitation. Reluctantly, politely, she took his hand and began to dance.

Satisfied, the earl turned away, only to face an angry, golden-haired young man. "Did you set him upon me like your watchdog?"

The earl stiffened. "If I'd done that, you'd be bleeding." What kind of arrogant young pup was this, and why was he so fixated on Arielle?

"If you let Arielle around Seth Taub, it will be she who's bleeding, if only from within. He's an emotional leech." And the golden-haired young man swung around on his heel and stalked out.

Peculiarly, the earl noted that his expensive evening slippers also made no sound, despite his high, agitated steps.

Good riddance. He turned back to watch Arielle and her partner, relieved to see that only the tips of their fingertips touched as they ducked beneath the tented arms of other dancers. Arielle's limp was becoming pronounced. She was getting tired.

Just as he'd decided to break up their dance, Seth Taub apparently reached the same conclusion. When the dance brought them together again, he gently took Arielle's hand, nodded his excuses to the dancers next to them, and led her off the floor.

The earl began to like this dark, somber-browed young man. He had a care for the female kind, who always needed the protection of those stronger than themselves. It was as it should be.

Arielle, however, apparently felt differently. When she rejoined her father, her deep blue eyes were almost black, so wide were her pupils. She glared up at Seth. "How prim and proper you *seem.* But if my be-

havior needs modifying, it will not be at your hand.
As Luke said, you are not to be trusted, Mr. Taub."

"Luke, is it? And he is a man you just met, who
was taking liberties with your person? I intervened
only at your father's request to stop wagging
tongues."

The earl looked at him askance. That was not
quite accurate, but he let the fact that Seth had offered his help slide. Arielle was already angry
enough.

"They can wag until they fall off, for all I care.
These people don't give a fiddle-faddle for me."
She looked around for her reticule and grabbed it
when Seth held it out.

How Seth knew which one, on a table piled high
with them, was Arielle's, the earl couldn't say. But
it was certain Seth had not only been watching
Arielle tonight but was also obviously interested in
her. And just as obviously, he knew this Luke and
was in competition with him.

The earl rubbed his aching brow and muttered,
"I'm calling for the carriage." And he hurried out
of the ballroom, thinking that next time he'd be
more careful what he wished for. His sweet, innocent, biddable Arielle certainly seemed different
out among a crowd. Perhaps it was best to keep her
at home, after all. Or did both of these young men
bring out the worst in her?

The moment he was gone, Arielle turned a cold
shoulder to the man who had ruined the only good
time she'd ever had at one of these tiresome affairs.

"Forgive me," Seth Taub said softly. "I only

feared for your reputation. Luke Simball is a rake-hell. He will ply you first with charm in a public venue, then with drink in a private one. Next . . ."

His pause was pregnant with a meaning that, innocent though she was, she understood well enough. She whirled back on him. "And what do I know of you?"

"Nothing. But I shall fix that soon enough."

"Perhaps I want to be . . . plied. Perhaps I'm tired of being good." Where the words came from, she did not know; she knew only that this man, as tall as Luke, but dark in every way where Luke seemed bright, irritated her beyond belief. Enough to make her bold in return, whereas she felt shy with Luke.

"Indeed? We shall discuss this topic at more length another time."

The response was proper. The expression was not. His amber eyes took on dancing glints of gold, making her wonder what they looked like in sunshine. With the hint of that smile on his face turning wicked, she realized abruptly that, in a very different way, he was as handsome as Luke. Those golden eyes trailed down over her figure with a lazy promise that made her wonder what he'd look like in an Egyptian-style sarong.

He offered his arm in a very proper way, his propriety spoiled by that glint in his eye. But he merely said, "Please allow me to escort you to your carriage."

Still miffed and off balance at her unwelcome attraction to this . . . this interloper, she debated turning away. However, her leg was aching from the unaccustomed activity, and at least with his support she could retreat gracefully.

She accepted his arm. They walked slowly to the front steps, Seth guiding her ably through the crush of departing guests. She gave him a curt nod of good-bye as they reached her carriage, where her father awaited.

After the earl helped her up into the seat, he turned back to Seth and spoke softly, so she could not hear. "Thank you, Seth. I shall see you soon at the club."

"I shall be honored, sir." Seth gave his polite, old-fashioned bow and then disappeared down the steps, blending into the night with his silent walk and dark dress and hair.

The earl noted that Arielle, despite her anger, stared after him curiously.

He tried to decide how he felt about that, but instead he collapsed back against the seat, gasping. "The next time you wish to go dancing, warn me in advance. I shall have to shore up my constitution."

Arielle did not answer, still staring into the darkness after Seth Taub.

Chapter Two

Two weeks later, a preternatural calm had descended upon Hafford Place. The ancient pile of moldering stone on London's outskirts had been built, Shelly was told, by the first earl, who was given his title by a grateful Queen Elizabeth in reward for his daring captaincy of one of the frigates that helped defeat the Spanish armada.

The structure he'd built followed the Tudor style with mullioned windows, dark cross timbers, and white stucco. But the turrets crowning both towers and the battlements bridging them with a walk bearing cutouts for archers betold an earl who didn't wear his new title comfortably. He was a fighting man, and so he remained to his dying day, when he was buried beneath the house in the crypt in which Shelly now stood.

She walked around his final resting place, glad for the sunlight shining through the high windows on each side of the crypt. She sought a smaller, less significant catafalque than that of the liege lord.

During these past two weeks in which Arielle seemed safe—troubled, but safe and free of nightmares—Shelly had spent her time trying to decipher the glyphs on the back of the amulet. She'd researched dusty tomes in the library. She'd even made a trip to the Royal Society asking for help, but the markings were not the royal Egyptian still being deciphered from the Rosetta stone. Nor were they Coptic, and certainly not Greek. They must be a more ancient version of text.

Today, after a luncheon during which the bewildered earl watched his daughter as if he expected her to sprout whiskers and lap at her Dover sole, Shelly had decided to follow a hunch down to the crypt. Perhaps the mother's final resting place bore some trace, some clue that would be the key to the amulet's deciphering.

Sure enough, Isis Blaylock's catafalque was smaller, less ornate than the others, obviously carved in haste. The poor woman had died in her early thirties, when Arielle was a child. Perhaps the distance of the years accounted for why the earl seemed somewhat indifferent to her memory. Shelly had seen no portraits of her, no cherished mementoes she'd left, either stitched with her own hand or painted with her own brush. Only Arielle, with that photo in her chamber, seemed to miss the mother she scarcely remembered. Even the servants refused to utter her name.

Shelly peered at the soapstone casket. Not granite, not marble. The very medium of her interment in this easy-to-carve stone hinted at her husband's lack of regard. Shelly shone the lantern in her hand onto the side of the tomb, trying to read the tiny markings carved there.

Words, but strange words. Familiar, but not quite . . .

"The Book of the Dead. Do you know it?"

Shelly almost dropped the lantern onto the shining leather shoes that had appeared at her side. She surged to her feet, glaring at the man who made her look up to him in a way she didn't like. She was taller than most men, but this towering beanpole resembled an escapee from a very bad nursery rhyme.

He was all arms and legs, but elegantly appointed arms and legs, and the fine figure he presented almost disguised his ungainliness. His waistcoat was severe black to match his black cutaway coat. His cravat was purest white, and he bore a diamond stickpin that matched the diamond-studded head of his walking stick. He had a prominent Adam's apple, and a deep dimple in his chin that somehow drew attention to the perpetually merry set of his mouth. Quite against her will, Shelly's gaze paused there. His mouth was wide, the top lip rather thin, but the lower lip bore an indentation that gave him a pout bespeaking either a truculent or a passionate nature; she wasn't sure which.

She straightened to her full, imposing height, not happy she still had to look up at him. "Who, may I ask, are you? And who gave you permission to invade the Blaylock crypt?"

His strange, slanted green eyes had begun to sparkle with interest. "I might ask the same of you."

"You might." Their eyes met.

Challenge made, measure taken. On both sides.

"Miss Holmes, I presume. Your reputation precedes you."

"You have the advantage of me, sir." She could have kicked herself for the trite response when she saw the rakish way he eyed her, end to end, as if he did indeed want to take advantage of her.

But he only replied mildly, "Oh, I am quite well-known too, in some scientific circles, and in my own modest fashion."

Shelly made a rude noise. She'd just laid eyes on the fellow, but she already knew he had very little modesty.

"No, truly." He clasped his hands to his bosom and raised his gaze toward the heavens. "May the dear Redeemer strike me dead on the spot if I lie."

They both waited a second, Shelly half hoping for a lightning bolt, whether she believed in its source or not. Meanwhile, the stranger was the picture of piety, but she knew it for a lie. She sensed in him a prodigious intelligence, a cool curiosity about the world around him, both seen and unseen, and a healthy skepticism very like her own. However, he differed from her in a marked way: He was a man who knew that a smile could open more closed minds than a scowl. That was a lesson she herself was still trying to learn, but she had no taste for him as tutor.

She turned away, ignoring his large, well-shaped

hands, which indicated both breeding and good grooming. "I make no doubt you are well-known in one place."

When he lifted an eyebrow, she finished, "The stage. But go find the Divine Sarah to practice your blandishments upon and leave me to my investigation." She turned a cold shoulder to him and knelt back to study the markings. To her irritation, the set-down that had overset richer, more powerful men than he didn't seem to affect him in the slightest.

The only indication of his feelings was that his merry tone had cooled. "You can either deprive yourself of a kindred spirit also wondering why Isis killed herself, or you can cooperate and hope that, if we compare notes, we can figure out the link between mother and daughter that marks Arielle's flesh and takes her on these strange astral projections."

Slowly Shelly turned back to him. Astral projections. Most people had never heard the term, much less knew Arielle suffered from it.

His mouth was solemn now. "I want to know why Isis killed herself. And I want even more to help save her daughter from the same madness."

I need to know why Isis killed herself. Shelly heard the words, not spoken, but implied by his tone of voice. "What concern is it of yours?"

"Let's just say that I have a fondness for her daughter and leave it at that."

Whatever "that" was went much farther than he admitted, but Shelly finally took pity on him, stood, and extended her hand. If she sensed a kindred spirit in him, a fellow quester and questioner, she refused to let him see it. She pumped his hand brusquely.

When she tried to pull free, he caught her hand between his much larger ones and warmed it. Nothing untoward or overly forward, yet Shelly felt a rush of heat rise to her cheeks and descend, more alarmingly, to an area of her body she seldom thought about.

"Ethan Perot, Viscount of Trent. And, of more interest to one of your bent, Royal Society member interested in physics, chemistry, and paranormal phenomena."

As she listened, Shelly eased her hand away, backing up a step before she could stop herself.

But that wide mouth only grinned, increasing her strange urge to stare at it. "And perhaps your greatest challenge, my very dear Miss Shelly Holmes."

Quelling the primitive impulse to flee both the look in his eyes and her own response to it, Shelly stood her ground and thrust the lantern at him. "Very well, make yourself useful and hold this. I shall let the earl decide what to do with you."

"A pity. I'd much rather you made that choice." His soft laughter warmed her cheeks as he knelt next to her. He held the lantern high while she began to copy the strange marks and words into a notebook.

After she'd sketched all she could, Shelly knelt down to study the markings again. "I need to get a thin piece of parchment and do a rubbing . . ." The words were scarcely out of her mouth when she saw him go to a black bag she'd not noticed earlier and . . . What was the matter with her? She noticed everything, normally.

Though she'd scarcely laid eyes on the man, she already knew he did nothing in the normal way. Steeling herself against the strange allure of his presence, Shelly stood, folded her arms over her formidable bosom, and watched him remove a long roll of parchment and a thick leaded pencil from his bag. He approached, a wicked gleam in his eye.

"You ask; I give. Rubbings are something I excel at, my very dear lady." As he passed her, he used one of those excessively large and capable hands to brush his fingers very lightly down her back. "And foot rubbings are my specialty."

She arched her back at him like a spitting cat at his innuendo, but her high dudgeon was for naught. He was the studious scientist again, bending to unroll the parchment over the inscription.

"Now, are you going to stand there grinding your teeth down to nubs, or are you going to help me hold this paper so I can do a respectable job of duplicating this devilishly intricate script?"

Still grinding her teeth in frustration, Shelly knelt again to help, trying hard to ignore the scent of his sandalwood soap and the far more exotic aroma so heady to her heightened senses—the scent of an aroused man.

How long had it been? She tried to remember,

and suddenly realized she had not been intimate with a man since Jeremy, several years past.

The strange feelings assailing her now, so similar to the ones she'd felt then, made her recall the scents and sights of that bleak Cornwall moor a bare few years ago—and the event that had changed her utterly and forever. For the better, or for the worse? She did not know herself.

Her eyes began to glow as she saw not the dim mausoleum and the man watching her curiously, but the alluring moonlight that had brushed the barren wastes with a strange golden beauty . . . right before the giant wolf bit her. Enough to make her bleed, though at the time she'd not been overly concerned, as she was still doubting herself the truth of something so fantastical as a being part man, part wolf, but all wild.

And then the change began . . . Shelly's nostrils flared as the scent of sandalwood filled her head, and suddenly she was hungry for touch and tongue. Only then did she realize that a large capable hand had closed over hers, and that this powerful rush of memories she usually squelched were all his fault.

"My dear lady, are you all right?" came a voice much more cultured than Jeremy's, though its effect on her was very similar. She wondered if he had rough edges, too, and how it would feel to smooth them.

She stared down at that well-shaped, sensitive hand, imagining it gliding over her skin. When the long fingers curled between hers, she felt a tangible lurch in her middle, her eyes glowing brighter as she longed to clutch back. To pull him into her arms, or better yet, fall into his.

And precisely because she wanted to be a woman again so badly, to forget the responsibilities and burdens of her "gift," she forced herself to jerk away. "Nothing is the matter except I have no predilection for forward men. Keep your hands to yourself."

He arched a brow at this, as if he'd sensed her inner battle, but he merely bent back to his work. Despite her inward catechism, however, loneliness, perhaps inspired by the look and scent of a man she knew instinctively was dangerous to her, battled for primacy with longing as, inevitably, their hands brushed again in the close quarters during the rubbing. But this time he kept things impersonal, only suggesting she hold the paper a certain way.

Damnation, would she never stop feeling the inconvenient instincts of a woman? Vowing to crush every vestige of these disconcerting notions, she moved her hands to the very edge of the paper and concentrated on the hieroglyphics appearing under the lead.

Inside his carriage, sitting before the curb at Hafford Place, Luke Simball stared up at the tiny patch of light visible between thick curtains on the second floor. Morosely, he wondered when he'd ever start feeling more like a man instead of like a cat on hot bricks. No matter how hard he tried to resist, he always found himself here at the same hour, like a tomcat on the prowl, the sun sinking before the night's dominion. Though he felt much more at home in the night than the day, only Arielle could make his nocturnal world complete.

No matter how many women he bedded in an effort to end this hunger, it was *she* who haunted his waking hours and tormented his dreams. From the time she'd become a recluse after her disastrous come-out several years ago, until the dance, he'd glimpsed her only once, getting into a carriage. Now the memory of holding her in his arms was as vibrant as she was herself. He didn't have to close his vivid green eyes to see her, so bright and strong was her allure. She was meant to be his, had always been meant to be his down through the ages.

She just didn't know it yet.

Despite her limp, her pale skin and shadowed eyes, she had a haughty aura of power, a grace of movement that made every hunting instinct he possessed go on full alert. The fangs he'd learned to suppress except when he was ready to feed formed of their own accord, beyond his power to control. Claws grew from his fingernails and soft pads began to form on his palms. The primitive urge to conquer her, to let her know him and learn him as he lavished her with delicate strokes of his claws and little love bites on her neck and shoulders, almost overcame him.

He enjoyed their dance of desire in their dreams, but he knew that if he took her then, he might lose all chance of winning her in the tangible world.

The time would come when she would choose him in both worlds.

Her dreams would be made reality . . . but only by her open, willful choice of him over the *other*.

When she'd paused on the step of the carriage, looking over her shoulder into the setting sunlight, as if sensing his heated stare, a primeval growl of response had come from his throat. Her eyes were so blue, exactly like her mother's. Her raven hair, even coiffed severely at her neck under netting, shone like the blackest panther's hide. Such would be her true form when she took her rightful place at his side.

Now, staring at that patch of light, he frowned, focusing his acute senses on the room behind the curtains. A flashing vision of the empty, neatly made bed came to him, and he realized she wasn't there. His glowing green eyes roved the windows and stopped on the broad terrace, its wide French doors half-open.

The faint sound of silverware clinking on china drifted to him on the breeze. She was at the table tonight, so she must be feeling better. Good. Soon she'd be ready for the more direct portion of his wooing. No more sitting alone, using the natural magnetism of his kind from a distance, urging her to him in spirit if not in body. He knew he was partly successful, because the psychic link between them was so strong that sometimes he saw her behind those barred windows, tossing and turning in the bed as she would soon toss and turn in his arms.

Arielle—lioness of God.

She alone was blood of his blood, joined to him by her ancestor, Cleopatra. She alone would be mother of his children when she finally stopped fighting him.

Tapping on the roof of his plush brougham to indicate to his driver he was ready to move on, he stared resolutely forward. His green eyes glowed amber in the gathering darkness when he whisked the carriage curtain closed. His glossy gold mane, brushing his starched shirt collar, shone even in the dimmest patch of moonlight peeking through the curtains. Impatiently he brushed it out of his face.

He leaned down and picked up the book he'd acquired a few days earlier. A knife fell from a hidden sheath at his hip. It was a wickedly long, thin blade of gold, inlaid with carnelian and lapis lazuli. It pleased him as it had pleased the pharaoh Akhenaton himself, who had once owned it. He stuck it back in the sheath and pulled his coat closed over it.

Then he turned his attention to the book. He read it in the dark without bothering to light the carriage lanterns. The title was: *Scotland Yard: Practices and Stratagems in Pursuing Persons of Ill Character.* In his other hand he ceaselessly rotated a small golden scarab inscribed with hieroglyphs on one side. As he flipped the scarab from finger to finger, balancing it perfectly without moving his eyes from the page, a lion stared out inimically from the other side.

* * *

Sitting at the dinner table with her father, her odd new companion Miss Holmes, and Ethan Perot, her mother's childhood friend, Arielle Blaylock tensed, her eyes going blank. Usually this feeling came upon her only at night when she was abed, but suddenly she felt that magnetic presence so close. Surely if she reached out . . .

"Arielle? Do you wish me to pass you something?" her father asked, automatically handing her the breadbasket.

Arielle blushed as she realized her arms were extended. She clasped her chair, mumbling, "No, Father, I was merely stretching." And yet her senses, so heightened of late, heard a carriage driving away from the gate. She knew one of them had come again. As the sound of the wheels receded, so did the feeling that all her nerve cells were being stroked by the tender-rough texture of a cat's tongue.

Her father had accepted the excuse and returned to his veal, but Miss Holmes gave her that direct stare that was increasingly unnerving to Arielle. Who was this woman her father passed off as her "companion"? She had none of the dull submissiveness of any companion Arielle had ever met.

Instead of ignoring the acute appraisal as usual, Arielle returned the unblinking stare. "When shall you return my amulet, Miss Holmes?"

"When I am assured your . . . malady is cured."

Arielle stiffened. "I have no malady. Everyone has bad dreams on occasion."

This won a raised eyebrow of polite disbelief, but no comment.

Ethan was not so forbearing. "Arielle, if you have no malady, how do you explain the scratches on your arms and bosom you always awaken to?"

"I . . . am too restless in bed. There's a splinter on my bedpost and I—"

A sputtering noise interrupted her. Her father had just spit his expensive Madeira back into his glass in a gauche behavior unusual for him. "My dear, I have stood beside your bed on more than one occasion and watched the marks appear from nowhere. Why will you not admit that something is amiss here? Something benighted. I cannot let you end as your mother did."

Tossing her napkin over her half-eaten food, Arielle rose with all the dignity she could muster when she felt like a speciman under glass. One these too rational beings found a bit fascinating, and a bit distasteful. "From all accounts, Father, you did nothing to get her help."

Her father blanched and half rose. "You don't even remember her, how could you possibly—"

"I see her nonetheless. She is watching over me and will guide me in the end. And she's warning me now that you're lying to me. If I find out you were complicit in her shunning by the ton, I shall never forgive you." She moved to sweep out of the room, her slight limp detracting not in the slightest from her regal posture and haughty chin.

The earl blocked her, his cheeks flushed, his eyes bright with anger. "How dare you . . . I did everything I could to help her, to protect her, but the madness took her away from me. And now, the same ailment affects you, and all you do is curse me and defy me."

He seemed to choke with rage and then he sank back into his chair, covering his face with trembling hands. "I see her when I look at you. When you tell me she guides you, how do you expect me to react, considering the way she ended?"

Arielle's own eyes grew bright. Unable to bear the widening rift between them, she moved to span it by kneeling next to her father and taking his hands in hers. "Tell me. Don't keep secrets from me anymore."

From his seat at the table, Ethan said gently, "He's only trying to protect you, child."

"How can I fight what I do not understand?" Arielle responded, still staring at her father. She sensed him weakening. "Please."

With a deep breath that seemed to steady him, the earl began, "Isis always had a strange prescience and sensitivity to the unseen world that intrigued me. I used to tease her about being a witch. At first we were very happy. But after you came along and you were both in the carriage accident, she . . . changed."

Unconsciously Arielle rubbed her aching leg. She remembered nothing of that night for she'd been but a babe, but she still had the remnants of that trauma in her scars and limp.

She squeezed her father's hands and he continued, "She was unconscious for over a month, and that was when the marks first began to appear. Tiny scratches, like yours, coming from nowhere.

And when she awoke . . ." He swallowed harshly. "At first I noticed little changes. More cream in her tea than was her wont. A restless inability to sleep at night. She began to wander the halls and disappear for hours. When she returned, she had grass stains on the hem of her night rail. One of our neighbors saw her one night, and that's when the talk began. At first I tried to ignore it, but it only worsened. And then . . ." He closed his eyes, his face twisted with pain, and when he opened them he was looking at Ethan. "I can't."

Ethan glanced at Shelly's intent, listening expression. "Is now the time for this? Do you want her to know, too?"

Shelly bristled, about to retort, but the earl said softly, "Miss Holmes has the right to know exactly what she's investigating, especially if there's some strange connection between Isis and Arielle."

Ethan came around the table and pulled Arielle to her feet. "There's no way to sugarcoat this. Isis grew increasingly wild and distant. I had formed a great affection for her as a longtime friend of Rupert's, but unlike your father, I had some experience with the arcane world. I believed the source of her ailment to be a psychic link Isis had not sought, but was, in some strange way, forced upon her."

Ethan's hands gripped tighter than he obviously intended, but Arielle scarcely felt them, so hard was her heart beating.

"I followed her that last night and saw, and saw . . ." Ethan swallowed. "A cat creature. A beautiful feline I've seen only in pictures that supposedly inhabits the Himalayas. White and powerful."

A flashing image streaked through Arielle's consciousness, a lithe creature of thick white fur spotted with dark, inky dots. Enormous feet like snowshoes. She closed her eyes, denying the image. Lies. Why were they lying to her?

"I believe it's called a snow leopard," Shelly said calmly. "And what was the creature doing?"

Ethan gritted his teeth but admitted, "Killing a girl from the neighboring village. The snow leopard was joined in her kill by a massive lion."

"How do you know it was my mother?" Arielle demanded.

He brushed a tender fingertip under her eyes. "Her eyes were yours, Arielle. And when she finally returned near dawn, she had blood around her mouth and under her fingernails."

Arielle swallowed. "That proves nothing. Perhaps it was her own blood."

The earl hurried to finish, as if now the tale was begun, he had to complete it. "It's true, Arielle. It cost me a fortune to hush it up. I paid the family a stipend I maintain to this day, not that there is ever any recompense for the loss of a human life. And that is when I locked Isis up, for all the good it did."

The rest Arielle knew. The increasing bouts of madness, the marks that appeared all over Isis's body, and finally, her suicide to escape the pain. Only now did she know that her mother had killed herself not only because she was mad, but to spare

her husband and daughter any more notoriety . . .
and to stop herself from killing again. If she were
to believe this fantastical tale.

She looked at the two men who had been most
influential in her life, and did not know whether
she could trust them. Were they trying to scare her
into compliance with this horrific account?

The earl brought his daughter to his bosom.
"That is why we must be so vigilant. Keep your
windows locked, and master these strange dreams,
and we will keep you safe."

Arielle straightened and pushed her father away.
"I am not my mother. They are only dreams. I feel
no urge whatever to kill anyone. And you should
have told me all this many years ago rather than expect me to accept such nonsense now as an adult."
She marched to the door, her limp scarcely evident.
"Now please excuse me. I am fatigued."

When she was gone, Shelly leveled her most dis-
passionate look upon the two men. "Why do you
not hit her over the head with a club just to get her
attention? Was that the best way to tell her such a
tragic tale, over dinner when she is already susceptible to nightmares? Of course she rejects believing
something so awful."

"She can't be healed until she admits she has a
problem, and every word we said was the truth,"
Ethan retorted.

"And she'll never admit she has a problem with
such heavy-handed treatment. Of course she
doesn't believe she's prey to the same impulses as

her mother, and frankly, I'm not sure I do either. She has quite a logical mind, and even if Isis became some sort of cat creature who liked to kill, Arielle has a deal of common sense."

"I see. So one is susceptible to the powers of the arcane only when one is weak-minded? I'll remember that for future reference," Ethan muttered as Shelly rose to follow Arielle to the door. She turned upon him at once.

"Future reference, my dear sir? You've already practiced your unique brand of coercion upon me to try to wrest my investigation from me. But I am not your typical simpering miss, and I am no more susceptible to the 'arcane' world than I am to male blandishments. Neither your height, nor your wit, nor your wealth impress me in the slightest."

"You've yet to see my best attributes. But that will come. No coercion needed."

Telling herself she simply would not grind her teeth, she simply would *not,* Shelly turned back to the distressed earl, her flinty gray gaze softening with sympathy for him. "Sir, there is one thing you must understand about the unique character of astral projection and shape-shifting. They are different from many of the psychic phenomena, wherein the victim is forced with a bite or a curse into a way of life that is anathema. Though these two abilities may seem like maladies to the rational world, to the sufferer, they are a gift. The afflicted person chooses to project, or chooses to shift—and they must also choose to resist. This is by far the hardest psychic ailment to cure. I can promise you nothing,

but I shall give you my all in the attempt." Shelly
swept out, unaware how impassioned she'd become as she spoke, as if this were not merely a
truth she voiced, but a reality she lived.

She left a very thoughtful Ethan Perot in her
wake, staring after her.

His thick black hair gleaming, Seth Taub leaned
back in his chair and blew tobacco smoke up at
the ceiling. He tried to keep his tone mild as he
disagreed with the marquess's appraisal of the female kind. "Women, my dear fellow, are more than
brood mares or chatelaines of a gentleman's
household."

"Yes. They are also bed warmers and decorate a
man's arm quite nicely at a ball," retorted Samuel
Hathaway, Marquess of Brackton, taking another
long pull at his brandy.

This brought laughter from some quarters at the
surrounding card tables, but frowns from others.
Lamb's Card Room and Smoking Club was situated in a quiet, out-of-the-way corner of Mayfair.
There was no expansive view of Hyde Park from
this nondescript town house; nor was there a picture window to display one. In Queen Victoria's
London, a man's appetites could still be satisfied,
but only discreetly.

And discretion was Mr. Cyrus Lamb's specialty.

He hovered at a little distance, close enough to
listen but too far away for the gentlemen who fre-
quented his establishment to feel his presence. His
pug-nosed face had the battered but compelling

look of a boxer who'd lost his share of fights but still lived to better himself—and those to whom he offered his loyalty.

Seth glanced over at him with the barest flick of his eyes. Cyrus disappeared and returned with a flamboyant black velvet cape lined in burgundy silk over one arm and an ebony gold-headed cane in the other hand.

Pocketing the substantial number of coins in the middle of the table, Seth rose. The polite veneer he'd forced upon himself evaporated as he shrugged into his cloak, looking down at the marquess. "Sir, unlike you, I find in myself the greatest sympathy for the female kind." Putting his top hat on at a rakish angle, he finished quietly, "Most especially for your wife."

The marquess spluttered his brandy back into his snifter and leaped to his feet, hands clenched. "Why, you scoundrel, you reek of anonymity despite your airs. No one knows anything about you and yet you criticize a man with ten generations of blue blood running in his veins?" This won some hear-hears from other quarters.

Cyrus quietly approached. His hands were not clenched.

But they didn't need to be. The look on his face made the marquess sink back into his chair. He blustered, "Show your face in my presence again and by God you'll hear from my second."

Seth's full mouth curved into a smile. "Pistols at dawn? How quaint. I should think we were past that, in this so-civilized company."

"Or swords. I haven't skewered any vermin lately. But then, I make no doubt you don't know the gentlemanly art of fencing."

Seth's smile faded. His honey-brown eyes took on a strange glow that gave them a golden tinge. Several of the men near him scooted their chairs slightly away. Taking the cane from Cyrus, Seth gave a quick turn and pull at the gold head. A wicked sword hissed with lethal menace as it came free. It was long and thin and gilded, slightly triangular in shape. It was so sharp it glittered, as if even the candlelight danced away in alarm.

Now the men didn't just scoot their chairs away; they scattered, all but bleating.

Even the marquess had gone pasty. To his credit he stayed put even when Seth whipped the blade from side to side as if testing its heft and straightness, his dexterity ruffling the marquess's hair slightly as he stirred up the still air.

Cyrus growled, "Sir, ye needs must keep yer temper or—"

As quickly as it was withdrawn, the blade was resheathed. "Forgive me, Cyrus. But Sheba gets restive when she's neglected too long. I was merely showing her off."

As the marquess's face returned to a normal color, he barked a harsh laugh. "Leave it to a . . . a . . . foreigner to do something so bloody stupid as to name a sword."

Cyrus put his considerable bulk between the two men, but Seth's lip only curled slightly. "It is named after a woman. And that, sir, defines the difference between us: I have respect for the weaker sex."

With a swirl of his cape, Seth was gone, the gold-handled cane firmly in his grip.

"Did you see it roar?" asked one of the men at Seth's table after he was safely out of earshot.

The marquess blinked in confusion, shoving the dregs of his brandy aside. "What in tarnation are you nattering on about?"

"The head of the cane. It was carved of pure gold into a snarling lion's head. I suspect you had a lucky escape, Hathaway."

"I say, have you all heard the rumors about those three girls they found in the Thames a few weeks apart?" inserted a pimply-faced young fellow at a different table.

Cyrus frowned, but he could hardly forbid the gossip that was as much the coin of the realm in his club as the pound notes littering the table.

The marquess grew thoughtful as he stared after Seth. "Yes, I did. And the bodies were . . ." He had delicacy enough not to finish.

The brash young man didn't even blush as he nodded eagerly. "Incised, they were. With strange markings some compare to Egyptian hieroglyphs. So deep and clear they had to be made with something confoundedly sharp. And tooth marks. Like . . . fangs. Pierced the carotid in each case and, ah, sucked at the blood. Or so it's rumored. Probably nonsense."

The marquess nodded absently, still staring at

the door where Seth had exited. "A lion-headed cane, you say? Interesting."

Feeling stronger than she had in ages, if still troubled by the horrid fate of her mother, Arielle combed her hair before her dressing table. Sitting as she was, her lawn night rail falling half off her shoulders, she could pretend she was what she longed to be: beautiful, passionately involved with a man she adored, and, most important, whole.

She rubbed her aching leg, trying not to think again of that awful night Ethan had depicted so vividly, of her mother transformed into a cat. Automatically, she reached for the amulet at her neck before she remembered it wasn't there. With a petulant frown that made her look like the miniature of her mother on the fireplace mantel, she rose, intending to find her dressing robe so she could march to Miss Holmes's room and demand it back.

This time she wouldn't take no for an answer. The heavy weight of the amulet made her feel grounded, her mother's daughter, linked to her by more than face and name. And she needed that sense of belonging, needed it with increasing desperation because with every night that was filled with dreams of lion gods who seduced her, she felt more alienated from the father she used to adore and was increasingly resenting.

No matter what face he put upon it, that ludicrous tale made it sound as if her mother had been a venal, bloodthirsty creature, and she simply did not believe it. The woman she saw in her heart and dreams was nothing like that.

She was about to shrug into her robe when there was a scratching at her window. She looked over at it, starting back in alarm. An enormous shadow of a rampant lion, reared upward on its hind legs, its full mane tossing as it flung its head back in a roar, loomed huge against the wall. But she blinked in disbelief as she looked again to find the shadow had shrunk to the size of a house cat, rubbing itself against the bars.

A meowing filtered to her on the night breeze coming through the window and wooden panels the housemaid had left open just a crack. Telling herself she was a silly goose, and she really must quit being so imaginative lest her nightly dreams start haunting her by day, she went to the window, opened the panels, and raised the sash so the supple feline could make its way through the bars. It sat on the sill, looking up at her expectantly.

Tentatively she reached out her hand for the cat to sniff, wondering if it was wild. It was a golden tabby with green eyes that viewed her with the ineffable cat wisdom that had made the creatures beloved companions of mortals since time immemorial. Why, her own mother was rumored to have had a treasured tabby that never left her side, and several cats were inscribed on her tomb in the family crypt.

Bast had been the protector of the household, and her image, snug around her neck on her mother's amulet, had always given Arielle comfort. Perhaps the odd bond she had with cats had drawn this pretty little creature?

The moment she touched the soft fur, the cat began to purr, rubbing against her hand. "You little darling," she cooed, picking up the cat to cradle it against her bosom.

It rubbed its head into the vee exposed between her breasts by the loose night rail. It licked her there, the roughness of its tongue sending a thrill of pleasure through her. If only . . .

Wondering at the strange eroticism of her own thoughts, and the flashing image she had of this creature as a golden-haired man in a lion mask nuzzling her in the same spot, she set the cat down at her feet. She was still enough of her father's daughter to realize that this growing obsession she had for cats had its unhealthy side. Sometimes she felt literally torn in two between the prosaic demands of her English father and the mystical allure of her Egyptian mother.

Immediately the tabby began to rub against her legs, side to side, as if it were famished for human contact. It looked up at her with those slanted eyes. Was it her imagination, or did they glow even in the bright candlelight? It gave a husky meow, as if it were hungry, but when she poured her nightly warm milk into a saucer, the cat only sniffed at the offering. It looked back up at her, and this time there was no mistaking that gaze. Like her, it was hungry. But not for food.

The unblinking green eyes were mesmerizing.

Catspell

*"Hold me, touch me, and I will succor you for-
ever. Come with me into the night in your true
form."*

Arielle heard the words clearly in her head.

In a male voice.

In a male voice she recognized, that of the
golden one of her dreams. The one whose face she
could never see beyond the gleam of green eyes.

Her pedantic half resisted. The dreams she understood, for they took her away from the unpleasant reality of her inadequacies to a place of magic
where all things were possible. There she could be
whole, and loved, and part of something born of
her mother's blood.

But this was no dream. And this was no normal
cat. Feeling both fascinated and repelled, Arielle
stood teetering in place, longing to touch that winsome, seductive creature and feel its warmth and
softness again, yet instinctively knowing that if she
did so, she served its purposes. And what were
those?

Fear overwhelmed fascination. Backing off another step, Arielle picked up the poker beside the
fireplace, retreating as the feline approached. "Go
away!" The sound of her own voice, stronger than
she felt, gave Arielle courage even when the feline's
shadow grew again against the wall.

A lion's ruff began to form, the chest became
massive, and the paws grew as big as plates.

But when she looked, the cat was sitting calmly
on its haunches, watching her with that hypnotic
gaze that pulled at something deep within Arielle,

something that was the source of her strength—and her nightmares.

"What do you want from me?" Arielle cried. The poker had sagged point-down to the floor in her loose grip, for she knew she could not hit the tabby, no matter how afraid she was of its alter ego.

The shadow grew larger on the wall, the lion now fully formed. The dark, forbidding shape began to stalk her as the cat moved toward her again. It was eerie the way corporeal and incorporeal moved simultaneously. A small tabby-striped foot moved forward. So did the plate-size paw seen only in shadow.

Arielle bumped up against the wall, unable to retreat farther. Still she couldn't raise the poker to defend herself, even when the tabby crouched, staring up at her, tail swishing.

"Come with me; transform to your true self. Let me show you the night as we were both meant to see it." The lion crouched, too, and glanced outside.

Arielle heard the words in her head in that husky, seductive male voice. The poker sagged further as she stared at the half-open window, curious to see what he saw. The night was beautiful. Even through the barely open window, she could see past the shadows to the horizon . . .

Though she did not know it, her eyes had begun to glow, too.

The bedroom door opened.

"Arielle, before I retire, I just wanted to see if you needed any—" Halfway inside the room, Shelly froze. With an all-encompassing glance at the cracked-open window, Arielle's defenselessness, the poker sagging in her hand, her eyes glowing, and the crouched cat and its counterpart massive shadow against the wall, Shelly took in the cogent facts.

The tabby's hair stood on end as she entered. It spit at her, fangs bared. So did the shadow lion, revealing massive jaws that could crush a skull without effort.

"Stand aside, child," Shelly said coolly. She picked up a large vase of flowers, tossed the blooms aside, and threw the entire container full of water at the tabby cat. Instantly the menacing lion shadow disappeared.

Still rapt, her eyes glowing, Arielle got drenched, too. She flinched as water splattered her in the face. The glow in her eyes died. She gripped the poker more firmly.

With a yowl, shaking vigorously from side to side, the tabby spit one last time, and then in a streak of striped gold, it leaped halfway across the room and landed nimbly on the sill, where it turned.

The look it leveled at Shelly could only be termed inimical. Shelly stared back coolly, pulling something that gleamed gold from her pocket. "You're not quite as strong as you would be if this were weighing her down, are you?"

Arielle and the cat both stared at the amulet with equal intensity.

Shelly strode to the roaring fire and flung the amulet into the flames.

Chapter Three

With a shriek of despair, Arielle ran toward the hearth, but Shelly held her back. The tabby leaped down from the sill, reared back on its hind legs, and began to transform. This time no shadow menace took shape from light's play upon darkness.

This time the stuff of nightmares became real.

Before their eyes the harmless house cat metamorphosed. Tiny paws grew to snowshoe size, as if to prepare the little frame for the weight to come. Then, fast as thought, the small body grew into a huge, muscular chest and legs. Finally the winsome ruff of orange fur at the house cat's neck became a bushy golden mane.

A very large, very real lion stared for an instant between Shelly and the softening amulet almost obscured in the flames.

Arielle was so distressed over her amulet that she struggled against Shelly's firm hold, uncomprehending at first even as the harmless tabby's true form was revealed in all its menacing glory. But when the huge cat leaped toward the flames as if to retrieve the amulet, Shelly shoved Arielle aside, grabbed the poker, and jabbed it toward the cat to keep it back, putting herself between the cat and the fire.

Liquid gold had begun to run over the wood, bubbling and bursting. Like glittering dreams. Like Arielle's dreams, hypnotic, mysterious, malleable, and forever out of reach.

With a furious roar that made the dishes on the table rattle, the huge cat turned its attention to the interloper. For an instant it merely appraised Shelly, head cocked to the side, as if curious about this weak human—a female to boot—who dared oppose it.

With a strength beyond normal human capacity, Shelly picked Arielle up in her arms, leaped the ten feet to the door, and deposited Arielle outside, slamming the bedroom door and locking it. Immediately Arielle began to beat on the door. "No, you can't! My mother's amulet! It's all I have of her. Please . . ."

The lion stayed put while she evicted Arielle, sitting on its haunches as if it, too, preferred a private confrontation. It watched Shelly with unblinking green eyes of an unusual emerald hue that would have been mesmerizing to one of a lesser intellect. For an instant Shelly leaned against the door, her own gray eyes taking on an eerie glow as she stared back, unimpressed.

Far from alarmed, the lion bared its menacing fangs in an almost lazy grimace, putting one massive paw over the poker Shelly had cast aside as if to emphasize her helplessness.

"I know you for what you are," Shelly said softly. "You cannot have her. Go, leave her in peace, or face the consequences." Somehow she knew the massive feline would comprehend every word. The spirit that inhabited this animal form was even more powerful than its physical manifestation. Perhaps more powerful than Shelly's own alter ego, but she gave no hint of fear as she faced the creature down.

With a very human-sounding snort of disgust at this foolish bravado, the lion began to stalk Shelly, step by step. She was pressed against the door, with nowhere to retreat. As if determined to terrify her, the lion gave another deafening roar that shook the pictures on the walls. Shelly merely watched him analytically.

They each heard Arielle's distressed voice asking for aid down below near the vestibule. Heavy footsteps began to climb the stairs.

They didn't have much time.

With arrogant certainty, as if he feared neither man nor beast, the lion stopped, lifted one paw, and extended his lethally sharp claws, turning them from side to side. He watched her all the while, as if eager to see her fear at her obvious fate. As if he fed on terror, and needed it more than meat.

Shelly merely lifted her own hand . . . except the appendage had undergone a curious transformation as well. It was brown, hairy, and, one by one, claws even heavier and sharper than the lion's were revealed. They gleamed in the gaslight as she moved her paw from side to side, mocking his movements. Her hand looked exactly like a wolf's paw, but a very large, very dangerous wolf's paw—controlled by human intellect.

The lion froze midstride, one foot still up, blinking in astonishment.

Shelly's other hand was transformed even faster, leaving her in wolf's form from her paws to her elbows, but otherwise very human. "It's all a matter of control, you see. You obviously have not yet perfected the art of shape-shifting."

As if to demonstrate, Shelly elongated her jaw into a wolf's snout as her gray eyes grew cold with menace. In the next blink, her face was human again. "And I suspect I've been doing this much longer than have you. I no longer even need such niceties as a full moon to shape-shift. I do so at will. You'll get the hang of it—but not with Arielle."

The lion sat down on its haunches, giving every indication that it was listening with total fascination.

The footsteps, wary, attempting stealth and failing miserably, had climbed the stairs and were approaching along the corridor.

"Two footmen, don't you agree? One carrying a blunderbuss, the other an ax."

The lion managed to look skeptical.

Shelly smiled. "Ah, that's right. Your most acute sense is sight. Mine is hearing. There's the slight scrape of metal against wood. He's keeping close to the wall."

The lion seemed to wait for the rest.

She didn't disappoint him. "The ax? That, I presume, is to open the door. It's kept in the butler's pantry for emergencies, and no one but the earl has a spare key to this room, so it will be the only way in."

The lion inclined his lordly head, as if in tribute to her.

But Shelly shook her head with regret. "Pity they're so ready to come to the weak woman's rescue. I was rather looking forward to testing you."

The lion gave a whuff as if in agreement. The cold menace in its green eyes had faded to what could only, in a human, have been termed a twinkle as he watched the "weak woman."

"Another time." Going to the window, Shelly used her werewolf paws to rip the bars from the casing as if they were dried kindling. Bowing slightly, she swept a paw politely before her. "A graceful exit will save us both too many confounded explanations, do you not agree?"

The knob rattled, and then the door shook. "Miss Holmes, be ye all right?" came the frightened but determined voice of the head footman.

The sound of an ax meeting wood echoed down the hallway.

Neither shape-shifter seemed rattled as they continued challenging each other with their gazes.

But the lion had apparently tired of the diversion

of meeting a truly worthy adversary. With a contemptuous look at first Shelly and then the easy avenue of escape, it sat stone-still, its head cocked to the side, and closed its eyes. As an ax appeared in the door and wood splintered, leaving a hole, the lion began to transform in a most curious fashion.

Before Shelly's eyes, it lost substance, becoming transparent. At first it shimmered, as if form resisted ceding itself to spirit, but by the time the wooden hole had become wide enough for a hand to wiggle inside and unlock the door, the lion was a silvery gray mist. As the door opened, the mist dissipated into a glittering whiff that floated away on the breeze issuing through the damaged window.

The corporeal was now part of the spirit world. At will.

"Damnation," Shelly muttered. "Now that ability, I envy." The vampire Serena, who had almost put a period to Shelly and her friends Max and Angel, had possessed the same ability. But Shelly had no time for recollection, for she had scarcely a second before the door burst open.

In that second she took one of her own claws and scratched the back of one paw until it bled. Then, faster than thought, because the skills were wedded now to her subconscious instincts as well, Shelly transformed her paws back into hands. She positioned herself as if half fainting on, appropriately enough, the fainting couch.

Someday, perhaps, she would get the dubious art of feminine frailty perfected, Shelly vowed as heavy footsteps entered the room. She tried to look helpless as the head footman warily peeked around the wall. In his hands he held a blunderbuss.

Outside, Seth Taub expectantly watched the whiff of mist gently float down to the ground. He was careful to be very still, to hold his breath, and to shrink back into the cloak of a weeping willow. Luke's senses, at times, seemed even more acute than Seth's own, perhaps because he suffered fewer pangs of conscience in using them. Luke had tried, so he claimed, since embracing his alter ego a year or so ago, to totally throw off the rags of remorse at the acts he sometimes had to commit in fighting the ancient battle of his ancestors.

Sometimes frail humans got in the way. Other times they fed growing predatory instincts. Instincts that became ever harder to control as each day faded into the limitless nights that ruled his kind. Seth still battled his instincts; Luke did not.

Seth watched the mist that was Luke take the form of a tabby and slink away into the darkness. Seth debated transforming into his favored shape, the lion, and trying to surprise Luke, but for now, he preferred that Luke not realize he had been observed in his battle and humiliating retreat.

Besides, the time was not right, for Seth's task here was not yet performed. As much as his deepest, most primitive instincts demanded he follow the tabby, Seth forced himself to calmly remember why he had come, why he had risked discovery a few nights ago when he'd broken into the crypt.

Catspell

He had hated violating Isis's rest that way, but he'd had no choice. With the original amulet confiscated, he needed the tangible link between mother and daughter to allow Isis's communications to counteract Luke's foul influence. Seth fingered the hard amulet in his pocket, feeling the calming raised image of Bast under his sensitive touch.

He'd had no choice but to melt down the breastplate and diadem Isis wore to recreate the amulet she'd left to her daughter. The jewelry had passed down from mother to daughter since time immemorial, back to the days of Cleopatra herself. Only its golden allure was strong enough to defeat the powers of death and darkness. As long as she wore it, Arielle would be safe, or so he hoped.

Two footmen peered out Arielle's window, interrupting his bleak thoughts. Because Arielle was not in the room, Seth's psychic link had been too weak for him to close his eyes and visualize what had transpired there to make Luke flee, but from his vantage he had certainly seen the bars ripped from the window with superhuman strength.

From the inside. With hairy brown, enormous paws that looked for all the world as if they were attached to female arms.

This woman, this companion of Arielle's, who and what was she? On mere reputation, Seth had already suspected she was not a normal woman. From recent observation, he knew so. Not only from the arrogance of her stride and bearing and intellect, but because she walked with a lightness that scarcely disturbed a blade of grass, and her eyes occasionally glowed in the darkness.

After what he'd witnessed, his last doubt faded.

She was one of them. A dweller of both worlds. How and what shape she took Seth did not know, but he vowed to find out. This night she had apparently risked her life to save Arielle from Luke's enchantment. While Seth was grateful to her for that, he was even more grateful that she had proved to be such a worthy adversary. Few beings, no matter which world they favored, had ever faced Luke in a fair fight and won.

Perhaps her ability could be useful.

The woman bore watching. At the right time, with the right handling, she could be made his ally. For the battle to come, he would need every ounce of strength he possessed, every advantage and weapon he could muster to win Arielle's love and send the other one permanently to the spirit world, where he belonged.

Luke, the enemy.

Luke, his brother.

The head footman peeked around the corner and then rushed into the room, his chest puffed out in self-importance. "Be ye harmed, miss?" he asked anxiously, setting aside the blunderbuss to help her up.

As if shaky on her feet, Shelly half leaned on him, careful that he noticed her bleeding hand. With a tsk-tsk of his tongue, he took a less-than-clean kerchief from his pocket.

Hastily Shelly dabbed at the cut with the tail end of her pristine white blouse. "A mere scratch. He did it on the way to the window."

Warily, both footmen inched over to the gaping window and looked down three stories to the ground, as if hoping to see a body. "Don't see anything." The footman turned to her. "He, miss? How do ye know the critter be a he? It were a lion, from the sounds of it."

Shelly looked back at the footman with closer attention. Not the usual dull sort. "A rather small lion, perhaps," Shelly lied. "But, ah, when he reared up, I saw his, uh, nether quarters." She gave a very good imitation of a blush.

The footman didn't have to imitate. Red as a new sunset, he circled the room, obviously looking for damage and proof of the lion's presence. But he found nothing, as Shelly well knew.

There was a scuffling in the hallway and then Arielle rushed in, followed quickly by a lackey who was rubbing his shin with a wounded look at her. Arielle scarcely glanced at the torn-open window, but she gave a quick encompassing look at Shelly.

Apparently reassured of her companion's relative well-being, she ran to the fire so fast she scarcely limped, staring down at the burning logs now spattered with glittering dots of molten gold, all that remained of her amulet. "Mother," she whispered.

The ache of loss in her voice made Shelly put an arm about her slim shoulders. "Arielle, it's for the best. That necklace was drawing you away from us."

"Perhaps I'd be happier there, and you'd all be better off."

Shelly turned her to face her. "Nonsense! And no matter what you think, or what the voices that call to you in your dreams say, your mother would not wish such a fate on you."

"How do you know?" Arielle shrugged her off.

"Happy women do not kill themselves," Shelly said with indisputable logic. "By all accounts, your mother was as torn between two worlds as are you."

"We don't know that! My father tells me very little of her."

"I suspect, dear child, he knew little of her inner turmoil. He cannot relay what he does not understand."

With a little moue of distaste, Arielle indicated her agreement. "Father has never been a person of much . . . imagination. I never understood why they wed. Except . . . except . . ."

Shelly nodded. "Yes, the drive to mate is primal, even among 'civilized' men and women."

Arielle looked at her. "Your irony is showing, my dear Miss Holmes. Am I to infer that you don't consider man civilized, or you doubt the strength of the primal need to mate?"

"You, my dear Miss Blaylock, are far too astute." Not wanting to have to answer the question even to herself, Shelly gave Arielle a brisk hug and then set her aside. "We can debate the continuation of the species another time, but one truth is immutable and indisputable: Your father loves you.

For his sake, if not for your own, you must fight this enchantment."

Arielle nodded, still staring at the amulet, and murmured, "I will fight."

"Would you find it . . . comforting if you knew why your mother had . . ."

"Yes! It haunts me, waking and sleeping. That is why I'm so drawn to her. I feel as if my spirit will not rest until hers does. And it's my duty to help her."

Unsurprised, Shelly continued evenly, "Have you any writings of hers? A diary, letters, even instructions to servants?"

Arielle shook her head, despondent again. "My father burned them all. Or so he said when I was twelve and asked for them." Then, going to the ewer on the stand, Arielle dabbed a clean washcloth into the water. Holding Shelly's hand over the bowl despite the woman's protests, she gently, thoroughly cleaned the wound. "I'm sorry you were injured trying to protect me, Miss Holmes."

"Shelly, my dear. Please. And this is nothing. Why, when I was seeking the yeti in Tibet, I fell down a crevasse and almost died. Had it not been for my Sherpa guide . . ."

The sadness faded from Arielle's expression as she listened. Task accomplished, Shelly inwardly cogitated on the immediate challenge. As she recounted the oft-told tale with enough verve to engross Arielle, Shelly eyed the window, thinking of the strange encounter with the lion that was obviously no mere lion.

Who was he? And even more important, why had he come?

Arielle wrapped her companion's hand in clean gauze, smiling at Shelly's tale of how one night, to stave off the bitter Himalayan cold, she drank her Sherpa under the hide table. Meanwhile, totally focused on different trains of thought at the same time, Shelly concluded two things from the current facts as she knew them.

When she'd entered this room, the tabby had been toying with Arielle, but had exhibited no sense of menace. The menace came only when Shelly had destroyed the amulet. But even more important, since the creature could perform a virtually instantaneous feat of astral projection, no bars, no walls, no device of man could keep it out if it wanted to come in.

And this was, apparently, the first time it had appeared to Arielle outside its dream form. It chose to appear first in a nonthreatening, winsome form, as a harmless house cat. And Arielle loved cats.

Therefore the creature came not to frighten or kill Arielle.

It came to seduce her.

And this certainty frightened Shelly more than outright menace, for it would be far harder to protect Arielle from seduction than death.

As the preceding discussion had proved, Arielle was at the transition in her life, as came to all young women, when the touch of a man was the last great mystery that would initiate her into womanhood.

Even as she made Arielle laugh with the funny

tale, Shelly despaired. How could she protect a girl who didn't want to be protected? A girl who seemed to want to embrace her mother's fate rather than escape it?

A long-nosed face popped into Shelly's head.

Ethan. She detested having to ask for help at any time, especially from a man who made her entire world feel off balance. But he was also the smartest man she knew, as familiar with the arcane world as she was, and most important, he had personally known Isis.

It was time, as the Indians used to say, to palaver. For Arielle's sake, she would swallow her pride and ask for help.

And if, in the pit of her stomach, there was a tiny flutter of excitement at the thought of seeing him again, well, Shelly told herself she was hungry. Fighting the spirit world always whetted her appetite.

The next night, human again, Seth waited until the lights dimmed in the window. Now that Arielle was in the room, he could see through her eyes because of their link: The bed was turned back invitingly. He saw the woman kiss his beloved Arielle's cheek and leave the room. He had watched the footmen clumsily try to block the broken window with wooden panels, but they would be easy to shove aside. Seth fingered the golden amulet in his pocket.

The same amulet he'd had made as an exact copy of the one the spirit world had warned him would burn. It had been finished this morning.

Only those golden tokens, passed down from generation to generation, had the power to overcome the distance between the spirit and real world, to allow Isis to communicate with her daughter. When she wore the amulet, Arielle was receptive to the spirit world.

And to both brothers . . .

Seth clenched the amulet even tighter, hoping he could be close to help protect Arielle.

Luke had broken the sacred vows they'd both made upon the transformation rites. For one year, Ra had granted each of them the powers of Mihos, his lion warrior god. One year for the brothers to battle and prove who was strongest. Only the one with the *ka* of purity, only the brother of *maat*, or truth, would survive. Forever. With Arielle, lioness of God, by his side, he would gain the gift every Egyptian pharaoh had squandered lifetimes and fortunes seeking: immortality.

Like their ancestors, Luke was obsessed with the thought of living forever, and the more he killed, the more merciless he became in the quest.

Seth, however, wanted Arielle in the now. Somehow he had to introduce her to the world of the cat and preserve her grip upon the world of man. Together then, in full control, they could defeat Luke.

A new royal dynasty would begin in the loins of the descendant of Cleopatra. A dynasty that would eventually return to the land of the scarab, the land that belonged to the ancient ways. Isis was his ally in this quest.

And the amulet would be her voice.

He whispered the sacred words from the Book of the Dead: "O ye Sons of Keb, overthrow ye the enemies of the Osiris Ani, whose word is truth, and the fiends of destruction who would destroy the Boat of Ra. Horus hath cut off your heads in heaven. . . . The Osiris Ani, whose word is truth, saith: Thou risest up for thyself, O Still-heart! Thou shinest for thyself, O Still-heart! Place thou thyself on thy base, I come, I bring unto thee a Tet of gold, thou shalt rejoice therein."

Closing his eyes and concentrating, Seth began the transformation, calling upon the rite of his ancestors to empower him.

Then, in the form of a civet, small but powerful enough to push the wooden panels aside, Seth climbed a tree next to her window and leaped the short distance to the ledge. Pushing the panel aside with his nose, he dropped down into her room, the amulet about his neck swinging with bright promise.

Chapter Four

At that exact moment, Shelly and Ethan entered the family crypt, lanterns held high in their hands. Even during the day the crypt had a moribund, neglected air. Now, at night, it felt deserted, not a bridge between two worlds, but a void. It was as if even the ghosts of the past had forsaken their ancient task of protecting their living descendants.

As if the good fight had already been lost, and they not only accepted, but embraced the fact that the last of Cleopatra's line would no longer walk the earth as human. She would suffer the fate of her mother and forsake the world of the living for the world of the half-life—neither human nor spirit, with no rest on earth or in heaven.

But Shelly Holmes shook off the foolish whim. She would not give up on Arielle. She had been hired to protect the girl, and so she would. As usually happened, however, no matter how she tried to lecture herself not to get emotionally involved with her clients, for a time they became the only children she would ever have. Thus her vocation had become a calling. No matter the cost, she would protect Arielle.

She stalked into the crypt, the lantern in her hand shaming the shadows into flight.

"Tell me again why we are doing this?" Ethan demanded irritably. "If there had been any evidence here of why Isis was so distraught, do you not think either the earl or myself would have found it by now?"

"His lordship has made a systematic, mostly successful attempt to erase every evidence of his wife's existence. But in doing so he's intensifying Arielle's fixation on her mother's fate, not demystifying it. When we can prove to Arielle that her mother's obsession with cats, and her fascination with all things Egyptian, were partially to blame for her . . . malady, then perhaps Arielle will begin to accept reason again. And even the earl is not ruthless enough to pry open his wife's casket to see if there's something there that would help us determine—"

Midsentence, Shelly stopped before Isis's catafalque, appalled. They both saw it at the same time. The lid, hastily shoved back in place, gapped slightly at one end where the seal had been broken.

Someone had desecrated Isis's tomb.

Shelly and Ethan rushed to the soapstone and hefted the lid aside. Shelly held her breath, expecting that smelly musk of decaying flesh and bones, but an odd, spicy scent was the only warning of the eerie sight that met her astounded gaze.

Shelly stepped back, gasping, almost dropping the lid on Ethan's fingers.

He pulled back in time, dropping his half of the lid, too. "What ails you, woman?" But the heavy stone lid, half-on, half-off the catafalque, lost the battle with gravity and slowly teetered over the side to the floor of the crypt with a loud crash.

The lanterns they had set on the ledge above cast a flickering light down on the casket's contents. Astounded, Ethan also took a step back.

Isis's remains had been mummified.

"Dear heaven," he exclaimed. "Do you know how many members of the Royal Society have been experimenting—to no avail, I might add—with mummification procedures? No one has even come close to preserving bodies as well as the ancients did. Who could have done this? Who has perfected such a sought-after art and yet not come forward to claim credit?"

For once, science was of little interest to Shelly. At this point her sole concern was how and why—and who would benefit from disturbing the poor creature's final rest. A rest she had paid for so dearly.

A couple of decorative gold threads remained in the shrunken earlobes and in the disarrayed lock of black hair still attached to the skull. But the skeletal hands that bore only a pitiable covering of flesh, peacefully crossed on the dried-up bosom, were bare of rings. Ethan had told Shelly that Isis had been buried with all her family jewels. A fitting tribute to a direct descendant of Cleopatra, as Isis had always claimed to be.

"Are you quite certain she was buried with the golden jewels she wears in Arielle's picture?"

"One of her last requests was to be buried with the golden diadem, rings, and earrings of her mother and her mother's mother, leaving the amulet for Arielle," Ethan rasped, his shock turning to rage. "Who would have desecrated her like this and taken her most sacred birthright? If anyone should have them off her cold, dead body, it should be Arielle."

They exchanged a look. Shelly had always found that when the motive was understood, the perpetrator was far easier to find. Whoever had taken this gold wanted it for Arielle. The shape of a lion who was not a lion formed in the shadowy corners of Shelly's worried mind. When she found the human form of that being, she would find the man-creature who'd raided this casket to further nefarious ends she did not yet understand. If anyone had answers, and knew more of Isis, it would be the shape-shifter who was trying to seduce her daughter into the same madness.

Without a word, she turned toward the exit. Moving as one they left the crypt as it was, the lid off Isis's casket, the lanterns on a ledge casting flickering, mournful light on the woman who had once been so lovely.

They hurried back into the house.

After they left, the lanterns flared higher in a

sudden draft of wind, despite the closed door. Shadows danced on the wall, shadows that made the place of the dead seem alive with that most powerful of human ideals: love. For the briefest instant, the withered hands might have clasped in a prayer; the ghastly lips whispered, too, from the Book of the Dead.

But there was no one to see.

And only one with ears to hear.

Inside her chamber, Arielle had just removed her night robe to climb into bed. Her eyes were still moist as she stared at the cold hearth empty of ashes, empty of the barest flecks of gold. Shelly had ordered the hearth cleaned, hoping to spare her pain.

But she was not empty of pain. . . .

Even memories of her mother had been stolen from her by her father's obdurate determination to see that his daughter didn't suffer her mother's obsession. Only now, with the beckoning bed her ship to the netherworld of dreams, was Arielle beginning to recognize the lure and power of the spirit world that Victorian society by turns scorned and embraced. Arielle knew of some fashionable girls who attended séances or card readings, and yet when her own nighttime visions followed her into the day world, she was the one called crazy.

What had her father's world of privilege and high morals gained her? A crippled leg, no memories of the mother polite society considered both amoral and deranged, rejection by the social climbers of the ton, a father who was more like her jailer than her protector. Worst of all, a cold loneliness she could escape only in dreams.

Torn between fury and despair, Arielle yanked the covers back to seek that forgetfulness when she froze, a chill running down her spine. "Mother," she whispered.

"*My child, beware. . . .*" The words came to her as clearly as if they were spoken in her ear, but when she spun in place, she saw nothing but shadows. Closing her eyes to use only her instincts instead of her mind, for an instant Arielle saw her mother clearly.

She was lovely and smiling, looking exactly as she did in the picture, but she seemed wistful, too. Her arms, laden with gold bracelets engraved with the Egyptian cat goddess Bast, reached toward her daughter with a love so powerful, the feeling brought tears to Aielle's eyes. Arielle reached back, but as their fingertips almost grazed, there was a scratching and then a thump at the window.

Her mother disappeared, but her last word lingered in the still, quiet air: "*Beware . . .*"

Arielle blinked back to awareness of her surroundings as the wooden panels blocking the window were scraped aside. She sensed more than heard the creature bound down into the room. She started to turn up the lantern next to the bed when she realized, strangely, that she didn't need it.

She could see despite the almost total blackness of the room.

The animal was small and lithe, and a cat such as

she'd seen only in pictures. What was it called? Ah, yes, a civet. It was indigenous to Africa, as she recalled, and this one couldn't weigh more than forty pounds. It had a black mask and black spots, and a rough, short mane, a frill of fur extending from its neck to its tail. When it was excited, as she recalled, the mane stood erect.

It stood erect now.

Beware, her mother had warned, but of what, or whom? Surely not of this beautiful creature. Arielle had always loved cats, and she was more drawn to them than ever now, in her loneliness.

Totally unafraid, she bent on one knee to pet it. It rubbed against her, and only then did she notice the heavy gold-link necklace looped several times about its delicate neck. She lifted the pendant to squint down at it. It was a bit beyond her newfound night vision to make out the strange markings clearly, but she thought she saw a cat. . . .

"My mother's amulet!" The civet bent its head, as if expecting her to unloop the necklace. "But . . . I don't understand. I thought it burned," she murmured as she put it around her own neck. Were there two amulets? Where did this one come from, and why was it wrapped about the neck of an exotic cat she'd seen only in pictures? Who, or what, was controlling these feline appearances?

Voices below disturbed her train of thought. The cat rubbed its head against her bosom a last time. Lithely, as if it had the strength and agility of a feline twice its size, it bounded out onto the window ledge and from there into a tree. The amulet a comforting weight at her neck, Arielle leaned out to watch it shimmy down the tree without a misstep. It paused at the edge of the grounds, visible only by its glowing golden eyes, looking up at her. For an instant Arielle felt a strange hunger that made her nipples harden and her breath quicken. Then, pausing to mark a tree with its scent, the animal was gone.

By the time the footsteps arrived at the door, Arielle had hidden the amulet under her pillow and had her covers demurely pulled up to her chin. When the knock came, she affected sleepiness. "What? Wh-who is it?"

With a scraping of the key in the lock, her door was flung wide. The earl entered, turning up a gas lamp on the wall and suspiciously surveying the room. Shelly inched past him and ran to the wooden panel that had been pushed down. She looked out the window, then turned to survey her charge with suspicious gray eyes that had their own eeric glow in the gloom. Ethan entered.

For an instant, glowing eyes met glowing eyes. The earl didn't notice the strange battle of wills, for he was too busy looking for signs of a break-in, but Ethan saw. When the earl turned, Ethan hastily flicked the gas lanterns up. Light chased the luminescence away as both gray eyes and blue blinked.

"Who was in here, my dear?" Shelly asked sweetly.

"No one. I had just fallen asleep." Arielle punctuated her lie with a convincing yawn.

"So the panel fell of its own accord? Odd. I saw the footman brace it firmly," Shelly said.

"Perhaps that's what woke me," Arielle said languidly. "How unsafe. Since you're so efficient, would you be a dear and fix it? I'm certain no one can fix things quite as well as you."

Shelly's eyes narrowed at the condescension. Ethan's lips quivered, but when he went to move the panel back in place, Shelly brushed him aside and did it herself. She not only braced it with a chair as the footman had, she picked up a marble bust and weighted the chair. "There you go, right and tight. Sleep well." She stalked out.

Arielle had a feeling Shelly suspected something, but when her father kissed her brow, this time her yawn was genuine. The amulet comforted her, taking away the bitterness and pain of her earlier thoughts to lead her back to the tantalizing prospect of her dreams.

There, in the spirit world, she was happy. There, all things seemed possible.

She was asleep before the door closed.

Down below in the salon, Shelly paced, certain beyond any doubt that the shape-shifter had come calling again. More than likely it had brought the spoils from Isis's raided tomb. But Arielle was far too bright to wear whatever gift she'd received. She'd hide it, fondle it when alone, but its power was no less devastating, whether acknowledged or secret.

The earl lounged back in a chair, watching her

with wearily drooping lids. "My dear Miss Holmes, do you never rest?"

Eyes narrowing, she was about to turn on him and inform him that if he'd been more diligent, perhaps his daughter wouldn't be forming a taste for raw fish, when Ethan stepped between them.

"You hired her for her unusual level of . . . energy, is that not correct, old chap?"

"Yes, but continual exposure to such intensity can be exhausting to a fellow," the earl said petulantly.

Ethan started to speak again, but Shelly silenced him with an imperious wave of her hand. "I can relieve your household of my enervating presence at any time, my dear sir, either at your behest or my own. And leave Arielle's protection to your proven, so-effective vigilance."

For an instant the earl's blue blood pulsed visibly in an angry vein on the side of his neck, but at her unbending gaze he slumped back in his chair with a self-deprecating laugh. "By Jove, no missish airs about you. You do call a spade a spade. Forgive me, my dear lady. It's my frustrations talking. I know you have a care for Arielle and are doing your best. But I feel as if I'm tilting at windmills and exorcising ghosts. Give me a man with a sword or a cutpurse ready to slice off my ear and I know what to do, but these continual forays into a world I've never believed in . . . well, they're more than a mite off-putting to a man of science."

Ethan went to the sideboard and poured a hefty serving of French brandy into a snifter, offering it to the earl. "Do you know what I do when I'm plagued by dismal thoughts of things I should control but cannot?"

"No, what?" The earl took the snifter, twirling the aromatic liquid and staring down into it intently.

"I curse the things I'll never control, like the usurious duties we pay on such niceties as French brandy." Ethan poured another snifter and clicked his against the earl's. "Excellent distraction, almost as effective as cursing that inimitable irritant every man desires but wishes he could live without—the fair sex." The two men grinned, in a perfect amity Shelly found perfectly annoying.

Of course, from the way those sparkling green eyes sliced her way, she knew Ethan fully intended her to be annoyed, if only to distract her and disarm her, so she was careful to keep her smile benign. "I believe men of your stamp would much prefer to control everything in their lives—wine, women, and no doubt song as well."

"You believe wrongly, then. Women who can be controlled are boring. But my fascination with the stronger variety of your sex doesn't mean I don't also find you . . . uh, them—irritating at times."

With a glance that said, *It's mutual,* Shelly nodded a regal good-night to the earl and stalked out. And Ethan Perot, little lordling, had the unmitigated gall to complain about her gender being irritating? If she didn't need his help with Arielle, she'd have sent him packing long ago. He was the biggest irritant she could imagine, a burr under her saddle, a rock in her shoe, a . . .

Shelly blew a deep, calming breath and paused

on the landing to look out at the moon. It was only half-full tonight, but always its lure pulled powerfully at her very soul. If she still had a soul, or a *ka*, as the Egyptians called it . . .

She knew what Ethan was doing. He was riling her anger, quite deliberately inciting her passions so she would be sensitized to him in every way. And dash it, his ploy was working. The strong sexual attraction she felt for him was obviously mutual. She did not understand why he wanted her, because with his money, his title, his intellect, and his charm, he could probably have almost any vapid but stunning creature in the ton.

The fact that he'd fixed his interest on a woman of little money, no birth, and less beauty . . . well, that spoke volumes about either him or her; she was not quite sure which. And she was also not quite sure she wanted to know the answer to that question.

She didn't need the complications of quickened breathing or prickly skin when she was facing the most difficult case of her career. The more Ethan distracted her, the less attention she had for the tiniest details that often made the difference between success and disaster.

What she needed was . . . dirt.

Dirt under her bare feet. Tree branches scraping her hide. She needed to feel alive to Mother Earth and know, as no human ever could, the true power of freedom. Freedom from thought, or woe, or hope or despair for the future. To know nothing but the taste of the night upon the tongue and the scent of the beckoning verdure visible only to her in the darkness.

In her lupine form the night didn't rule her; she ruled the night. And instinctively she knew the creatures she battled felt the same temptation. Who better to catch a shape-shifter than another shape-shifter?

Shelly went to her room to remove her clothes.

Below, Ethan made his good-byes to the earl and exited the house. However, instead of calling for his carriage as he normally did, he looked around to be sure he was unobserved. The guest quarters faced the back lawn, and the earl had informed him he'd given Shelly the best guest suite in the house.

Walking quietly to be sure he was unobserved, he kept to the shadows and the trees, finally reaching what he recognized as the guest quarters from the dark blue curtains. Then . . . he climbed the tree directly opposite Miss Holmes's room. He cursed softly when his foot slipped, and he lurched sideways before catching himself. He heard a tearing sound and knew he'd ripped his tight formal pants at the rear seam. The things he did to prove a theory to himself . . .

Settling comfortably in the tree, careful to remain hidden beneath the leafy canopy, he waited, watching the closed curtains through a pair of opera glasses. Gaslights had come on in the room shortly after he reached his perch, but he was hoping they'd go off and the curtains would be whisked aside.

Shelly was a nocturnal creature. He'd noted that her unusually acute senses seemed to grow razor-keen with nightfall. A couple of times he'd seen her lift her face to the night and sniff the air, somewhat like a dog testing his territory for danger. As ludicrous as the image seemed, it was the only one that fit.

A few times he swore he'd seen her gray eyes glow green in the darkness, but then she'd looked away, as if trying to hide their peculiar radiance. When she looked back, her eyes were gray again.

On more than one occasion he'd also seen her look up and wait for the entrance of someone into a room well before Ethan heard the approaching footsteps. Sometimes she stroked a silken pillow or velvet bolster with an innate sensuality that made his every tiny hair—and another uncooperative appendage—stand on end. From the first time he saw her, Ethan had sensed a wildness beneath her steely will and brilliant mind. Urges she controlled, but with difficulty.

And the more they sparred verbally, the more he longed to touch her physically and learn for himself the source of that wildness. Every man wanted a passionate lover. Beautiful, sensual women were abundant in his world.

But Ethan had tired of their shallowness. He wanted more, a woman who could meet him toe-to-toe and match him in bed and out of it. He'd searched his entire life for a mate of equal intellect, will, and curiosity about the world and never found her.

Until now. But the inimitable Shelly Holmes hid something from them all, a secret that went beyond her natural reserve. He had to solve the mystery of that core of wildness if he were to win her for his own. He knew it as surely as he knew that when they made love, his own world of boring routine would quake to a cataclysmic end. The man who won Shelly Holmes would always be challenged, but he'd never be bored.

As he trained his opera glasses on that tiny, bright crack of light, Ethan thought back to his own quiet investigation of the investigator.

Discreet questioning of Shelly's maid, on loan from Arielle, had yielded the information that sometimes, when the woman took Shelly's nightly sherry to her room, her mistress was gone. The clothes Shelly had worn that day were neatly draped over the clothes stand for her to clean and press, and yet the night rail and dressing gown awaited at the foot of the bed, unworn. But Ethan had not really needed the servants to verify that Miss Holmes was a most unusual woman with even more unusual proclivities.

The question was . . . why? What had made her so unique? He sensed that the answer lay in deducing her nightly activities. Since he much doubted she'd taken the earl for a lover, which could certainly account for her absences, she must be leaving the house. Because of his fear for Arielle's safety, the earl had the entire house bolted at bedtime. It turned into a veritable fortress with key locks for which only he and the housekeeper had copies.

If Shelly were leaving the house, she was doing so through her own window.

His thoughts were interrupted when the lights in her room went out. He held his breath, hoping, waiting, wondering if he could even see her if she did open the curtains, but then the half-moon, which had been hiding behind the clouds, obligingly peeked at just the right angle into the room as the curtains were flung wide.

Through the glasses Ethan could see a tall, white form standing there. She was hidden in the dark shadows, but he saw the pale gleam of skin and realized, with a thrill of excitement, that she was nude. As he watched, she stepped closer to the sill, and he almost dropped the glasses when he caught a good look at her stunning figure from the waist up.

She was well-endowed, her large breasts firm for a mature woman, with rosy areolae. They were so firm he had to assume she'd never been with child. Her skin was so pale and creamy that his mouth watered just for the taste of it. His trembling fingers tightened on the glasses, bringing them slightly more into focus, but when she leaned outside, her arms flung wide to embrace the night, his throat choked up. She threw back her head and sniffed the air.

She was all healthy, sensual woman. A female who enjoyed the night air on her bare skin. There was nothing strange about that.

He was about to lower the glasses, feeling like a Peeping Tom, when her long, powerful arms, lifted to the moonlight, began to change. Ethan blinked rapidly, thinking he was seeing things. He focused again, but the hair on her arms was growing longer as he watched. Her musculature was changing, too, the human arms bending like a canine's leg, and the hands . . . why, they had developed paws.

"Holy Mary, Mother of God," Ethan whispered. And he was not a religious man.

Surely he was imagining things. It must be the moon shining more brightly than ever on that window, tricking him into seeing not a woman, but a, but a . . . Ethan couldn't say the word. While he believed in many strange phenomena, including astral projection, he'd never believed in something so fanciful as . . . as . . .

Ethan pulled the glasses away and rubbed his eyes, but when he looked back, he saw her face changing too. The rounded jaw grew long, with a snout and menacing fangs. The feminine bosom now boasted a powerful rib cage. Numbly, Ethan let the glasses drop, for he no longer needed them.

Then, with the moon shining beatifically on every inch of her now hairy form, as if on a chosen one, the only woman Ethan Perot had ever been drawn to in mind, in body, and in spirit completed her transformation into an enormous wolf. Her greenish-gray eyes luminous in the moonlight, she effortlessly leaped over the windowsill and landed lightly on the grass three stories below.

She shook from head to toe, like a dog shaking

off water, but he sensed she was casting off her frail human form with the act. Then, like a puppy, she rolled over and over on the ground. Her thick brown fur matted with leaves and dirt, she crouched on her forelegs, her hindquarters in the air. Tail wagging, she threw back her head to howl. But curiously, she caught herself, cautiously looking around.

Instead she trotted into the trees, walking right beneath him. He went very still, holding his breath, aware how acute her senses were, but then, with a bound that didn't so much as rustle a single dead leaf or twig, she disappeared into the shrubbery.

Ethan rested his swimming head against the tree trunk. Of all the answers he'd expected when he set out tonight, this revelation was the least likely. A white witch, perhaps, or some other practitioner of the occult, or even a scientist such as himself playing with vials and chemicals, he'd theorized.

But . . . a werewolf? And a werewolf who could think, by the looks of it. A werewolf who could control her changes. Ethan knew the myth. Werewolves were supposedly afflicted only at a full moon, and the moon was only half-full tonight. Furthermore, Shelly Holmes seemed totally unafraid of her deformity. She reveled in it, in fact.

Ethan shimmied down the tree, his thoughts making him unwontedly clumsy so that he skinned his knees and both hands. Was it possible she could control the transformation at will?

It certainly seemed so. When she opened the curtains, she had paused to look around carefully in all directions before she began changing. Such a skill would certainly explain how she could face down what was, by Arielle's garbled report, a lion. Who better to battle a shape-shifter than another shape-shifter?

And yet, Ethan decided as he walked around to the stables with knees so shaky he wondered how he remained erect, if she had these skills, she could well be as unpredictable and potentially dangerous as the creatures she battled.

On a more personal level, he had to wonder what sort of man would willingly bed a were-woman. And yet, the mere memory of her standing there, her arms thrown wide in the empowering glow of the moon, bosom firm and begging for the touch of male hands, made him grow stiff. As he climbed into his carriage, he realized his own hunger was as basic and animalistic as hers. His body, whether his mind approved or not, answered her elemental call with primal needs that made a mockery of rational doubts.

Those needs, empowered as they were by primitive instinct, feared her in neither form. Those needs wanted to touch her in both shapes and learn her without fear. To win that power for their own mutual pleasure.

Leaning weakly against the squabs of his carriage as the yawning coachman took them home, Ethan stared out at the sly grin of the moon. This night had answered the questions that had haunted him since he'd met Shelly, but the answers only raised more tormenting dilemmas.

Should he tell the earl the truth? No, for Shelly could be in danger. They'd likely cart him off to Bedlam anyway, but he could not bear the thought of any creature who reveled so in freedom being penned up and poked and prodded and tested. So what should he do? Was Arielle safe in the protection of such a creature?

Equally important, somehow he must hide his feelings of trepidation mixed with fascination the next time he saw her.

More to the point, if she realized he'd discovered her secret, would she kill him?

Chapter Five

Rupert Blaylock, the Earl of Darby, was a man who believed that if variety was the spice of life, then routine was its glue. Without it, households, empires—and father-daughter relationships—could not function. When his rigidly managed estate operated as he dictated, he accounted life good. Given the threats to that normal routine since Arielle had taken ill, Rupert had formed the habit of reviewing the previous day's events with his butler over morning tea, especially if any were unusual.

The following morning Rupert enjoyed his customary tea and scones, nodding as the butler reported an uneventful night. Arielle, for once, had been sleeping peacefully when her father checked on her, her hand curled under her pillow but her dreams apparently blissful. Miss Holmes had retired early and told her lady's maid she did not need her services, locking her door, and Ethan

Perot had left shortly afterward.

The earl was nodding his satisfaction, hoping things were back to normal, when a stable lad hurried into the dining room, his face pale. "S-sor," he said, dipping a quick, awkward bow before the butler's stern gaze. As he looked around nervously at the fine room, he stammered, "The g-game warden . . . h-he sent me to f-find ye. He says ye m-must come right smart. . . . There be a susp—suspicuous—"

"You mean suspicious, boy?" the butler inquired loftily.

"There be weird goings-on hereabouts last night. This morning we found a deer from your park, its th-throat ripped out and most o' its ass—that is, its rear parts missing. Eaten, they w-was. By some-thin' big. And hungry, by the looks o' it."

"A dog?" The earl folded his papers aside, sigh-ing. So much for peace and quiet.

"A large wolf, I suspect," Ethan Perot said, en-tering the room. He lifted the lid on the teapot to sniff. "Hmmm, Darjeeling, my favorite." He poured himself a cup and commandeered the *London Times* from the earl's pile.

The earl eyed him irritably. "Good morning to you, too. Why not have the entire plate of scones while you're at it?"

"How kind of you. Normally with only two left, I'd leave one, but since you insist . . ." Ethan put the last two scones on his plate and buttered them lavishly. He had the temerity to wink at the staring butler.

"If you can quit stuffing yourself long enough—what were you saying about a wolf?" the earl demanded.

Ethan wiped his mouth on his napkin. "As I left last night, I heard what sounded remarkably like a wolf howling."

"There haven't been wolves this close to London in years, Ethan. Must have been a large dog. We shall examine the carcass."

The boy was squirming from foot to foot. "Sir, there be . . . someat else."

"Yes? What is it, lad?"

"Someat else . . . someone else, was found."

Ethan froze in wiping his mouth and the earl froze with the paper half raised, half lowered. His voice was hoarse. "What? Out with it, dammit!"

While the terrified lad still struggled for words, there came a pounding at the door.

The butler answered and they heard muffled voices shouting.

Ethan twitched the curtain aside. The front drive was jam-packed with carriages, and men in bowler hats swarmed up the stoop. A couple lugged heavy photographic equipment.

The earl sank back into his chair. "Dear God, this is a nightmare."

Ethan stuffed the last of his scone into his mouth. "We don't know yet what's amiss, so don't think the worst. Might I suggest Miss Holmes go with us? Her powers of deductive reasoning are formidable, if indeed there is a body."

"Of course, of course. Send for her, Jennings. And tell those blasted news hounds to get away from my property or I'll call the dogs on them."

The butler exited.

Decisively, the earl put aside his tea cup. "Capital idea, Perot. Miss Holmes is always a woman of unflappable practicality, exactly what we need in this situation. I make no doubt that the whole thing is a tempest in a teapot."

"I hope so, Rupert."

As they readied themselves for the carriage ride, Ethan remembered how "unflappable" the indomitable female had been last night when, in her werewolf form, she'd rolled in the grass like a puppy. He couldn't wait to see her expression when she had to pretend no knowledge of the kill she herself must have made after she disappeared into the bushes. Of the deer, of course.

And if there were a body? Ethan's tiny smile faded in sheer horror at the thought.

No, surely she could not kill a human. And yet, she was a werewolf. Ethan's heart began to knock against his ribs. It was certain she was a dangerous woman to unmask, and perhaps an even more dangerous woman to pursue.

It wouldn't hurt to goad her a bit, to test her mettle, perhaps to even hint that he was suspicious of her nocturnal activities. Even before last night, he'd been determined to delve into the real Shelly Holmes. But since last night, when he'd seen how special her powers really were, he'd formed a veritable obsession with this . . . creature. When he'd awakened this morning after the revelation, he took with him into the daylight strange, erotic dreams. What would it be like to make love to such a being?

Like Shelly, Ethan Perot needed stimulation, challenge. He had to thrive, not merely survive. And Shelly Holmes—in both her personas—was challenge incarnate. If he could win that secret, guarded heart by challenging and stimulating her in turn, then she would never harm him, no matter what form she took. As she'd proved last night by her cautious behavior and measured, controlled transformation, incredibly, Shelly Holmes was master of her malady.

If there was a body, Ethan was confident the killer was someone—or something—other that Shelly Holmes.

Upstairs, in Arielle's room, the "unflappable" Shelly and her charge were arguing as their shared maid removed the breakfast dishes. Arielle had circled an advertisement in red on a London rag sheet her father deplored.

"But we *must* try this. With no written records to follow, and my father's refusal to discuss her, how else can I understand my own mother?"

Shelly glared down at the advertisement. It read: *Mistress of the spirit world Madame Aurora invites the distressed, the grieving, or the curious to join with her in communion with their dear departed ones.* And in smaller type, *Séance in your domicile for a mere ten pounds.*

"Ten pounds! What nonsense," Shelly scoffed.

Arielle pleaded, "I know the dreams I have, the torment I feel in my mother, will be settled only when I understand why she killed herself. And if this . . . Madame Aurora can make her spirit return and answer questions, then I shall be at peace."

"Or perhaps be forced to face the same demons that drove your mother mad." Shelly shoved the paper away. "People who advertise such things are almost always charlatans preying on the grieving."

Arielle's blue eyes filled with tears. "I am grieving. Every day of my life I sense her sadness, her attempt to reach me from the beyond. But something stands in her way. Something I have to understand."

When Shelly stared at her, unyielding, that stubborn set returned to Arielle's mouth. "I am going to do this, even if I have to . . . to rent a room somewhere disreputable."

"And what do you think your father will say of this?"

"What he always says. No. But as usual he will change his mind."

Arielle sat down before her dressing table to finish her toilette herself. She made a dismissive movement with her hand. "You may go."

Shelly's eyes narrowed and, for the merest instant, glowed grayish green in the shadows, but then she swiveled on one heel and exited. As soon as Shelly was gone, Arielle went to her closet and removed her hooded cape of emerald green lined with white silk. It was not a conservative garment, but it was the only one she had that bore a hood.

She was not going to waste time with missives or messengers.

She was going to find and engage this Madame Aurora herself. Arielle folded the cape into a square and stuffed it inside her most capacious handbag, but it was still a tight fit. On rare occasions, her father allowed her to go to the apothecary for powders to help her sleep and for beauty aids, for she'd told him she trusted no one but herself to select them. Last night she'd poured the last of her powder into her cold tea and stirred it up, hoping a hungry scullery maid didn't decide to partake of her dinner remains.

Arielle looked at the tiny address marked on the advertisement, where checks were to be sent. It was, interestingly enough, near the apothecary. She could sneak out the back of the shop and walk there herself. Her heart beating fast and joyously, she picked up her mother's tiny portrait and traced the vibrant features so similar to her own. For the first time in a long time, she felt positive and hopeful that in healing her mother, she could heal herself.

"Mother," she whispered. "Come to me. Show me how to help you." She patted the amulet in a hidden pocket

It was even easier to leave the house than she'd expected. She'd gone below to find Shelly, her father, and Ethan piling into a carriage and careening out of the paved drive toward the estate's park. With no difficult questions to answer, it had been a simple matter to call for the town carriage and coachman.

She was totally unaware of a rider on a massive black stallion following her from a discreet distance. Or of the glint of a looking glass trained on the carriage window, or that when the coachman stopped before the apothecary's establishment, the black Arabian stallion also stopped. A man with a distinctive lion-headed cane dismounted and ducked into a doorway to watch her reach her destination.

When she entered, he entered.

As was her usual habit, she browsed the latest exciting finds from Paris and Brussels, but her selections were more cursory than normal. When, her arms laden with purchases, she went toward the man taking coins at the front of the shop, she stepped on the shiny black shoe of a gentleman reaching toward a top shelf.

She stumbled a bit, tipping the top canister of perfumed powder in her precarious pile. It fell with a clatter, showering them both with scented powder. She sneezed, the packages wobbling more in her arms as she shifted her weight accidentally onto her bad leg.

The packages were removed and her arm was braced by a hand in a gentleman's white glove. She looked up, way up, her eyes watering, to see a very handsome and familiar face. "Mr. Taub! Forgive my clumsiness. I was just in a tearing hurry and did not see you moving into my path."

Setting the packages down on a vacant shelf, Seth Taub removed a pristine linen handkerchief, complete with the initials ST in ornate script, and used it to dust down her clothes. Gently, gallantly, avoiding her most intimate areas.

The light stroke of the fabric was still pleasurable, sending tingling heat to her nerves everywhere it brushed. She stared up at him, tongue-tied. She had been miffed at his officiousness at the ball, but secretly she'd hoped to one day see both him and his blond rival again. And here he was, patient as she virtually accosted him with feminine fripperies. Her cheeks reddened. No wonder he saw her as a child to be protected.

"Nonsense, my dear Miss Blaylock. Had I not planted my great foot in your path, we would not both be smelling of lilacs." He leaned down toward her, his golden eyes glinting like the sunlight winking slyly on the diamond-paned windows. He sniffed very discreetly, his breath stirring the hair at her temples. "Though it smells much better on you than on me."

He used the kerchief to brush off his own white-spattered clothes, grimacing his distaste.

This most confident of gentlemen, so confident he tended to make her feel painfully awkward, was still subject to typical male predilections such as scorn of female cosmetics. This indication that he was, despite his uncommonly powerful presence, after all, just a man, somehow tickled her own sensibilities.

She grew bold enough to tease, "You should try

the bath scents next. They leave one wondrously soft and fragrant."

His startled gaze leaped back to her face.

When she realized the suggestiveness of her innocent remark, she went magenta this time. "Oh, dear, oh, my, I am so mortified," she stammered. "I did not mean . . . that is . . ." She trailed off with a gasp when he covered her mouth with a fingertip. When had he removed his gloves? The slight contact jolted through her like a lightning bolt, firing her lips with heat.

"Shhh . . . don't apologize. The image of you in the bath shall warm me for a very long time."

She felt totally at sixes and sevens, not sure where to look. It wasn't safe to stare at that strong mouth with the sensual dip in the center, for she wondered what it would feel like pressed against her own. It wasn't safe to fix her gaze on his broad chest, for she so longed to feel it against her cheek. But when her eyes went lower still, imagining . . . She knew she must be purple now. Finally she bowed her head and stared down, since the only safe spot in the store, with such an enticing object looming in her path, seemed to be her own feet.

That masterful fingertip tilted her chin back up. He lowered his gleaming dark head until his mouth was even with her ear. "You are delectable. Every time I smell lilacs I will remember this moment."

His breath tickled, so close did he come to kissing her.

But then he set her aside and put on the charming smile of a gentleman as he propped her boxes in one arm, complete with a fresh canister of powder, and offered her his other arm in support.

It was then she noticed his cane, which he had hooked over the arm carrying her packages. He led her toward the counter, where the clerk was eyeing them suspiciously. She tried to lean around to see the strange cane more clearly. It looked as if the golden head were in the shape of a lion.

When he set the packages down on the counter, she saw clearly that the ornate carved head was indeed in the shape of a lion. While the clerk totted up the purchases, she ran an admiring fingertip over the carving. "Your family crest?"

"You might say that." He offered the cane to her. She examined it. "You like it?"

"Yes. I love cats."

"I've heard that about you. So do I, as a matter of fact."

They shared a smile so warm the clerk had to clear his throat—twice—to get their attention. After Arielle paid the bill, she asked the clerk to keep her purchases behind the counter until she returned for them.

Then, looking outside to be sure the coachman still awaited atop the carriage, she offered her hand to Seth Taub. "It was most enjoyable seeing you again. Please excuse me, but I have another errand to run."

"May I assist you?"

"Oh, no, this is something of a rather private nature."

He raised a curious brow at that but was far too well-bred to probe. "At least let me walk you to your destination."

She hesitated. She saw no harm in his walking her to the flat, which was very close by. She nodded.

Offering his arm again, he turned toward the entrance, but she tugged on him, leading him to the back. "My coachman is out front."

His brow went even higher at this. "I apprehend you don't wish to be seen by him entering this . . . this . . ."

"Flat. I wish to retain someone's services."

"Someone not necessarily respectable. This would explain your caution."

The quickness of his brain, especially combined with such a handsome form, was both appealing and off-putting. Removing her hand from his arm, she exited before him, finishing evenly, "She lives close by at 221 Drury Lane."

They stepped outside the back door into a narrow street that stank of garbage. Two urchins digging in a refuse pile turned to look at her. Their faces were wan, hungry, their eyes old far beyond their years. They flinched back as if from a blow as she and Seth approached.

Arielle tried to force herself to walk by, knowing she had just enough money to pay Madame Aurora for the séance. She had heard London was filled with such waifs, children with no parents, no homes, and no hope. But this was the first she'd seen any of them. Being a recluse had its advantages, as she was beginning to realize.

A gentle tug on her arm stopped her. Seth pulled a couple of bills from his pocket and walked slowly over to the waifs, his movements deliberate and unthreatening. "Here, lads, eat well tonight."

They warily looked from the money, to him, to the pretty lady, and down both ends of the alley, as if suspicious of the price of such beneficence. Two dirty paws reached toward the bills. A noise down the alley startled them and they jerked back, but it was only the closing of a door.

Seth smiled gently, and for the barest instant Arielle thought she saw moisture haze his magnetic golden eyes. "Come, lads, it's not often you get offered good English pound notes. I promise not to bite."

Startled, Arielle looked more closely at the money. Indeed, he held out to them a pound apiece, probably more money than they saw in half a year. Snatching the bills, they bolted, obviously afraid he'd change his mind.

But when safely out of reach, they both stopped, dipped a little bow as they tugged greasy, bedraggled forelocks, and then disappeared, lost among the invisible poor.

Arielle felt a great rush of admiration for this strange man. She tried to imagine any other male of her acquaintance being so kind, even her own father. Her mind boggled. When Seth offered his arm again, leading her out onto Drury Lane, she found her voice huskier than was usual. "Why did you give them so much?"

"Because they have so little." Golden eyes beamed

down into hers, as golden as the sun, and for an instant she felt a stab of familiarity. She'd seen these eyes before and she wasn't thinking of the night she'd met him at the ball. He'd been so austere and proper then, very different from the way he was now, beaming down at her with a warmth and humanity that drew her like tide to moon.

The memory teased at the back of her mind as they stopped outside a bleak, unmarked flat, but since he'd been counting the numbers, she knew this must be right. "I'll be only a moment," she murmured, filing that disturbing familiarity into the back of her mind for later perusal.

But when she rapped the tarnished brass knocker, he only held more tightly to her other arm. "I am not going to allow you to enter this place alone."

Arielle stiffened. "I do not recall asking your permission."

"You are an innocent. You know nothing of how cruel the world can be."

"You, sir, do not strike me as a protector of innocents."

"Oh, yes? Do you see anyone else showering orphans with pound notes?"

They were talking about very different types of innocence. Arielle didn't know much about this man, but she'd heard of his reputation with women. And any man who could ooze charm one minute and danger the next was not a fitting protector of women of good character.

However, he might be an excellent protector of women off on foolish quests. Arielle eyed the grimy windows and the generally disreputable flats around them. She nodded shortly. "Very well, you may accompany me," she said loftily.

"Thank you, your highness."

Her gaze jumped back to his face. Oddly, there was no sarcasm in his tone. He gave her the title as if she'd earned it, long ago in a past she didn't remember. It was almost as if he had called her by that title and she had worn a crown. That sense of familiarity tugged at the back of her mind again, harder this time, but she could not give it precedence until she'd accomplished her goal.

She rapped the door knocker louder, and finally steps approached. The door was flung open. A rat-faced man stood there, his ugly features emphasized by flamboyant crimson pantaloons and a green velvet vest over a beaded shirt. He put his hands together and gave an obsequious bow. "May I help you?"

His accent was odd. He had dark hair and dark skin and had the look of the East about him. His shoes even curled at the tips like Aladdin's slippers.

"I wish to see Madame Aurora," Arielle said, pulling the circled ad from her reticule. "I'm here to inquire about engaging her services."

"Excellent, excellent. Please, come into the parlor and I will tell her you are here."

He led them into a lush parlor totally at odds with the building's derelict exterior. The room was filled with expensive furniture of eastern influence. Griffin-winged tables, plush round divans, and an enameled, embossed demitasse set on a table inlaid with Moorish designs of moons and stars.

Seth set her packages down and looked about, his mouth curving. "All we need is the Turkish water pipe and a belly dancer."

"At your request, I can supply both," came a heavily accented voice from the door.

They both turned toward the entrance. What Madame Aurora lacked in breeding, she made up in bulk. She was an enormous woman whose size was emphasized by the diaphanous garments she wore. She had rings on every finger, rings that sparkled with the pure fire only precious stones emitted. Her eyes, buried in rolls of fat, were still piercing and observant, of a brown so dark they looked like onyx.

Her calling had made her prosperous, obviously. Arielle also hoped her success meant she was genuine in her ability to commune with the spirit world. Arielle cleared her throat, wondering why she felt so nervous. She was here more or less upon invitation. "M-Madame Aurora, I w-wish to discuss with you the possibility of a s-séance."

Arielle felt Seth's immediate wariness. His hand, still on her arm, jerked slightly, and his body went stiff. He frowned down at her as if to dissuade her, but his disapproval only made her more determined.

She continued, "I'm having dreams, strange and tormenting, of my mother and of other, ah, figures who call to me and try to get me to join them."

"Join them, my dear? Where?" Madame Aurora waved a chubby hand toward a divan.

Seth sat down, patting the seat beside him, but Arielle chose a round ottoman instead. She was not certain why she felt such a fierce need to do this on her own, but at the moment she didn't question the reason; she only yielded to the impulse. "Somewhere that feline creatures hold sway. One is good, the other evil, but I cannot tell which is which. I can see them, but they are masked as lions."

Seth had gone perfectly still now as he listened.

Attuned to him, even with her back turned, Arielle sensed that for some reason her nocturnal visions were of supreme interest to him. Why, she could not fathom, but that too would have to wait for later pondering. She rushed to finish, her heart pounding so hard she could scarcely hear her own husky voice. "And always my mother is there, trying to talk to me, to warn me, to show me the truth and the light. But I cannot hear her. I want you to help me hear her." Arielle pulled the ten pounds from her purse and offered the money.

Madame Aurora rose and set her great bulk down on the generous ottoman next to Arielle, adroitly pocketing the fee in one voluminous pocket of her pantaloons. "Poor child. Sometimes the veil between this world and the beyond has to be torn before it can be opened. Are you of strength enough to hear this truth? Your mother may not be the one calling to you, after all. Perhaps it is someone else. Someone you know and are meant to follow, though you do not realize it yet."

Those gleaming dark eyes glimmered in Seth's direction but were as quickly back upon Arielle's troubled face. The woman gently tucked a loose tendril of hair behind Arielle's ear. "I accept. When do you wish to engage me?"

"Tomorrow night."

Madame Aurora went to a desk and removed what appeared to be a map. But when she spread it out, Arielle saw, even from her sitting position, that it was a guide to the constellations, more of a work of art with gilt engraving and lovely blue and purple stars and yellow moons. Each calendar month showed the phases of the moon and the positions of the stars.

"Hmmm . . . Jupiter rising and Mercury in retrograde. Not a propitious time."

"Please. I cannot wait much longer." Arielle's eyes filled with tears. "She needs my help. I can feel her calling to me. Every night."

Sighing, Madame Aurora put back the guide. "As you wish. But I cannot promise you will like what you hear."

Arielle rose, her nervousness gone, her doubts washed away by a cascade of relief. "Thank you, thank you!" She gave the woman her address, they settled on the time of nine o'clock, and then she and Seth were at the door.

As the manservant ushered them out, Seth pointed at a picture of Cleopatra holding an ankh, the Egyptian symbol of eternal life. "Lovely portrait, that." Arielle turned to look.

Indeed, the painting was titled, *Cleopatra, Eter-*

nal Ruler of Egypt, Goddess of the Underworld. Arielle moved closer to study it, feeling a chill slither down her spine like a snake.

The goddess had shiny dark hair, deep blue eyes, and a certain tilt to her chin that was very familiar to Arielle. She saw it whenever she looked into a mirror.

While she was occupied staring at the painting, Seth put a hand in his pocket and then he dropped a gold coin in Madame Aurora's hand. Black eyes met golden, both showing varying degrees of satisfaction, and then Seth took Arielle's arm and escorted her outside.

As he walked her back to the apothecary, through the shop to her coachman, he was silent, seeming somewhat somber as he gave the coachman the packages. While the servant loaded them in back, Seth said quietly, out of the man's earshot, "I will be there by eight thirty to help you prepare."

"No, it will be difficult enough to convince my father to allow me to do this without . . . without . . ."

"A rake present? Rake I might be, but I have one sterling quality in such matters that your father lacks." He brushed that vagrant tendril back behind her ear, his touch sending a shiver of pleasure through her from her scalp to her toes. "I believe in the spirit world. If your mother is trying to contact you, please let me be there to help you hear her."

Arielle's eyes darkened as she looked up at this man. Even as her instincts warned he was not to be trusted, that there was a reason those golden eyes seemed so familiar, she found herself nodding permission. "I shall be honored to have your assistance."

Seth bowed his shining dark head to kiss her hand. She longed so to brush that thick hair away. He had, after all, already breached the rules of polite society by touching *her* cheek and hair. But Arielle was never overly troubled by society's niceties. Far more troubling was her instinctive knowledge that too much contact with this man, whether physical or emotional, would exact a toll on her she was only beginning to understand. He was not safe for women of good character, but it was not his rakehell reputation she feared.

When he rose again, his smiling golden eyes fixed on something in the distance behind her. The smile vanished instantly, replaced by a hatred so complete and vicious that she was shocked. She blinked and turned to look, seeing only a tall man with golden hair striding rapidly away.

When she looked back at Seth, he was smiling again. "Until tomorrow."

As he stepped back and waved, Arielle lowered the curtain so she wouldn't have to see him being swallowed up in the crowded streets. Without the distraction of his presence, she was aware that, despite his powerful physical charisma, it was his inner life that drew her so strongly. They were surprisingly alike. They were both solitary creatures, drawn to the spice of the unknown. They were both passionate and sensual.

She already felt a strange bond with him, and

she'd met the man only twice. It was thus dangerous to her state of mind to have him at the séance, for she would be at her most vulnerable.

But somehow she knew she had no choice. Somehow she knew he was meant to be there. Even if she denied him, he would find a way.

Destiny was gaining on her, as surely as Jupiter was rising and Mercury was in retrograde. And just as surely, she also knew that Seth's blond counterpart, the gentler, kinder Luke, would also be there.

She only hoped that Madame Aurora truly could not only call up the spirit world, but help her navigate its treacherous waters. Somewhere in those misty dreams lay the truth that would comfort her mother's troubled soul and illuminate her own dark wanderings between two worlds.

No matter the danger, she had to learn that truth, for only it could set Isis free.

Comforted for the first time in weeks, she leaned her head back against the squabs and closed her eyes, sleep drifting over her like a peaceful blanket.

Chapter Six

The minute she was out of sight, Seth hurried
through the crowd, using his cane to brush people
aside, but by the time he reached the shadowy entrance where he'd seen Luke spying on them, his
brother was gone.

Had Luke been close enough to hear his conversation with Arielle? Did he know of the séance?

It was not in Seth's interest—hell, it was not in
Arielle's best interests—for Luke to be there, too.
Luke didn't just want Arielle for his mate. He
wanted to own her, to take her feminine power and
turn it back upon her in subjugation. And if her
mother were indeed trying to contact her, Arielle
would be in thrall and unable to defend her far
weaker psychic abilities from Luke's onslaught.
Seth's hand tightened on the lion head of his cane.

No matter what, he had to be certain Luke was
barred from attending, in whatever form he fa-

vored. The two of them had chosen far different paths to transformation, taking their inherent skills and characteristics as boys into the feline world with them. Just as they'd been as brothers, Seth was direct, demanding, and able to persuade with the sheer power of his personality. Smaller, gentler Luke, with his angelic looks and rotten heart, was guile incarnate. Seth believed that his brother had not yet perfected the form of the lion, which was Seth's own second skin now, though Luke's ability to astral-project and turn into mist was stronger than Seth's.

Remembering his younger brother as he'd been when they were growing up, rambling about the countryside in Devon, where their father was a minor baron and their mother a student of history and psychic phenomena, Seth felt a tinge of sadness at what he knew he'd ultimately have to do to win Arielle for his own.

But he had no choice but to kill or be killed. Only one Mihos could survive.

For all his laughing demeanor, Luke Simball was as amoral and pitiless as the cats he favored, a lethal predator upon young women. If he succeeded in seducing Arielle to his dark ways, Arielle could well end up like one of the young women Luke toyed with and cast aside.

As Seth crossed the street, the front page of one of the more strident London dailies drifted by on a gust of wind, plastering itself to a window. The garish headline ran: *Fourth Body Found at the Earl of Darby's Estate!!!* And in smaller print, the article continued: *Is there a new Jack the Ripper afoot? Attractive young females of straitened circumstances are dying in the most horrid ways. . . . peer recruits world-famous detective Miss Shelly Holmes to protect his daughter. Scotland Yard is mum.*

Staring out the carriage window at the parkland moving past, "world-famous detective Shelly Holmes" felt rather small and defensive, like a sparrow, in fact, under the eagle eyes of Ethan Perot. She felt a difference in him this morning. He'd always been intent upon her, as if she riled his deepest curiosity, but now she felt that acute analytical ability focused with deadly accuracy.

What had set him off? Shelly was mystified, and since she was very seldom mystified, she was all the more uncomfortable for it.

When they stopped in a corpse of trees not far from the dirt road that bisected the earl's small parkland, Ethan leaped out first and held the door for her, unctuous as a butler. "Careful of your step, Miss Holmes."

Pretending not to see his offered arm, she leaped down the two carriage steps in a bound, glad she'd defied convention this morning by wearing her breeches. She'd intended to ride, not analyze dead bodies. However, as was her wont, she kept her inner turmoil private with the ease of long practice. There had seldom been a confidante in the life of Shelly Holmes. And the fact that this lord of the long nose obviously aspired to that role made her all the more determined to keep him at arm's length.

Thus, the moment she stepped down and smelled that ghastly but all too familiar smell, Shelly took care to keep her expression objective. She would not have Ethan Perot, or even her employer, know how much she hated the mingled odors of decaying flesh and the last defecation of a body cleansing itself as if in preparation for its final journey. No matter how many murders she probed, she never got used to the stench that betold, in this case, the final terror and passing of a life too young.

What a terrible waste.

Only when they grew close enough to see a pitiably small lump of what appeared to be ripped fabric and piled leaves did the two lords remove their kerchiefs and cover their noses. Appalled, Shelly came to an abrupt stop. She'd expected the gory condition of the body, but not the mangled condition of its surroundings—and of any clues the perpetrator might have left.

Innumerable boot prints had tromped the decaying leaves into the mud. The young woman's body had been turned over, for the copious blood staining everything around it was absent from the patch of earth next to her. The scene had obviously been well visited by the gamekeeper, numerous lackeys, perhaps even the constable, who had already alerted Scotland Yard.

"Why was I not told immediately?" Shelly demanded, glaring at the earl.

He removed the kerchief from his nose to retort, "I was not informed myself until this morning. My household is run with order, and this . . . this . . ."

"Desecration?" Ethan supplied helpfully, his tone nasal as he kept his kerchief over his nose.

"Precisely. My estate manager thought it best to keep it quiet until we knew more, but an overeager stable lad told a neighboring estate's head hostler, and he told—"

"I quite understand." With supreme effort, Shelly managed not to add, *They'd rather give you the illusion of order than deal with your temper tantrums.* She held Ethan and the earl back with a commanding look and an outstretched arm. "Stop here. I need to examine the manner of death before this area is disturbed even more."

Shelly adroitly managed to step into the earlier boot prints as she circled the body, seeking clues. Blood was everywhere, blackened now and drawing flies. It spattered the leaves in a ten-foot half circle around the still form, the marks close together and resembling a starburst farthest from the body, then fainter closer to where the poor girl lay.

Shelly had seen such marks before. Indeed, she'd made them herself many times, albeit only in animals. Shelly pulled a small notebook from her pocket and began to write, but Ethan held up a larger notebook.

"Please, dear lady, allow me." He poised a pencil above his notebook.

When she eyed him doubtfully, he said, "It will make you more efficient and me of more use. We both are working to the same end: saving Arielle."

Since Shelly could hardly argue that point, especially with her employer nodding his approval, she grudgingly agreed and continued her examination. Gesturing toward the odd starburst pattern of blood sprayed in a half circle on the adjacent trees, she said judiciously, "At least one artery was severed, likely two, and this person was young and healthy."

Ethan merely wrote, unsurprised, but Rupert expostulated, "How in the name of heaven could you possibly know that? You have not looked at the body yet."

Shelly continued her examination, not even glancing at him. "Only a severed artery expels its contents violently enough to leave such a pattern. At roughly waist height and head height, it was probably the carotid artery of the neck and the femoral artery of the upper thigh that were punctured. The extreme distance"—Shelly stepped off ten feet—"of the spray marks indicate young, healthy arteries. According to the latest medical theories, the aged usually have arteries that move blood sluggishly, though modern science does not yet know why."

Rupert Blaylock, Earl of Darby, was for once in his life speechless.

Ethan was not. "Bravo, dear lady."

Shelly said through her teeth, "The next time you call me dear lady, especially at such an inopportune time, I shall . . . I shall do you an injury."

"How intriguing. May I inquire which body part you most want to turn your attention to?" He looked at her, eyes twinkling. "Just so I'm at my best, you understand, should you decide to subject me to the same exhaustive examination."

This time, for her sanity, Shelly pretended deafness and concentrated on her task. Very carefully, stepping into the many footprints of the earlier "investigators," Shelly approached the body. She knelt and gently turned the remains back over, as if in death she could offer the poor creature the kindness she should have had in life. The head flopped unnaturally as she turned the corpse, falling sideways like a rag doll's.

The earl gagged and turned away, but her acute senses heard Ethan scribbling as she intoned, "Female. Blond. Nineteen to mid twenties, I should say. No taller than five feet." Shelly's voice got stronger as her anger grew. She checked the nails. "Broken fingernails encrusted with blood. She fought back."

"She was the daughter of the village apothecary," the earl said, his voice muffled in his kerchief. "But what was she doing in my parkland? Surely not poaching."

"An assignation, perhaps?" Ethan suggested.

"She had no suitors that I'm aware of. Her father kept her under his thumb." The earl's eyes misted. "I have to tell him. And since it happened on my land, I'll make remuneration to him."

"Poor mite." Ethan's soft tone almost brought tears to Shelly's eyes, but she controlled herself and glared at the earl.

"Money does not solve everything, sir. Besides, other than the fact that this happened on your estate, how do you know there's any connection between this poor unfortunate girl and Arielle?"

The earl backed away a step. "I said no such thing."

"But you were thinking it." She turned back to her work, too busy to wonder over much about the strange, speculative look Ethan gave her.

"As we supposed, her carotid artery was severed." Missing, more like. The bite mark on her neck was so huge and savage, the entire side of her neck was gone. That explained why the blood marks faded so quickly. The attacker must have thirsted for her blood and gone to the richest source immediately. The ragged clothes were torn and bloody, but it was easy to see that the second bite had indeed severed the femoral artery of her left leg.

Again Shelly saw the imprint of very large fangs. For an instant she was haunted by a fear that her transformation last night had not been as controlled as she'd thought. The size of these fangs was similar to her own in lupine form. But her leaping heart slowed in her breast when her keen gaze speared the darkness and saw antlers a good fifty feet away, the remains of the deer she'd killed and feasted on.

No, whoever had killed this girl had done so after she'd returned to her room. She wondered if the location of the murder was itself a challenge to her. But who knew of her abilities, save that cat creature she'd faced?

No one. Redoubling her efforts, Shelly arrayed the body as decorously as possible and began to reconstruct the murder by the clues of the footprints left behind in the soft ground. It was difficult, even with her experience, because of the contamination of the crime scene.

Here the entrance of hobnailed boots, probably the gamekeeper, there a more refined boot print with a higher heel—the constable perhaps. She'd defined several other marks, all made by small, coarse clogs that probably belonged to the stable boys, before she spotted what she was expecting.

A paw print near a tree.

There, almost obscured by a pile of leaves, as if someone had deliberately tried to cover it, was a shallow depression of a very large paw print. Again like Shelly herself in her lupine persona, the cat had moved much more lightly than the size of the print would indicate. But curiously, when Shelly tried to track the print, she found no others. She looked up at the tree.

Gashed deep into the oak's dark bark was a fresh scratch, such as a claw would make. And very near the scratch, caught on a splinter, was a coarse wisp of hair. Deep golden hair.

Hair the color of the great lion she had encountered. Shelly pocketed the evidence, but Ethan, damn his watchful eyes, caught her.

"I say, dear lady, how can you expect me to keep an accurate account of this examination if you hide things from me?"

Reluctantly, Shelly showed them the tuft of fur.

The earl turned it over in his hands. "Coarse."

Ethan snatched it. All mirth drained from his face as he handed it back and made a notation. "Lion fur found at the site of the killing."

Blanching, the earl expostulated, "How could you know from such a small sample? It could be a dog, or a small alley cat—"

"Both have softer fur," Ethan disagreed. "We shall not know for certain until we compare the tuft under a microscope to a known sampling, but I have hunted in Africa and touched a lion's pelt before."

While they argued, Shelly was climbing the tree.

Ethan blinked up at her through the leaves. "What the deuce are you doing now?"

Shelly tracked the claw marks, trying to get an idea of the size of the animal by placing her hands on each mark. She could not stretch far enough. The chill of intuition froze into certainty. A lion very similar to the one that had faced her the other night, at least of similar size and color, had made these marks.

Shelly traced the path of claw marks to the end of a branch and looked down. Again, a pile of leaves had been raked over the evidence, but when she dropped down and gently pulled the leaves away one by one, she saw . . . a man's footprint. A bare footprint, also lightly imprinted. When she tried to track it further, she found a sweeping mark where the footprints had been erased by a branch, no doubt. It led to a rock outcropping and disappeared.

Ethan said over her shoulder, "Well? What has that acute brain of yours concluded?"

Shelly longed to set him in his place with the dire nature of her conclusions, but she had no interest in frightening the earl even more, or perhaps stirring up the press if they heard rumors of her suppositions. Shelly said only, "A brutal murder of a young woman was committed here last night. Mostly likely by a large feline, perhaps a lion."

"And?" the earl and Ethan said simultaneously.

"The other facts I will convey when I have more evidence." And had figured out how to safeguard Arielle from the lure of the cat-man who wanted to entice her into his dark world.

For Shelly had seen enough to draw one definite conclusion from this chain of evidence.

A lion went up this tree.

A man came down.

Ethan arched an eyebrow and smiled as he put the notebook back in his capacious greatcoat pocket. "Keep your cards close to your chest, if you will."

"Is there any other way to play?"

"Not for the two of us." His green eyes absorbed the sight of her.

She looked away, but her gaze snapped back to his at his next comment.

"I call your bluff, my very dear lady. If you wish to find further evidence to substantiate your theory before you tell all, what do you make of the remains of that deer a mere fifty feet away?"

Shelly didn't need to make anything of it. She'd killed it herself last night. As a werewolf.

He continued, "Do you suppose the same creature killed it? Or perhaps there are two very large, very dangerous animals loose in the earl's parkland. I examined both sites earlier, you see."

Kicking herself metaphorically, Shelly looked at his boots. A slight heel. The expensive footwear was his. "Did you also contact the newspaper?"

He scowled. "Of course not. While your conclusions were more thorough than my own, they are exactly the same. This poor child was ripped apart by a large lion. But did the same creature kill the deer?"

Challenge, pure and direct, gleamed from his eyes now. He swept an arm before him, much as she'd done with him on occasion, and invited her to walk deeper into the trees.

As she did so, she could not escape the uncomfortable notion that she was also walking deeper into a trap.

Luke Simball felt Seth long before he saw him. Instinctively he began the transformation. His hands formed into claws, his pupils narrowed, and a tail began forming.

However, since he sat alone at a table in his club surrounded by gentlemen, supping on perfectly sautéed Dover sole—which he would have preferred raw—he marshaled his natural urges. The tail receded and his hands, human again, used knife and fork with perfect etiquette.

When Seth appeared in the large bay window, walking fast, his cane over his arm, Luke was prepared. He merely cut another bite of sole while he waited, his expression totally neutral. Despite the artful show of indifference, however, now the sole tasted like grass—with a liberal peppering of hatred to add spice.

That was a familiar taste. And an addictive one.

He knew why Seth was here. He'd been spotted after following Seth and Arielle to the psychic's abode. Though he had not been close enough to hear the subsequent conversation between the two, a few pound notes had loosened the fat woman's tongue. The only question remaining was whether he should wangle an invitation, as Seth no doubt had, from Arielle, or simply sneak into the room in his alter ego. It was untenable that Seth, with all his ferocity, ruthlessness, and guile, should be sequestered with the woman they both hungered for at such a vulnerable time in her psychic development.

Luke had taken one look at the fat woman and known that however laughable her style of dress and affectations, she was a genuine channeler to the arcane. If she succeeded in calling up Arielle's mother, Luke needed to be there. He had felt more than once that the spirit of Isis did not look kindly upon him.

A shadow loomed above him. The room quieted as gentlemen of all stripes and status paused in their smoking, drinking, and talking to watch the coming confrontation. No one knew they were brothers, but all of London branded them new-comers who were accounted to be in competition with each other in all things. Cards. Women. Money. Wagers abounded on who would first challenge whom to a duel.

If they only knew, Luke thought wryly, wiping his mouth as he looked up at Seth's angry face. The duel had already begun. No gentlemanly conduct or seconds would regulate it.

Luke waved a polite hand to the chair opposite. "Really, old fellow, you shouldn't loom above one like a mighty oak in need of trimming. It's most disconcerting."

Seth remained standing, though he kept his voice low, obviously well aware of the surreptitious stares. "Do not make the mistake of coming to Arielle's séance. Consider yourself warned."

Luke wiped his mouth. "Ah, subtlety. Your strong suit."

Seth leaned down over Luke, his hands flat on the table, so only Luke could hear. "I prefer honesty over malice, deceit, and treachery, unlike some."

"Did I deny knowing about the séance?"

"No, but only because you knew I saw you skulking about."

His appetite totally gone now, Luke shoved back his half-full plate. "Odd how the patterns of the past always drive the vicissitudes of the present."

"I'm trying to play fair in deference to the familial connection between us, but—"

"Not on my account, old chap. Playing fair was never part of our relationship, even when we were boys. To the winner go the spoils."

Seth straightened again, and for an instant as he stared down at his brother, Luke saw a flicker of sadness in his golden eyes. A year ago, even six months ago, something instinctive in Luke might have responded. But now it was too late. Now Luke's instincts were those of the cat. Predatory. Ruthless. Brother or no, Luke wanted to take Seth's neck between his hands and squeeze, to bite the sensitive point where brain stem met spinal column and . . .

Claws popped out of his fingertips. Folding his hands in his lap, Luke looked down so Seth couldn't see his changing pupils or note that the bright light hurt his eyes. The same instinct made him purr, deep in his throat, "Arielle is mine. Accept it and I may let you live."

Seth looked genuinely pained. "You shame me. You shame our common parentage and our ancestor Mihos. Even when we were boys, I could never trust you to watch my back. Now . . ." Seth's voice, too, lowered to a dangerous rasp. "You are worse than the felines you claim to love. Even cats kill mainly to eat, to defend territory, or to mate. You kill for enjoyment."

"And you? You were not ruthless when you confronted all those poor dead young women?" Luke took care to raise his voice just enough for those straining to overhear. "You will pay for your

crimes, and I will win Arielle for the best reason—
I am more worthy." When Seth merely looked at
him evenly, Luke made his voice pitying.

"Really, Seth, can you never get over your juvenile competition with me?"

The taunt almost worked. Only Luke could see
that Seth's eyes, too, now had diamond-shaped
pupils, or note that hair had begun to grow on the
backs of his hands.

Seth took a deep breath, the golden hairs receded, and he sounded almost normal. Almost.

"If you come to the séance in any form, I shall
kill you." He turned on his heel and left.

Chapter Seven

"It looks like perhaps the same animal did this," Shelly lied without compunction as she, Ethan, and the earl stood over the deer.

"Nonsense. The other kill was feline. This one is canine." Ethan watched Shelly appraise the dead deer and said helpfully, "Look at the fang marks. A lion's mandibles leave a much wider bite radius than the narrow jaw of a wolf."

"Who is the expert here?" Shelly pretended to examine the bite mark, all the while recalling the delicious warm rush of blood in her mouth as she'd eaten the deer. She had indeed made a quick, merciful kill. One massive bite on the back of the neck had severed the deer's spinal column. She'd not eaten much before she trotted back to the house, her wilder appetites sated for the nonce. But as she stared at Ethan, she felt them returning. . . .

"I, madam," he said loftily, "am also a student of

anatomy and science. I have killed lions before, skinned them myself, and dissected the remains to study them. Also with wolves. Can you say the same?" He watched the way she looked at him and gave the ghost of a laugh. "I infer I may be your first human dissection specimen if I do not desist, but . . . I am ever persistent." And whispering for her ears alone, he added softly, "And vigilant."

Proving it, he pulled a string from his capacious coat pocket, making her wonder what else he hid there, and measured the neat bite at the base of the deer's skull. Then he stalked back to the human remains and did the same, making notations in that infernal notebook. When he returned, he showed her the much longer length of string he'd measured for the lion's kill.

"Facts do not lie."

"No," she snapped back, "but their interpretations are manipulated according to the theory espoused."

The Earl of Darby looked between the pair, one his friend and the other his employee, with a thunderstruck expression, as if he'd finally picked up on the undercurrents between the two. However, the combatants ignored him.

"How would you explain this kill, pray tell?" Shelly challenged him. "A very large dog, I opine. Wolves have not hunted in the woods so close to London for many years."

"No, the bite patterns of a dog and a wolf are somewhat different, and the fangs on this creature are abnormally large, even for a huge wolf."

"Monsters, then," Shelly said evenly. "I shall let you explain that to the reporters on their way here and see whether such sensational speculation helps us calmly gather the facts we need to solve these murders."

"Reporters? They do not need to know—" He broke off as he, too, seconds later, heard the approach of a light carriage and saw two men in bowler hats careening toward them. Even from this distance, he could see that one had photographic equipment. He looked back at Shelly. "My very dear lady, you have uncommonly excellent hearing. Better than any . . . human I've ever met."

Alarm bells rang in Shelly's head. He'd been hinting that she knew more about the killing of this deer than she was letting on, but this comment bordered on overt challenge. Was it possible he'd seen her transform last night? Surely not. She'd been so careful. As always, she'd looked in every conceivable direction. She kicked herself mentally for revealing that she'd heard the carriage a full five seconds before he did, but the damage was done. She could only bluff her way through.

"Some of us of the female persuasion seem to be more sensitive to aural and tactile sensations," she blurted, then wished she hadn't. Why did he make her reckless even when she should be most on her guard?

Ethan's green eyes darkened in that disconcerting way of his. This time, however, his thoughts were very obvious because his gaze wandered over her, centering on her full bosom pressing against the staid male shirt. To her fury, her nipples hardened under that caressing gaze. "That is something I shall be delighted to ascertain in a very . . . tactile experiment at a later date." He kept his voice so low that Shelly knew the earl couldn't hear him. "But I suspect your sensory abilities spring from a source other than your sex."

Fortunately, the carriage arrived, saving her from the most unwise retort trembling on the tip of her tongue. She walked rapidly into the trees, hearing the rude questions from the reporters raining down on the earl and Ethan as babble over her own heartbeat.

Was it possible Ethan himself was the lion creature? He had toyed with her so expertly, with the cruelty and confidence of a cat. What better disguise for a predatory shape-shifter than an old family friend pretending to protect Arielle? He'd have access, he'd have opportunity, and it could well be he had motive if he were as obsessed with the daughter as it seemed he'd been with the mother. Arielle looked exactly like her mother, after all.

No matter the evidence, she didn't want to give credence to these suspicions. In the privacy of her own thoughts she could admit that, as much as he exasperated her, Ethan also powerfully attracted her. But why else would he goad her about her "abilities," trying to catch her in mistakes, if he didn't suspect her prowess?

Troubled, for the last thing she needed was to be the subject of an inquiry herself even as she tried to conduct one of her most difficult investigations ever, Shelly climbed into the cart for a solo trip back to the mansion.

She found an uproar in Blakely Hall. Arielle, her cheeks red, arms akimbo, cobwebs bedecking her shining dark hair, and dust on her gown, glared at the army of servants her father employed. And they glared back.

Maids scampered toward the stairs, arms laden with dusting cloths and beeswax. Footmen carried brooms of every length and type, but a few of them looked as if they'd as lief use them on their mistress as on cobwebs. One said, "But miss, your father banned us from ever cleaning that room."

Arielle scowled, looking a bit like her imperious father at that moment. "I am sole heir to this house, and very near my majority, so I have some say in that too. And I say you are to clean my mother's salon. Immediately!"

Shelly glanced around for the butler or the housekeeper, but both were missing. Several footmen looked at her pleadingly.

Arielle stamped her foot, perforce putting most of her weight upon her bad leg. She was so agitated, however, that she scarcely seemed to feel it. "It *shall* be my mother's salon, and it *shall* be ready by nightfall, all the dustcovers removed and every scrap of furniture shining, or by heaven, heads shall roll!"

Shelly gawked at her. Arielle had always had a streak of wildness beneath her demure, innocent exterior, but now she was a veritable virago. She put a gentle hand on Arielle's shoulder and felt the girl's trembling. When Arielle turned to her hopefully, Shelly nodded at the head footman. "Please do as she asks. We shall get the earl's approval upon his return." And with a wink she added, "If any heads roll it shall be my own."

Grumbling but obedient, the small army of servants marched upstairs.

As soon as they were alone, Shelly patted a lower stair and sat down. When Arielle sat beside her, Shelly said gravely, "I presume we have Madame Aurora conducting a séance tonight?" At Arielle's nod, Shelly sighed. "Your father will be most displeased with you, and I cannot say I blame him in this instance. To retain her you must have gone alone to her place of residence."

Arielle grabbed Shelly's hands. "Make Father understand, Shelly, please? If I can only speak to my mother, find out why she haunts my dreams and why she . . . she . . . I know I can sleep better and not feel so agitated."

Squeezing Arielle's hands, Shelly said gently, "Quite apart from the dangers to you personally, my dear, you must be aware that the odds of actually encountering your dear departed mother are very slim indeed. I have been to six of the seven continents. From voodoo priests in Jamaica to shamans in Africa, closer inspection always revealed some sort of mechanism or hypnosis used to make the participants believe they were seeing the incarnation of a loved one. I have personally participated in several séances since my arrival in England, and always there is some sort of projection method involved."

Arielle pulled Shelly to her feet. "I am aware of that, but there will be no curtain, no tablecloth on the table, no hidden compartments. Just a plain bare table in the middle of the room. I'm even having the drapes removed. Come. See for yourself."

And that was where the earl and Ethan found them, watching as the servants removed dusty, sun-bleached velvet drapes and cleaned the diamond-paned windows until angels seemed to dance upon the now-gleaming hardwood floor.

The earl stopped upon the threshold, stunned, with Ethan on his heels. He glanced around at the formerly grim and darkened salon, now trans-formed into a place of light and life. The apoplectic rage began to fade from his face as he stared at his daughter. She stood in a patch of that sunlight, ra-diant as the rays themselves, staring down at her mother's picture, which she'd pulled from her pocket.

Such joy and hope in a face that seldom ex-pressed either. Shelly was touched to see the trans-formation in the earl. If ever she'd harbored one niggling doubt about his regard for his daughter, it was banished by the look on his face.

He walked to Arielle and pulled her under his arm, kissing her brow. "If we do this thing, allow this woman into our home, will you leave it be? Will you put your mother's picture away and get on with your own life? Go to the occasional ball and meet young men?"

"Yes, Father." She stuck the picture back in her pocket. "I promise."

And perhaps it was Shelly's imagination, but it seemed to her that the angels dancing through the diamond-paned windows skittered faster in a dance of joy. She looked toward the window, glimpsing a small cat, one that looked remarkably like the tabby that she'd seen earlier, staring into the room from a tree outside. For an instant their eyes met, its green gaze inimical, and Shelly knew beyond any doubt that it was not an ordinary cat and had, in fact, used its acute hearing to eavesdrop.

By the time Ethan turned to look, too, the cat had disappeared and Shelly was checking the window locks and verifying that the doors had stout locks. They exchanged a look. Despite herself, Shelly asked softly, "You will be here tonight?"

"Of course, my very dear lady. Of course."

For once Shelly didn't mind being called his very dear lady. Despite the touching tableau between the earl and his daughter, and the thorough cleaning of the grimy room, Shelly had a feeling that tonight would be a turning point in Arielle's fate.

For good. Or ill.

Shelly would need all of the help she could get to help protect Arielle from her own untapped powers . . .

In the lower salon off the soaring vestibule, the night certainly began merrily enough. While the earl, dour in black, was merely grudgingly cordial to the outlandish Madame Aurora, who was attired in virulent purple with a turban swathed in the signs of the zodiac, Arielle was so eager and welcoming that her enthusiasm spilled over onto the others present at the gathering.

Smiling at her gaiety as she chatted with the psychic, Ethan stood quietly watching in that objective, observant way of his, his brandy snifter whirling in his hand. He occasionally sniffed the aroma of the aged French brandy, as if the fumes gave him inspiration, if not illumination.

Shelly had forced herself, for once, into a semblance of propriety for a matron who supported herself as a companion. She wore gray serge trimmed demurely with white lace cuffs and even carried a matching kerchief. She inserted a "la" here and there in her part of the conversation, and even managed a small shriek as Madame Aurora told the tale of her last séance.

"The dead duke was the same in death as he'd been in life, more's the pity, leering down the bodice of every attractive young female at the table save his own wife."

Shelly simpered, "Ah, men will be men even in the afterlife, it seems, the poor dears."

The dimple at Ethan's mouth deepened. He lifted his glass to her in a toast at her playacting ability. The way his gaze wandered over her, however, seemed to justify her remark.

Madame Aurora nodded sagely. "We carry our hopes and dreams, however venal or foolish, into the world beyond. That is why it is so vital to make the present as clear as possible so we can see our way as we enter that golden palace."

Shelly fanned her kerchief before herself, nodding in agreement despite her urge to slap the silly woman.

"Yes, yes, very fine and all that," the earl interrupted with a harrumph, "but let us proceed with this . . . this event."

The entire gathering, including Madame Aurora, heard the true appellation he'd suppressed: charade.

Madame Aurora swigged the last of her sherry and set her wineglass down with a snap on a Chinese lacquered commode. "I shall be happy to give you references. I have performed a séance for the royal family."

"Yes, well, we all know the queen is so besotted and foolish over her Albert that she'd hire the devil himself to commune with her dear departed." The earl glared over his daughter's head at Madame Aurora, who was so affronted that the feather on the front of her turban was quivering.

Arielle put a hand on her father's arm. "Please, Father, you agreed to let the séance take place. What purpose does this antagonism serve but to make things more unpleasant?"

Bravo, my dear, Shelly said inwardly, pleased at the growing maturity in her charge. She also had noted that of late Arielle's limp was barely noticeable. In a strange way, the more the marks of her astral projections marred her flesh, the stronger she seemed to become.

The earl, too, seemed impressed at his daughter's gentle set-down. "Quite right, my dear, quite right. I can excuse my churlish behavior only by saying that I'm very worried about you." He turned to

Madame Aurora. "My apologies, madam. I meant no offense."

She nodded regally. "None taken, sir. It is both admirable and right that you should worry about your daughter's well-being. But if I may reassure you, while sometimes the spirit world can be malevolent, I have never in all my years of conducting séances seen a mother wish her own child harm. However, I do make one caveat: Consider me a conduit only. I do not sit in judgment nor offer redemption. I merely interpret what I am told by your dear departed, whether the news is welcome or unwelcome."

The earl nodded shortly and turned to lead the way upstairs. Shelly and Ethan moved to follow, but Arielle kept anxiously checking the mantel clock. "Not yet, Father. We have another guest."

Shelly noted that Madame Aurora also made no move toward the stairs, glancing surreptitiously at the door. When a knock sounded, she seemed to relax so slightly that only Shelly observed it. So it was with extreme interest that Shelly watched the butler answer the door and usher in Seth Taub.

As always he carried his lion-headed cane, and as always he was immaculate in white cravat and black tails. Now that she thought of it, Shelly realized she'd never seen him dressed in anything but black. He doffed his top hat and offered his cloak to the butler, but when the man also went to take the cane, he hooked it over his arm.

When he entered the salon, he made a slight bow to all present. "Please forgive my tardiness."

The earl glared at him. "What the devil are you here for?"

Arielle went to offer her hand to Seth. "Thank you for coming, sir." She lifted her chin, looked at her father, and said, "I invited him, Father. He was a wonderful help to me in finding Madame Aurora." Her father harrumphed his appreciation of that, but Arielle had eyes only for Seth.

He held her proffered hand a bit longer than propriety required, so much taller and stronger than Arielle that his presence seemed to fill the huge salon. Indeed, as Shelly narrowed her eyes, for the barest instant it seemed as if his shadow grew against the wall, elongating and . . . Shelly blinked rapidly and the lion disappeared. She glanced at Ethan, but he was intent on the man and girl, and had obviously noticed nothing unusual. Shelly gazed at Madame Aurora, wondering if the woman had somehow planted the notion in her brain. She sensed that the medium knew Seth, but if so, what was the connection? More to the point, Seth Taub obviously stood to gain something from this performance.

Wary anew, she looked back at Seth, but he was carefully appraising his surroundings. He examined the windows, the curtains, even the ledges outside and the trees brushing against the panes. Almost as if he expected someone—or something—to sneak inside.

The earl looked as if the words tasted bitter, but he forced himself to be the proper host. "Might I get you something to drink, Mr. Taub?"

"Seth, please. And no, since I was late, I, too, prefer to proceed with the séance."

Nodding his appreciation, the Earl of Darby led the way upstairs.

Seth offered his arm to Arielle. She took it, smiling radiantly. As she walked at his side, Shelly noted that her charge scarcely limped. She should have been pleased by this fact, but somehow it troubled her. Madame Aurora followed the pair up the stairs, leaving Shelly and Ethan to bring up the rear.

"They make a handsome couple, do they not?" Ethan murmured.

"Handsome is as handsome does."

He curved that sensuous mouth as he did when he teased her. "I had not thought you subject to clichés, my dear. You are a true original."

Shelly speeded up ahead of him, vowing not to let him distract her with his teasing. If ever she needed total concentration it was now. She had long ago learned to trust her instincts, and those shouted that Arielle's blithe determination to commune with the netherworld was dangerous, certainly for the girl, but perhaps for all of them.

As they traversed the second set of stairs to the third story, a closet door off the entryway that had been not quite shut creaked open. A tiny, furry paw shoved the heavy door ajar with uncommon strength for the scrawny orange tabby kitten that stood there. It sat on its haunches for a moment, licking its paw to clean its face.

After grooming its sides and belly, as if it wanted to look its best, it stretched languidly. Only then did it look up the stairs. Even in the brightly lit entryway, the tabby's eyes glowed bright green. Then, so fast it was a blur, it streaked up the stairs, the shadow cast upon the wall much larger than its kitten form.

More menacing.

The shadow of a lion . . .

The small salon was isolated in the guest wing of the house on the third story, but its recent cleaning and the removal of all the drapes had chased some of the gloom away. The sparkling diamond-paned windows allowed in some light from the gas lamps in the courtyard below. However, that gas lighting had not been extended to this seldom-used part of the house.

Ethan noted that candelabra flickered brightly on the huge round table in the room's center, and sconces glowed from the walls. But despite the servants' best efforts, the high-ceilinged room could not be polished or lit enough to disguise its true ambience. Shadows lurked in its farthest reaches, as if the room itself were determined to maintain an aura of mystery immune to the best human stratagems. *My tragedies*, it seemed to whisper, *might be long forgotten, but my secrets will also remain untold.*

Up until this moment, Ethan had viewed the séance as something of a lark. But taking in Arielle's excitement, the earl's grimness, Seth's wariness, and Shelly's foreboding, Ethan began to feel a bit of trepidation himself. He'd always believed séances were just smoke and mirrors, but somehow he knew this night would be different. Instinctively he moved closer to Shelly.

Madame Aurora looked around, spinning in a slow circle, her eyes closed as if she felt more than saw the room's checkered past. Her eyes open again, she touched the round, gleaming table situated in the middle of the large room. She arched an eyebrow at the bare windows. "The drapes?"

The earl looked puzzled, so Shelly answered shortly, "Removed at my request."

"The tablecloth, too, no doubt, trying to ensure that I use no tricks."

The two women exchanged a hard look.

"A true medium between the spiritual and earthly planes would need no aids," Shelly said with her usual inescapable logic.

"A skeptic. Marvelous." Madame Aurora clapped her plump hands, rings sparkling. "I do so enjoy transforming skeptics into believers. Shall we sit?"

"Any particular order, madame?" Arielle asked.

"Any seating arrangement is fine, my child. It is the combined energy of our thoughts, the buried dreams of our childhoods, and the unfulfilled longings of our adulthoods that entice the dear departed to succor to us. As long as we hold hands, that energy will swell enough to rip aside the curtain between our two worlds and let us glimpse your mother."

Ethan glanced at Shelly and rolled his eyes. She almost smiled, but looked quickly away to examine the room again. Why was she so wary? Could it be her own paranormal senses felt a danger none of the rest of them had yet ascertained?

While the bustle of scraping chairs and rustling clothes was under way, Ethan noted that Seth discreetly checked the locks on the windows. Following Seth's gaze, Ethan looked outside at the tall tree rubbing sylphlike fingertips against the panes, and his trepidation increased. Seth was also very nervous. But why?

Persuaded that perhaps this little lark could be dangerous, Ethan stepped in front of the earl and took the seat next to Shelly. She sat next to Arielle, who sat next to the medium, followed by Seth and the earl.

"Hold hands with me, dear child." Madame offered her plump hand to Arielle, who took it eagerly.

She closed her eyes and whispered, "Mother," with such longing that Ethan's heart ached for her. Seth's wary golden eyes went dark as his pupils expanded, and even the earl's hardness eased somewhat.

Her father said, "She loved you, Arielle. With every fiber of her being."

"I know, Father. I feel it every night when I'm almost asleep. But I have to know why she cries. She needs me somehow. Please help me do this. Only then can we both be at peace."

"So be it," said the earl, willingly completing the circle by taking Seth's hand, love for his daughter making his eyes glisten.

Catspell

"Shhh . . ." whispered Madam Aurora. "Enough talking. Listen . . . but not with your ears. Do you hear them? So many, calling to us, trying to reach us across the ether. They are there. Open your hearts and minds."

And rocking from side to side, she shut her eyes and began a strange humming.

Slowly, quite without conscious effort, the others began rocking gently with her, instinctively, as if they were on the same ship seeking port in stormy seas, with Madame Aurora's firm hand on the tiller. Her murmuring took on sound and pattern, yet still the words were strange, hypnotic. They had a lovely cadence that was both soothing and invigorating.

Ethan's eyes drifted shut right after Shelly's, and he wondered if she was wrong. Perhaps the woman's gift was genuine. With the thought came a strange release of something in his gut, as if a door had opened only when the skeptic began to believe.

The candles guttered, and then—*whoof!*—went out all at once. The sconces flickered as if in a strong gale, but there was no wind coming through the casements. In fact, the tree outside was still. Ethan opened his eyes to see twin green eyes glowing at his feet under the table, but when he blinked, they were gone. He was about to peek under the table when the murmuring became words he recognized, in a voice very different from Madame Aurora's.

141

Ethan froze, his hand going slack on Shelly's.

Even as the sconces began to go out, one by one, as if snuffed by an invisible finger, Ethan recognized the voice. The soft lilt of a gentle accent, speaking in Arabic, which Ethan spoke fluently.

It was Isis.

Chapter Eight

There was a stirring at the table, a shocked inhalation of breath from the earl and Shelly. Arielle merely sat like a stone, her huge blue eyes fixed on the distance, not on the woman next to her, for they all knew Madame Aurora was only the mouthpiece. Her plump hand squeezed Arielle's, as if reassuring her, but Arielle was not afraid.

She was spellbound. "Mother . . . I knew you were watching over me. But I don't understand what you're saying."

Ethan forced himself to concentrate, for it had been years since his travels in Egypt and the Holy Lands. The words were familiar, and finally he realized Isis—or at least an astonishing semblance of Isis's voice—was reciting a quote from the Book of the Dead, the Egyptian scroll that held the sacred beliefs of the ancients about the afterlife.

Isis's voice singsonged, " 'The Osiris Ani, whose

word is truth, shall not tarry; he shall not remain motionless in this land forever. Right well shall he see with his two eyes; right well shall he hear with his two ears, the things which are true, the things which are true.'"

What riddles were these? Was Isis's spirit warning them or was this all a gigantic hoax by a talented medium? In the flickering of the last lit sconce, Ethan warily looked around for a logical explanation of the unexplainable. They all cast enormous dancing shadows on the wall. The sconces flickered in the still room as if a high wind buffeted them. Were the participants too insensate to feel the breeze or was something spiritual, visible only in its effect on the sconces, among them?

If this was a hoax, it was a very clever one, for there was nothing that could hide any type of device. Bare walls. Bare windows. A bare table. Then again, near Arielle's feet, Ethan's searching gaze glimpsed gleaming green eyes. He bent to look under the table and thought he caught a glimpse of orange in the shadows, but he wasn't sure. He heard a very slight rustle from the hem of Arielle's taffeta gown, and then nothing.

Ethan considered calling a halt to the proceedings, but Arielle was so rapt, her head cocked on one side as she listened to what sounded like Isis's voice, that Ethan hadn't the heart to protest. For the moment the girl seemed fine. What harm could a kitten do, anyway?

Ethan looked around the table again and noted

that Seth, alone among them, had stiffened. He, too, searched his surroundings, not focused on the eerie voice at all. For some reason Ethan's wariness increased. It was as if Seth sensed something the rest of them could not feel. As if he trod both earthly and spiritual worlds at will.

Shelly whispered next to him, "What is . . . she . . . saying?"

Before Ethan could respond, the singsong tenor of the words began to change. They quickened with urgency, becoming staccato. "That which is held in abomination to me is the block of slaughter of the god. Let not this my heart-case be carried away from me by the fighting gods. . . ."

Across the table, Ethan stared at Seth. Tension shouted from Seth's very posture: head erect and eyes darting between Madame Aurora's face and Arielle's rapt expression. Ethan also suspected that Seth understood the strange language, and not for the first time he wondered about the man's ancestry. Ethan suspected that if the man had not been invited, he would have found a way to inveigle himself into the séance.

"Hail, thou lion god!"

Removing all doubt about his comprehension, Seth nodded very slightly as if acknowledging Isis's greeting. The sconce flared and then began to go out.

Ethan's breathing quickened, and his trepidation became fear. With a wild flickering, the flame went out just as the disembodied voice, filtered through

Madame Aurora, said with soft admiration, "Hail, thou who dost wind bandages 'round Osiris, and who hast seen Seth."

In the darkness, Ethan felt Shelly tug fiercely at his sleeve. "Interpret! Tell me what's going on!"

But Ethan was frozen in panicked comprehension. Seth . . . in the ancient Egyptian myths, Seth was the jealous brother of Osiris, who so resented his brother that he killed him. Isis was Osiris's wife, and she had to battle Seth to bring her husband back to life so he could rule the underworld.

But this wasn't ancient Egypt; it was the queen's England. Such ancient tales were just that—folklore. But a chill shivered down Ethan's spine at the irrefutable similarity between legend and fact. The fact was, Isis's voice had just warned her daughter, Arielle, of warring gods. Then she hailed a man named Seth as a lion god.

A match flared to life, and then the earl, his hands shaking, had lit the central candelabrum. "Enough of this nonsense," he grumbled. "All right, madam, how did you do it? How could you so perfectly imitate my dead wife's voice and speak in that savage tongue of hers—"

A strange purring sound interrupted him.

He trailed off as he stared at his daughter. "Arielle . . ."

"Oh, my God!" Next to him Shelly leaped to her feet, starting around the table, but Arielle spit at her and backed away. Shelly froze, watching the transformation.

Ethan stared between Arielle and Seth. They'd

all been so worried about Isis's effect on the girl that none of them had considered a more dangerous influence. Seth sat rigid, his total attention on Arielle. His eyes had begun to glow golden in the dimness, with diamond-shaped pupils, and they were brilliantly hypnotic. . . .

Just as he leaped up to manhandle Seth from the chamber, Ethan belatedly realized that Arielle wasn't looking into those hypnotic eyes. She wasn't looking at any of them. Her eyes were slitted, glowing, becoming cat's eyes as they watched. Her fingers, clutching the table, had begun to grow fur, and tiny baby claws, looking dewy and unused, began to sprout from her fingertips.

For a moment they were all frozen in fear, unsure what to do, even Shelly. And then the disembodied voice came a last time, wailing, a lament so sad it brought tears to Ethan's eyes.

"Hail, thou who returneth after smiting and destroying him before the mighty ones! My heart weepeth over itself." And with a soft sobbing, Madame Aurora began rocking again, cradling her ample bosom as if she held all the sins and sorrows of the world.

Whiskers poked from the sides of Arielle's nose, and then the metamorphosis became more rapid as the sobs increased. Finally Isis's voice spoke her only words of English. "Daughter, beware. Know always that I love you and go to make a place for you."

Madame Aurora groaned and slumped sideways. Shelly rounded the table toward Arielle, but Arielle swiped at her with growing claws. A tail sprouted underneath her dress, switching beneath the back of Arielle's gown. Arielle looked down, licking at the whitish hair growing on her hand, purring. She made a sudden movement that twitched her skirts away from her feet.

They all saw it at the same time: a tiny marmalade kitten sitting at her feet, staring intently up at her with glowing green eyes.

Unblinking. And somehow, small and scrawny as it was, the kitten emitted a strange sense of power. From the look of horror on the earl's face, Ethan realized he wasn't the only one who felt the danger in the tiny creature. It regarded her as if it wanted to own Arielle, to bend her to its will.

This was the source of Arielle's hypnosis, not Isis's spirit or Seth's strength.

Her blue eyes taking on a tinge of green, Arielle stared back at the kitten. Thick white fur, spotted in places, began to cover her face and arms as the transformation became more rapid.

The earl tried to take his daughter in his arms, but with an angry yowl exactly like a great cat's, she scratched him. Holding a hand to his wounded cheek, he backed away a step, looking at Shelly pleadingly.

Her own eyes glowing in a strange way, Shelly moved toward the kitten, but Seth was faster. Shoving Shelly aside, Seth kicked the cat with his foot, breaking its concentration on Arielle. The kitten turned on Seth, spitting, but he kicked it again. Toward the window.

Shelly ran and opened it.

Seth whispered something even Ethan couldn't catch. The words sounded Arabic, yet different. With the next kick the kitten latched onto Seth's ankle with all four paws and its teeth, biting viciously.

Arielle stood frozen, blinking as the cat's hold on her wavered. The hairs began to recede, the whiskers shortened, and the sharp claws became tiny and dewy again.

"My cane!" Struggling with the cat, Seth glared at Shelly.

Shelly grabbed the cane still hanging on the back of Seth's chair and offered it to him. Seth swung the lion-headed tip toward the cat still clinging to his leg. Releasing him, the cat streaked toward the open window. On the sill, it arched its back and hissed.

The earl had relit the sconces and candles, so the brightly lit room cast the kitten's shadow on the tree outside.

Ethan inhaled sharply. Here was all the proof needed of the tiny creature's true strength. A lion arched its back at them, a full mane flowing as the kitten flung back its head and roared.

The sound that came out of the tiny throat was a lion's roar.

Without mercy or compassion, Seth used his cane like a golf club and whacked the cat out of the window into the tree. The cat ducked the worst of the blow and landed on all fours on a tree branch. For a moment it hung there, staring in at all of them with a purely human hatred and a promise of retribution that made Ethan instinctively move to pull Shelly away from the window.

Then, with a final lion's roar, it bolted down the tree into the darkness.

Arielle, who had collapsed into her father's arms, fully human again now that the psychic link with the kitten was broken, began to cry. "What happened? I heard my mother sobbing and then . . . nothing." She looked around at them with lushly lashed, dewy blue eyes, latching onto Seth's grim face. "Did I do something?"

Seth shook his head. "Nothing you could help."

The earl patted his daughter's shoulder with a shaking hand, looking over her head at Seth with a mouthed, *Thank you.* To Arielle, he said, "Well, my dear, have you had your fill of toying with the spirit world yet?"

Arielle hid her face in his shoulder, mumbling, "Mother was here, wasn't she? But what did she say?"

"Deuce if I know. Except . . . she wanted you to be careful."

Arielle peeped up at him again. "Of what?"

"Of . . . demons. Gods of the underworld." For once there was no mocking tone in the earl's voice as he spoke of such "nonsense." Just gravity. And worry for his daughter. Again he looked at Seth. "My deepest thanks, sir. While we all stood stunned, you acted and sent that . . . that thing out the window before it totally bewitched Arielle."

Seth nodded, but Ethan noted he rubbed his lion-headed cane repeatedly, as if he found either comfort or strength in the feel of it. Seth smiled at Arielle. "How do you feel?"

Madame Aurora snored gently, her head resting on the table, as if being the medium had drained more than psychic energy from her. Arielle glanced at her, then back at Seth.

She cocked her head to the side in that thoughtful way of hers, then said solemnly, "Two steps down a very long road. A lonely road that only I must travel. Perhaps the same road my mother traveled?" She addressed the question to her father.

The earl looked away from her searching gaze, but with a newfound strength Ethan had noted in her in the past week or so, Arielle crossed her arms over her bosom, brooking no denial. "Enough prevarication, Father. If tonight has proved nothing else, it has shown that there are things in this world and the one beyond that are trying to influence the course of my life. How can I expect to make the right choices if I do not understand my own heritage and the details of my mother's death? Stop treating me like a child if you truly wish me to become a woman. I want to know the truth. The whole truth—not that pabulum you fed me."

Over the earl's consternation, Shelly smiled broadly. "Bravo, my dear. And truer words were never spoken." She lifted an inquiring eyebrow at the earl.

With a mixture of pride and sorrow, he recovered himself to brush that rebellious lock of hair away from Arielle's flushed cheek. "You win. But may we have this conversation on the morrow, after we've both had time to recuperate from this draining event?"

A loud snore from Madame Aurora seemed to punctuate his point. They all laughed.

Shelly came forward. "Come, my dear. Your father is right. We've had enough truth for one evening. We could both do with a warm cuppa by a warm fire. I trust you will see the woman home." Her tone, as she looked at Seth and Ethan, added, *never to return.* But she was all motherly concern as she escorted a tired Arielle down the stairs, leaving the three men alone.

Immediately the earl rounded on Ethan. "What in blue blazes did that woman yammer on about? You speak that heathen tongue—used to converse often with Isis, in fact—so I know you must have understood."

"Nothing made much sense," Ethan said grimly. "I believe the voice was quoting from the Book of the Dead, a sacred scroll that details ancient Egyptian beliefs about the afterlife. It was intended as something of a map on how to get to the underworld and live forever. Isis's voice, or what sounded like Isis's voice, said something about truth, and a lion god, and a battle. But whether she was warning of something or trying to tutor Arielle in preparation for her own journey, I do not know." Ethan chose not to mention the connection he'd made to Seth. He evenly met Seth's probing gaze, and it was finally the younger man who looked away.

The earl stared out the window at the spot where the cat had clung. If they'd doubted their own sanity, and believed themselves now to have been subject to mass hysteria, there was proof enough of the demon's existence in the fresh claw marks on the tree. "I never thought I'd have to suffer that horrid sight again, of a creature part cat and part woman. But it must be true. These dreams, the scratches on her arms, that ghastly kitten. Heaven help us all, but despite my best efforts, the sickness of the mother has passed to the daughter."

The verification of Isis's ailment did not surprise Ethan, for he had glimpsed her in that form himself. Seth also showed no surprise, merely rubbing his cane more thoughtfully.

The earl turned on them, his teeth clenched with determination. "But it ends here. No demon will seduce my daughter into becoming a ruthless creature of the night. I do not want Arielle to be alone for even a minute." He turned so Seth. "You have already proved you are vigilant and concerned for her welfare. Sir, will you help guard my daughter?"

Seth bowed his shining dark head. "I am honored by your trust. I will do my utmost to deserve it."

Ethan bit back a protest. *Trust, my eye*, he thought. Seth had his own plans for Arielle, and while he hoped they were kinder than those displayed by the cat that killed the girl in the woods, Seth's own capacity for ruthlessness had been proved in the vicious way he kicked the kitten and clubbed it out the window. Well, he certainly didn't seem to have harmed the creature. Indeed, this evidence of unnatural strength in a sickly-looking kitten only increased Ethan's foreboding that solving this series of murders would prove dangerous indeed. He wanted to warn the earl about Seth, but Ethan had no smidgen of proof to counter Seth's undeniable gallantry in protecting Arielle.

Yet.

As they all went downstairs, Seth escorting a weakened Madame Aurora by the arm, Ethan recalled the myth of Egyptian creation, and the titanic battle between good and evil brothers over who would rule the underworld. If that fiction were playing itself out in real life as some surreal puzzle they had to solve, Ethan wondered what sort of pitiful protection he, the earl, and Shelly could offer Arielle against such powerful beings.

Especially as it appeared she'd already begun the transformation that would turn her into their kind.

An hour later Arielle was in bed, and Shelly stood at the front salon window, looking outside. Ethan and the earl were entertaining Seth and the medium in the dining salon with a light, late supper. The earl had invited Shelly but she'd demurred, unable to contemplate food with the sick feeling in her stomach.

She'd been worried from the first time she saw the girl writhing in bed that Arielle's strange link with the other world was among the strongest she'd ever seen—thus among the hardest to break. After tonight, she felt almost a sense of desperation. The change had begun in earnest, and worst of all, Arielle apparently felt no warning and had no memory of her transformation, so she could not defend herself against it.

As for the earl's charge to Seth to help guard his daughter . . . well, Shelly intended to discuss that with him at length. She couldn't fully deduce why at this point, but quite simply, Shelly didn't trust Seth despite his outward gallantry.

The thought had scarcely left her head when a block of light pierced the drive outside as the front door was opened. She heard the murmur of good-nights, recognizing both Seth's and Madame Aurora's voices, and then both of them came into view on the drive. A barouche clattered around, and Seth offered a hand to help the medium into the carriage.

The woman stopped, looking up at him, mur-muring something even Shelly's acute hearing could not detect. But then, with a stealthy look around, the woman held out her hand. Shelly stiff-ened, easing back into the drapes in case they spied her at the window. Seth, too, turned to look over his shoulder, his caution another warning, and then he pulled a small leather money case from his pocket to remove several notes. Shelly cursed un-der her breath, wishing she could see the denomi-nation, but Madame Aurora certainly seemed well satisfied as she pocketed the bills.

As the carriage rattled away, Shelly knew her in-stincts, as usual, had been right. Seth Taub, as gal-lant as he seemed on the surface, was not to be trusted with Arielle either. Arielle had already paid the woman for the séance, and the fact that Seth had given her a healthy bonus meant she must have performed a service for him as well. Perhaps it had all been a hoax to disguise his own manipulation of Arielle, from the kitten to the voice.

Asking Seth to guard Arielle was asking a rake to protect a beautiful virgin. Even more alarming, Shelly would stake her reputation that despite his intervention tonight, Seth, too, wanted to see Arielle turn into one of those ruthless cat creatures. Shelly had to watch him, following him if need be, to better understand his motives. Ethan would help. . . .

Shelly quashed the thought, not sure she trusted him either. She certainly didn't trust her own behavior when he deliberately provoked her. He'd soon be gone from her life, like the others, and off she'd be to her next adventure, where she would have only her own strengths, of both the human and lupine variety, to trust. And that, she told herself as she closed her chamber door, was exactly the way she wanted it.

But when she fell asleep, finally, an hour later, she didn't dream of saving Arielle, battling cat creatures, or sweeping off to grand new adventures. She dreamed of a tall, slim man who made her laugh, who made her angry, who even made her cry. And she, who had a very high threshold for pain, tossed and turned as if on a rack, feeling torn in twain.

She wanted to reach toward that outstretched hand; truly she did. She wanted to trust that wide, knowing smile. She wanted to lose herself in those bright green, inquisitive, and oh-so-intelligent eyes. She wanted to lie with that slim but wiry form and feel again, if only for a stolen hour, what it meant to be a woman.

She wanted.

And she, who feared nothing, was terrified of that wanting. . . .

In her room, Arielle was subject to similar, far more erotic dreams, but unlike Shelly she did not resist them. She embraced them, quite literally, her arms out to meet the half-lion, half-human creature who purred, deep in his throat, as soon as he touched her. But this time when he came to her, a golden mask over his face, he bore the thick black hair of a man, not a lion's mane. When he touched her, only the hands of a man stroked her. No claws extended to leave marks, and only the strong muscular curvature of a man's broad chest and shoulders met her exploring fingertips.

And she found this creature every bit as mesmerizing as the other, golden one. He, too, made her strong, forgetful of her infirmity, made her feel in every tingling sinew the hope and promise of the unknown, not the dreary certainty of the boring present.

Then she was pinned in her own bed, limbs askew, her night rail twisted about her waist, writhing in ecstasy as he touched her in ways no one had ever touched her before. She could taste the sweetness of his lips through the mask, and he was elixir of the gods.

He *was* a god. . . . She opened for him, to know him and learn even more in the knowing. To pay him fealty even as she earned a richer reward for herself, for all women, in the giving. Passion swirled between them, and when he buried his head against her, he nipped, leaving tiny marks that gave more pleasure than pain. In her dream she rubbed them as if they excited her, her nipples going erect.

A soft scratching at her window penetrated the sexual haze. She awakened, her heart pounding against her ribs, pulsing between the legs, to find her hand at her woman part. She blushed in the darkness, flinching away from her own intimate touch, wondering what had awakened her from the sweet dream.

Then it came again. A scratching.

She realized there was someone at her window. Easing out of bed, she slipped on her robe and padded silently over to it, taking care not to alert the guard outside her door. Her father had insisted, over her protests, on posting a footman at her door. She would never, he informed her loftily, be alone until these nocturnal killings were solved.

She also knew, though he would not admit it, that he was afraid she'd harm herself in her delusional condition. She knew on an instinctive level that she had done something shocking that alarmed them all at the séance tonight.

She had proof enough of her own transformation, for, as she moved she realized that her leg, which always ached, didn't even twinge. Her steps were almost totally even. But she wasn't afraid; she was elated. She felt as if she could face anyone, defeat any enemy. Perhaps, as her father warned, she should be wary of this strange sound at her window in the middle of the night, but in her new-found strength, she wasn't wary.

She was curious. Like a cat.

And rebellious. Like a girl on the brink of womanhood. She was tired of being smothered, tired of being treated like a child. She was a woman grown, and she had the right to direct her own destiny, even if meant embracing danger. What harm could it do just to see who came to her so late? She had only to call out to fetch help.

Outside her window, half on her sill, half in the tree, Luke Simball smiled at her. When she opened the sash after a moment's hesitation, he offered his hand. "Come out and play."

Uncertain, she eyed him, astounded anew at her ability to see in the dark. She saw that his long golden hair was tied back in a queue, but the old-fashioned style was pleasing. His eyes glowed green in the moonlight, and his face was a harlequin mask of light and dark as the tree limbs danced in the brisk breeze, veiling and revealing his winsome features. But the darkness was as compelling to her as the brightness. . . .

"Even children are allowed out to play for an hour," he said with a teasing smile that offered no threat.

"I'm not a child!"

His assessing gaze dropped to her bosom, and then he delved into her eyes again. "No, I can see that." His hand beckoned to her. "I want to tell you of your mother's land, what it was like to be born in the bosom of the Nile. I want to help you understand her."

"You knew my mother?"

He nodded.

The last of her wariness faded. He could not have said anything more calculated to tempt her outside. Besides, seeing this golden-haired man who looked like a god in the flesh after dreaming of someone so similar . . . She had to investigate whether her crazy imaginings were harbingers leading her to the man who was her destiny.

She took that strong hand, stepped onto the window ledge, and, with an adroitness that amazed her, as if she had claws, she climbed onto the huge tree and down into the grounds, every foot precisely placed for balance.

If this new adroitness and strength were madness, then so be it.

With a laugh of joy at the touch of wet, warm grass on her bare feet, she lifted her hems high and followed him into the night.

Chapter Nine

Tossing and turning in bed, Seth finally threw back his covers and arose, knowing he'd get no peace until he was sure of Arielle's safety. Rupert, the Earl of Darby, had assured him over their late supper that Arielle would be fine that night because he was posting his brawniest footman outside her chamber door. Quietly, out of earshot of Madame Aurora and Ethan, he'd added that he would appreciate Seth's assistance the next morning in guarding his daughter, for she'd insisted on visiting a mortally ill former governess who lived on the outskirts of notorious Whitefriars.

Such a personal task needed the chaperonage of a gentleman, not a servant, and no one, including the earl himself, had Seth's proven ability to recognize and intercept danger from seemingly innocuous sources. Or, as the earl concluded, "You've a mean right with that cane of yours, and you don't hesitate to use it."

Seth had accepted with alacrity. Now, after seeing firsthand how easily Luke could seduce Arielle, even in a most unimpressive form of feline, Seth knew that no matter how many guards the earl posted, Arielle would never be safe—until Luke was dead, or she was, by her own choice, Seth's consort instead. As he dressed, Seth looked at the inky black horizon behind the buildings lining this posh part of the Thames, and wondered how he'd gain entrée to the house so early, invited or not.

Perhaps he'd take advantage of that tree outside Arielle's room. Perhaps it was time for Arielle to meet his true alter ego, too. . . .

The last of Arielle's wariness faded as she followed Luke deeper into the park. The moon was a sylph above, shy and virginal, yet even in the dimness Arielle could see as if it were daylight. Though her newfound powers were somewhat disconcerting, they were also enlivening, for never had the sounds and seductions of the night been so powerful.

There, the rustle of a bird in its nest. Here, under her feet, the soft feel of decaying leaves and moss. She felt as if she walked on air, unimpaired by any infirmity. And the smells . . .

Arielle lifted her nose, enjoying the mixture of fecund earth and something even more enticing. She blushed as she saw Luke staring at her, realizing that most exotic scent emanated from him. A mixture of man and a spicy aftershave that was unlike any she'd ever smelled. Instinctively she moved two steps closer to him, inhaling more deeply.

He smiled and offered his wrist to her. "You like it?"

"It's wonderful." She breathed in, and a pleasant spinning began in her head.

"It's an ancient Egyptian mixture of myrrh, peppermint oil, and a few other spices."

She took another step closer to his warmth, drawn in some inexplicable way to touch him. She tentatively traced a fingertip over that strong wrist, feeling the pulsing of his life force. Not for the first time she realized that when she was with him, she was attuned to the most basic, primitive forces of nature. The senses of touch and smell. The need to feel, and laugh, and taste of all that life could offer.

In short, just like the golden lion-man in her dreams, he made her feel alive. . . .

He pulled something from his pocket and held it under her nose. She sniffed the bonbon, scenting cloves and nutmeg and something else sharper, spicier, that she could not define. She looked between him and the treat, suddenly wary again.

"It's a delicacy I can find only in Egypt. I adore them." He popped one in his mouth and chewed. When he offered another one to her, she licked it. It was wonderful, sweet yet spicy and entirely delicious. She ate it in one bite.

"Delicious," she said. "May I have another?"

After the second one, suddenly her clothes felt confining. Recklessly she unbuttoned her night wrap to give herself room to breathe. Luke's hands were there to help. She blushed as she felt the light brush of his fingers against her bosom, but allowed him to unbutton her wrap the rest of the way. She half expected him to shove the fully open robe off her shoulders, and her fingers curled in automatic rejection, but instead he stood back.

"Dance with me. Learn what it means to be a woman like your mother. I know your father's intentions are for the best, but he is smothering your true self."

That she certainly couldn't argue with. Power seemed to pulse through her veins, making her capable of miracles. She took his hand, flashing back to the memory of the first time she had danced with him, and how strong he'd made her feel then, too. He pulled her into a clearing and began dancing a slow waltz with her. He was even easier to follow in this primitive ballroom than he'd been the night of the dance. He was tall, strong, warm, and charming, his mouth close to her ear as he told her of Egypt, just as he'd promised.

"The sight of the Nile at dawn is one you will never forget. Then you can see what the ancients saw, and why they believed the Nile to be the source of all life. The sun itself seems to bless her, kissing its way across her shoulders"—and his mouth brushed against the curvature of her collarbone—"to warm her for the new day. Life is eternal there, Arielle. Death has no meaning, for it is only a new beginning. Your mother saw that. Someday soon you'll see it, too." His steps quickened, but still she followed, around and around the clearing, and it was the most lovely drawing room she'd ever enjoyed. No stuffy rules to follow, no prying eyes.

Only the man, the moment and the movement.

"You have the blood of Cleopatra in your veins, Arielle. She dared anything, refused to be conquered by anyone. She had herself wrapped in a carpet and dropped naked at the feet of the great Julius Caesar to forge an alliance with him and save her country from interlopers. You have that bold spirit, too. Listen to that part of yourself, not your father. This moment was meant for us. Somewhere inside you know it, and your dreams have led us here, to the promise and magic of what we can be together. Forever. And ever."

Her open wrap kept flapping about her knees, almost tangling in her feet, and finally she paused long enough to shrug it off. When he held her close this time, only two thin linen layers—his shirt and her night rail—kept modesty secure.

That intoxicating scent he wore felt like champagne bubbling up her nose to sparkle and churn through her veins. The heady rush forbade fear, or want, or pain. There was only sheer joy in what she could be if she embraced the becoming this man fostered.

She had dreamed of a being just like him, of bright boldness, and reality was even better. He felt so good. He smelled so good that when his soft, hypnotic murmurings, which reminded her of a cat's purring, were muffled against her lips, she felt no start of maidenly embarrassment. Only familiarity, as if she had known him first in her dreams, exactly as he said.

Was he the chosen one? She had to know, to test him. And herself . . . Lifting her face to him, she invited his kiss.

She didn't have to ask twice. At first he was gentle, his lips persuasive and tasting of the treat they'd shared. He continued to sway them side to side, and somehow her night rail got twisted, baring one hardened nipple to brush against his bare chest.

His bare chest? She realized he'd unbuttoned his shirt, but the feel of skin on skin was so pleasurable, she had no will left to resist. Curious and hungry for more, she opened to him, offering him the sweet interior of her mouth. He gave a little growl and stopped dancing to hold her away, his hands curling into what felt like claws at her shoulders. The strange marks that had appeared only in her dreams began to etch themselves into her skin.

Scratches, tiny at first, reddened her shoulders. They stung only slightly, and when he bent his head to lave them with a rough tongue, purring his pleasure into her heated skin, the pain became delight.

The whirling in her head went faster and faster until her entire world was spinning. The moon and stars were mixing into a sparkling garment of velvet and diamonds. It wrapped about her, warming her, stealing away her will to resist.

She barely felt the ground beneath her hips, but oh, through her very marrow, she felt the sweet strength of his body over hers. When he kissed her more deeply, tongue probing, a throaty growl came from him that sounded remarkably like a cat's yowl in heat. He rubbed his chest against her, baring her bosom even more, and the tingling in her nipples was answered by that familiar thrumming in her lower quarters. The scratches on her arms and shoulders deepened, even where he did not touch her, and dotted with blood.

It was as if he touched the most primitive parts of her with his thoughts and instincts, and physical contact were not required.

From somewhere deep inside Arielle a similar, more feminine feline growl answered. . . .

Then temptation was gone, snatched away from her. She heard a scuffle, men's curses. Her eyes opened, and the bubbly champagne that had surged through her veins began to pop, leaving a bad taste in her mouth as she saw why—who—had lifted Luke away.

Seth. He held the somewhat smaller man now like a dog, shaking him by the nape of the neck. Luke's open shirt flapped around his shoulders, impairing his movements as he tried to swipe back in defense. Finally he lunged free and turned, his back arched, hissing like a cat. His eyes narrowed to strange diamond-shaped pupils, and Arielle thought she saw hair growing on the backs of his hands, and sharpened nails poking from his fingertips.

But then he glanced at her, and the hair receded, the nails disappeared. Lowering his head on his shoulders, he charged Seth, throwing both arms around the taller man's chest.

But Seth was stronger. He planted his feet, meeting Luke's force with his own upper-body strength. The sound of the men slapping together echoed through the clearing. Arielle winced, but part of her exulted in the sheer primitive power exhibited for her benefit. Then the men were shouting at each other in the same strange tongue her mother had used at the séance. She knew now that it was the Egyptian version of Arabic.

The sensual haze cleared further at the shocking sight of two suitors, one very blond, the other very dark, fighting over her. She had no illusions about the reasons for the battle, for the look of jealous fury in Seth's expression as he pulled Luke from her had spoken volumes, as did Luke's interrupted seduction. Astonishing as it was, both these handsome young men wanted her, a cripple, a shy girl with few social skills and fewer friends. She'd never had a suitor in her life. Both these men were the talk of London, with apparently sizable fortunes, and they could take their pick on the marriage mart.

But why? Why were they both so attracted to her?

Scrambling to her feet, her head clearing further, Arielle stood poised between the combatants, one bright, the other dark. They battled like boxers who had no patience with Marquess of Queensbury rules. They were vicious, merciless, punching each other in the nose, the face, the private parts, whatever they could reach. The thought came, nonsensical at first, then stronger as she watched them move in and out of the trees: There seemed a weird kinship between them, a similarity of purpose and resolve. It was almost as if they were twin halves of a whole, incomplete without the other.

Without light, there was no dark.

The most frightening connection logically followed: Without evil, there was no good. . . .

But who was good and who was evil?

She did not know at this moment, was not sure she even wanted to know, for she was drawn to both of these men. Seth was the more serious, the steadier one, but Luke was so alive, so full of power and confidence. Torn between them, Arielle winced as a blow was followed by a curse from each side.

She had to stop this. "Please, no more. Not on my account." She started to say, as she would have of old, *I'm not worth it.* But the words would not come.

Things had changed in the past few weeks since the dreams began. *She* had changed, and though she didn't understand this becoming, she knew it had made her stronger. Like her ancestor Cleopatra, she was worth this battle, and many more. But for now, she knew only that she couldn't bear to see them fight so viciously, drawing blood on both sides.

The strength to act came from instinct. Grabbing her robe and holding it like a shield above her head, she ran between the brothers. "Stop!"

A fist on each side of the blanket glanced off her as the powerful blows were retracted barely in time. Even then, she staggered from the brunt of them.

Panting, Seth ripped the robe away. "Get out of the way." He glared at the marks on her shoulders. "Why did you let him do this to you? You are mine."

"She's mine, by her own choice. If you hadn't interfered . . ." Luke glanced at her sagging neckline. Arielle pulled it back up, but it was far too late for false modesty. Luke, too, tried to move her aside. Gently. Unlike Seth, Luke was always gentle and kind.

Seth caught her other arm.

Suddenly she was furious at being naught but a trophy, first for her father, now for Luke and Seth. Her back was arched and her teeth grew to pointy incisors. She slapped at both men, each trying to pull her aside, and was astounded to see claw marks on the backs of their hands. Then each of them was smiling, backing off, as if enjoying this primitive side of her. They merely watched.

She was staring down at her own hands, enraptured by the claws and the nascent pads on her fingertips, when a bouncing torch flared into their battleground, blinding them all. Arielle's transformation stopped in the brilliant light, a fact that Shelly's quick gaze noted as she hurried into view. The earl was right behind her, carrying the torch.

Shelly said urgently, "Arielle? Are you all right?"

Shelly and Arielle's father were both in disarray, clothes buttoned askew, as if they'd hastily dressed.

They froze in the clearing, staring at the guilty trio. The earl looked from Arielle's bare, scratched shoulders to the blood on the backs of each man's hands. "Arielle?"

Arielle thought of lying, but the facts spoke for themselves. She said coldly, "Luke invited me to dance with him in the clearing, and Seth . . . stopped it." Arielle turned a haughty shoulder on the lot of them, not sure what to think and suddenly unutterably weary now her excitement had ebbed. "Think what you like; do what you like, Father. As always. I hope you all go to blue blazes." Grabbing her robe from Seth's unresisting hands, Arielle shrugged into it and stomped off, her limp evident again.

The torch trembled in the earl's hand. His free hand clenched and unclenched as he glared at Luke. "You . . . profligate. Wastrel. How dare you try to seduce my daughter?"

Sighing, Luke pulled his shirt back on and buttoned it. "If Arielle is starved for male contact and fun, you have only yourself to blame." Luke nodded curtly at Shelly. "Madam." Seth he didn't acknowledge at all. He stalked away.

The earl blinked rapidly, as if unsure what to say to Seth. Finally he managed, "Once again, in the space of a day, I'm in your debt." He offered his hand.

Seth shook it, but peremptorily. "How did you know to come?"

"Ms. Holmes heard Arielle screaming," the earl replied.

Seth looked speculatively at Shelly.

"I sleep with my windows open," she explained.

"Very brave of you, considering there is a killer loose," Seth responded with what might have been sarcasm. "Not to mention wonderful hearing, given the distance from this copse to your window." He straightened his clothes and moved to walk off when he noted something white on the ground. He picked up a piece of paper and sniffed, his expression hardening again.

Shelly moved to see what he held, but he stuffed it into his pocket and looked at the earl. "Do you still wish me to accompany Arielle on her visit to Whitefriars tomorrow?"

Ignoring Shelly's discreet shake of the head, the earl smiled. "Of course, of course. We shall expect you for breakfast. Thank you again for your assistance this eve."

When he was gone, Shelly opened her mouth to argue, blew a frustrated breath instead that ruffled the loose hair over her forehead, and led the way back to the house. "But I will find out what he took," she promised herself under her breath.

In his carriage on the way home, Luke smiled. Arielle was like a ripe plum about to fall, plump and juicy, into his waiting hands. He'd nurtured her, showered her with the sunlight of his desire, tantalized her with kiss and touch, appearing to her as both man and unthreatening cat. Soon she would be his; she would bend her enormous but untapped powers to his will.

He had seen it in his dreams, long before the wild civet bit him and the change began. . . .

Delicately he licked the back of his own hand, his tongue curled like a cat's, and scented her sweat on his flesh. The taste of Arielle, his lioness, was elixir of their gods, his ancestors and hers, back to the time when Ra, the sun god, was born of Nu, the sea.

Soon he would more than taste of her. Together they would kill Seth. He would become the sole heir to Mihos and take for his obedient consort the descendant of a queen, just as the legend foretold. Forever would he rule the night, killing at will with his mate beside him, both on the hunt and in his bed. Like the pharaohs Mihos once served, he would be worshiped as a god.

That morning Seth arrived early, dapper as always in severe gentleman's black. He was quiet through breakfast, and when Ethan walked in, he asked if they could retreat for some privacy. The earl, Ethan, Shelly, and Seth all trooped into the study.

Forestalling Shelly's request, he showed them a bonbon still in its wrapper, pulling an exact matching wrapper from his pocket. "As you can see, the wrappers are identical. I thought I recognized them. This explains much about Arielle's behavior. Luke didn't just offer her candy," Seth said grimly. "This treat is spiced in the ancient Egyptian way. Cloves and nutmeg with one potent addition . . ."

When he trailed off, the earl's eyes narrowed. "Well?"

"Catnip. It was in the treat, and probably his scent as well."

At the earl's bewildered look, Shelly said baldly, "An aphrodisiac. Especially in Arielle's current vulnerable state."

Outraged, the earl leaped to his feet. "I'll have the wastrel jailed, I'll have him flogged, I'll—"

"For what?" Ethan interrupted. "There was no violation. He only danced with her. And given Arielle's condition, even if there had been consummation . . ." He trailed off.

"Consent," the earl said grimly.

"Precisely," Ethan concluded with the ghost of a laugh. "If Scotland Yard goes around arresting all the men in London who try to seduce women into consent, half the men in the city will be in jail. Besides, if Luke is angling to marry her, announcing his behavior will only abet his ends."

"Thank God you found them in time, Seth," the earl said with a shudder. "But I can certainly make his wastrel behavior known so that he is not accepted into polite company."

"You can try," Ethan agreed. "But that does us little immediate good. Seth, how is it that you were warned when your flat is halfway across the city, especially when all of us thought her safe in bed?"

"I know Luke," Seth responded after a brief hesitation. "He will never give up. And Arielle is . . . vulnerable to suggestion at this point in her development."

"So it would seem," Shelly said.

"One more thing," Seth went on. "I am also certain Luke was the cat creature at the séance."

Deflated, weariness in his strong face, the earl sagged against the wall as if he no longer had strength to stand erect. "But why? Why does he want my daughter so badly?"

Seth looked away, shaking his head.

Shelly persisted, "Yes, Seth, you seem to understand Egyptian matters and legends very thoroughly. Perhaps you can tell us why Arielle is so important to Luke. It seems to go beyond want. To need. To . . . obsession."

Removing his pocket watch, Seth checked the time. "Arielle shall be late for her engagement if we don't leave."

The earl frowned. "I'm not at all certain I should allow her to go. Not now."

"Now it's more important than ever," Seth pointed out. "Arielle needs every connection she can find to her humanity. The more she reaches out to people she cares about, the less influence Luke shall have on her." At their expressions, he hastily amended, "That is, if he is the cat creature."

The earl started to protest again, but Shelly gently squeezed his arm and smiled at Seth. "Of course you are right. We'll have the carriage brought around for the two of you."

Nodding, Seth hooked his cane over his arm and exited.

After his steps receded, Shelly and Ethan exchanged a look. Ethan volunteered, "I'll have my closed carriage brought over from my flat. Seth has never seen it." He also exited.

Bewildered, the earl expostulated, "Dash it, I never understand what in Hades is going on. Why is Ethan fetching his carriage, and why do you want Seth to take Arielle on this confounded visit to her old governess after trying to dissuade me from letting her go with him?"

"Evidence, my dear sir. We shall follow him and see if he plays guardian or seducer." Shelly ticked off on her fingers. "One, Seth Taub is hiding the fact that he speaks fluent Arabic."

When he gave her a look that said *How on earth do you know that?* she responded baldly, "I made inquiries at his club, his flat and most importantly, his barber."

The earl blinked. "His barber?"

Shelly gave him an impatient look. "Surely I need not tell you that a barber is the closest thing a closed-mouth man has to a mother confessor. Besides, this particular chap seems to only speak Arabic—his shop's in the Muslim section of London. When I tried to speak with him he understood me not, yet I saw him not five minutes before chatting merrily away with Seth through the window."

The earl expostulated, "You didn't let him see you, did you?"

"Of course not. But that's becoming immaterial. I'm quite sure Mr. Taub knows we're investigating him. Now where was I? Ah yes . . . Two, he always seems to materialize when Arielle needs protection most."

"Precisely why I asked for his help—"

"Three, he has a greater understanding of the arcane matters in this case than I do, after all my many years of research. But he is always very close-mouthed about it rather than forthcoming, as he surely would be if Arielle's safety were his sole motivation. Four, he paid Madame Aurora a handsome sum after the séance, above that which Arielle had already paid the woman, obviously for the performance of some service. Why would he be bribing her to help bring Isis back to life?"

When the earl went to interject, Shelly concluded with grim satisfaction, "And five, and most troubling, I have of late received the most damning piece of evidence regarding Seth's sincerity in matters concerning Luke Simball: Seth and Luke are half brothers."

Stunned, the earl collapsed into a chair, almost missing the edge, and he had to grab the arms to pull himself back up. "Where did you hear that?"

"I have a compatriot in the Cairo area and asked him to look into recent young male emigrants of good birth from Egypt to London, one tall and dark, the other tall and blond, both very handsome and strong. Here is what he sent me by courier a few days ago." Shelly went to a packet inside a hidden drawer of the desk and brought back handwritten copies of birth certificates. "Luke Tresall and Seth Tresall. Born two years apart, both the sons of an English nobleman of great wealth attached to the foreign office in Cairo. They were born to two different Egyptian women of high birth, but I cannot tell if they grew up together. Both were educated at Eton and Oxford by their father, and left considerable fortunes, though he apparently never married either woman. He has since died. Horribly. A year ago, around the time both Luke and Seth returned to England."

The earl closed his eyes, seeing the truth in Shelly's face. "How did he die?"

"He was attacked, according to the doctors who viewed the body, by a pack of wildcats."

Over the ponderous silence, Shelly stashed the birth certificates back in the hidden drawer. "With four additional murders in the past two months, it's evident time is running out. We must have some type of trail to follow to catch this creature."

"But Arielle—"

"We shall not let their carriage out of sight, I assure you. Though I agree it's dangerous leaving Arielle alone with Seth, he has proved himself too smart and too patient to overtly threaten her. Or so I believe. But if he tries to seduce her or kidnap her, we shall have proof enough of his baser motives. At that point I intend to have him taken in chains, if need be, to Scotland Yard and have him questioned. By the time his barrister arrives to express outrage, I hope that Ethan and I will have elicited some kind of useful information from him as to what is actually motivating both him and his

Catspell

brother to single out Arielle and encourage her . . . instincts."

"But if he's alone with her in the carriage, how will you know she needs help?"

As if in answer, the door opened and Ethan stood there. He wore a deerstalker cap pulled low over his face, and the coarse hobnailed boots, dungarees, and patched shirt, topped by a worn driving coat, of a coachman. He dipped his cap lower and said with a thick Cockney accent and a ribald gleam as he appraised Shelly, "Cor', it's a bloomin' fine figure of a lass, it is."

Sniffing, Shelly swept past him. "Keep to your place, me lad. And that is on top of Arielle's barouche. I shall change and be inside your carriage before you leave. I'll be sure we keep our distance." The door closed behind her.

As he appraised Ethan, the earl felt his despair lighten with a smile. "The two of you make quite a team, old chap."

"Agreed," Ethan said, resuming his refined accent. "If only I can convince the redoubtable Miss Shelly Holmes of that, I shall die happy."

When the earl glared at him, Ethan said hastily, "Bad choice of words."

So it was that thirty minutes later, Seth helped Arielle, garbed from head to toe in a black velvet cape, into her father's plainest barouche. "You know the route, my man?" Seth asked as he paused on the carriage steps to look up at the coachman. He could see only the back of the man's hatted head.

The coachman nodded, his head still turned away, but his reply was respectful. "Yes, sor. Familiar with the area I be. Too much so." He shuddered. "I'll be careful, me lud."

"Very well." Seth started to get in the carriage, but paused on the steps. "Have I seen you before?"

"No, sir. The usual fellow got sick."

"I see. Well, slow and steady, that's the ticket, even through Whitefriars." Seth pulled up the steps and got in, knocking on the roof with his cane. They were off.

A mere thirty seconds behind them, another, smaller carriage wheeled around from the back, driven by the usual Darby coachman. The side window was open and a glitter of a lens sometimes caught the light as it remained trained on the rear window of the other carriage.

The two coaches wove into the thickening traffic on the country road leading into London, Shelly's carriage several vehicles behind the barouche but keeping it in sight.

Chapter Ten

Arielle studiously avoided looking across the carriage at Seth. Two times in as many days this man had "rescued" her from what her father considered a pernicious influence. First at the séance, in an event Arielle could not even remember properly, and then in typically brutal male fashion, trying to beat up Luke, who had only been flirting with her. And now her father insisted that this interfering bully accompany her on a most sensitive visit that was sure to leave her in emotional tatters.

The fact was, Arielle was tired of being protected. There had been some mysterious change within her during all her strange, erotic dreams. Then, when she awakened in her father's arms after the séance, the world had taken on new colors. It was as if she'd been wearing blinkers to the beauties and possibilities of life, and now she could see.

She was tired of feeling like a cripple. Tired of

trusting her father, or anyone else, even Shelly, to look after her. She wanted to become a woman in full, in every way: independent, strong, and passionate. And last night, climbing down the tree, not feeling even a twinge in her leg, seeing so well in the darkness, and then dancing, with Luke's strong body brushing against her, for the first time in her life she'd felt like a woman grown. A flush overtook her as she recalled those sights and scents, especially that marvelous cologne he wore. She fanned her face with her hand, wondering when she'd see Luke again.

Seth turned from studying the passing view, which showed increasingly smaller and poorer houses as they neared Whitefriars, to catch the look on her face. His blank expression darkened as he examined her flushed cheeks, quickened breathing, and dilated eyes.

Arielle felt a strange tingling sensation at her temples, as if the power of his intellect could probe through her outer defenses to the core of all she was and hoped to be. Shrinking against the squabs, Arielle said, "Do not look at me so!" She spoke louder than she intended.

Unseen by either of them, a tiny panel opened above their heads, and the tip of a listening horn peeked through.

Intent on Arielle, Seth crossed his arms over his chest. "I shall look at you how I please, and before long it shall be as often as I please, in great . . . detail."

Well, really! She knew it—his white-knight performance was an act to ingratiate himself into her father's good graces. For all the good that would do him, because he irritated her extremely, and she was not about to let herself be bamboozled by his obvious attractions. Luke was much more appropriate for her. Truly he was.

Trying to convince herself, she scowled at Seth, but he scowled right back. Again she felt a psychic reaching in him that both mystified and frightened her. "Why have you appointed yourself my protector?"

A smile deepened the sensual tug of his mouth. "I didn't. Your father did. And you yourself did long before we met. You just have not realized it yet. I forgive you for being so confused."

Her gaze fell to his lips, then skittered back to his face as she blustered, "Poppycock! I'd as soon be a hen guarded by a fox as your ward. It mystifies me that my father cannot see the threat in you."

"*Protégé* would be a better term than *ward*. You have much to learn, Arielle, but you have natural gifts you have not begun to use. Someday you will not only match me in power; you could well surpass me." He leaned very slightly forward for emphasis. "However, unlike Luke, I am content to wait upon your pleasure." His gaze raked her form in the black taffeta. "Again, unlike Luke, I will take nothing from you you do not want to give, and I will not seduce you to make you mine. What we can and shall have together will be reciprocal."

This time she shrank so close into the squabs that her bonnet went askew. Her heart thudded so frantically in her breast that she wondered if he heard it. The strange feelings of last night as she was torn between the two men returned to her: desire and fear, mixed into some heady brew that settled low in her abdomen and incited a strange ache in her nether regions.

What manner of man was he? How could he make her so angry and so . . . She fanned herself again with her hand. She had never been so confused in her entire life, and the fact that he obviously knew that only irritated her more. Sheer defensiveness made her retort before she could stop herself, "I think I know when a man is trying to seduce me."

He lifted a skeptical eyebrow in a way that infuriated her.

"I do, I tell you. Besides, Luke is good for me. You are not. He makes me feel as if I only have to stretch my wings to fly. You make me feel as if I have to be cautious at every step."

A strange expression flitted across his face, and in a lesser man she might have believed she'd hurt him, but then it was gone. "Most young girls fear their first strong attraction. I will not castigate my rival, save to say that one day you will apologize to me when you realize that I am thinking of you and your happiness in all my actions. Luke is thinking only of himself. I just hope you do not realize it too late and that I can protect you, from yourself if need be, until that day." And as if the subject were closed, he tipped his hat over his head and leaned back, giving every appearance of drowsing.

Of course, that condescension only made her more eager to continue their argument. "Does it not occur to you that perhaps I find Luke more appealing, and that your grizzly-bear tactics last night were neither needed nor appreciated?"

"Grizzly bear." He tipped his hat back again to eye her with that devilish look of amusement that she found totally infuriating and . . . fascinating. She watched his mouth as he talked. "What an interesting turn of phrase, though it's somewhat discomfiting to me to be compared to a creature that kills its own young."

"So do cats." Now where did that come from? But in a strange way he reminded her of a great cat, with his soundless movements, his golden eyes, his agility, and his acute senses. Luke exhibited similar tendencies, for that matter. The amulet she wore hidden in her garter seemed to burn against her skin. She had noted that often of late, the amulet seemed to be attuned to her emotions— particularly when she was in the presence of a cat. What it meant she did not know, but she sensed that only solving the mystery of her mother's death could explain her curious attraction to all things catlike.

As if her head were made of glass transparent to his perusal, Seth appraised her with those mesmerizing golden eyes. He said softly, "A male lion kills the cubs of a pride only if he's a rogue trying to take over. If they are his cubs, and he is the king of the pride, he will defend both his infants and his lionesses to the death."

"That may be, but the lioness does all the work while he lies around grooming his mane."

That irritating smile returned. "Quite so. But if you've ever observed lions in the wild, as I have, you'd also realize that the lioness doesn't mind. Do you know how a male and female lion bond? Not so dissimilar to human beings, if you think about it."

At his look, Arielle swallowed and stared out the window, her heart skipping in her breast.

"They mate. Repeatedly. Nothing bonds male and female faster or more completely, in any echelon of the animal kingdom, than sex. That, too, shall be my personal delight to teach you. But only when you are ready, with the laws of God and man binding us, and your father leading you down the aisle."

Stunned, she stared at him. Was this his concept of a marriage proposal? As if she would accept. Even if he asked with candy and flowers and candlelight, which he wouldn't. This man obviously had an overeager sense of duty and obligation, and none of Luke's sense of daring and fun. Yet the rogue thought came—why then was she still so attracted to him? But she couldn't let him know that. Since he was staring at her with those enigmatic and wonderful eyes, she knew she had to answer something or be damned by her silence.

"If it's up to you, I shall have no right to wear white," she snapped, blushing when his eyebrows arched until they disappeared beneath his hat.

For a moment she thought she'd won, but then a long hand reached out to toy with the collar of her cape. "You could be right," he said without shame. "But unlike Luke, I will consummate our future relationship only with your full, enthusiastic cooperation."

Well, that was plain enough. And the flush in her cheeks seemed to spread through every inch of her body as his fingertip brushed against the throbbing vein in her throat. His gaze seemed to focus there as his voice went husky.

The words seemed torn from him. "You know the legend of the lion god Mihos, yes?"

She shook her head, scarcely hearing him over the pounding of her own heart.

He brushed the soft velvet over her knee. "He was commander of the pharaoh's armies, a very powerful, virile leader versed in the ways of men, a warrior of such courage and wiliness that they called him the lion. When his tomb was prepared for his death, he was even depicted as a man with a lion's head. But his *ka* was out of balance when he died and went before Anubis, for in his original earthly form he had broken the hearts of untold women. He took his enjoyment and cast them aside, going on to the next, and the next, very like his kindred spirit the lion. So when he died, he was condemned by Anubis, Osiris, and the council of his elders to wander the ages until he found his missing half, the only female who could counterbalance his urges and give him peace. She would be a descendant of the Ptolemy, like Cleopatra, also versed in the way of the cat, and when they joined as one in human form, the legend goes, they would both win immortality. If they so chose they could rule the earthly night forever as powerful felines, and never die."

That gentle fingertip trailed higher, to the curve of her thigh. She caught his wrist and removed his hand, only to have him turn his large palm upward and capture her fingers in his.

She tried to pull away as she scoffed, "A fairy tale. I do not believe in reincarnation."

He continued as if she hadn't spoken, his luminous golden gaze fixed on the gentle curvature of collarbones and arms revealed by her slipping cloak. He ran an admiring hand over them, finishing quickly, "Or they could join as humans in body and spirit, keeping their feline powers under a balance that would allow them, after one normal lifetime, to join the pantheon of the gods in the afterlife."

While she was still digesting the amazing legend and wondering about her mother's place in it, the carriage jolted to a stop. Pushing his hat back in place at a cocky angle, Seth climbed down as the carriage was opened and the step was lowered. He gave a polite thank-you to the coachman, who had his muffler drawn close to his face under the low cap, and then he offered a hand to Arielle.

Scorning the courtesy, she leaped the three steps to the ground with an adroitness that pleased her. She had no idea why, but since last night she felt stronger, more alert. That strength had given her wit enough to argue with a man who had always intimidated her, ignore a dubious declaration of intentions that dumbfounded her, and it now allowed her to view her abysmal surroundings with equanimity.

Never had she seen such poverty and filth. The sewers around St. James didn't look like this. Refuse, and what seemed to be human waste, drifted by in the gutters lining the cobblestones. None of that new macadam street covering was invested in this part of the city.

Ancient, tottering houses, more like huts for the most part, were interspersed with decaying taverns. And everywhere signs offered every type of human defilement and temptation, from a simple alehouse to something far worse.

Arielle stared at a slatternly woman with a half-revealed bosom, standing on a street corner, and she did not need Seth's abrupt taking of her arm to know what she was. "Come along," he said brusquely. "This is not the time to dawdle."

The coachman removed a blunderbuss from the carriage seat and moved to follow them.

"That is not necessary, my good man," Seth said. "I suggest you stay with the horses or we may be missing a carriage upon our return."

The coachman pointed. A husky lad, big for his age, held the reins of the horses while he fingered the gleaming gold coin in his dirty clasp and glared a warning in every direction.

"For safety, sor," the coachman told Seth. "Me master insists I go along."

His voice sounded a bit hoarse, but when he coughed, Arielle assumed the man had a cold, which was why he was so closely wrapped in the muffler.

Seth sighed and nodded grudgingly. "Very well. But look sharp. I don't want to stir up any more attention than we already have."

And that was plenty. Eyes shadowed them, watching from the curb, from boarded-up and broken windows, even from a balcony or two where scantily clad women leaned against rickety railings. Two men in unsavory attire began to shadow them, but when Seth removed his sword from the cane just enough to show the glimmer of very sharp steel, they slunk away into the shadows.

Looking down at the note the earl had given him, Seth led the way up what seemed more of an alley than a street. For once Arielle was content to let him lead and be her protector. When he pulled her under his arm away from a staggering drunkard, she did not complain. Had she not been so determined to tell her old nanny good-bye, and so determined to prove her newfound strength, she would have turned back into the carriage before ever getting down. She was glad, as overbearing and arrogant as he was, that Seth was here. And the sight of the coachman, stepping very alertly with a surprising grace for his height, also comforted her. She glanced over her shoulder at him, thinking she caught a flash of unusually bright green eyes, but then he was looking down and she dismissed the odd thought.

Of course he was familiar. No doubt he'd driven her many times.

It felt none too soon when they finally stopped at a nondescript hovel, so ancient it looked gray rather than painted. The address posting was virtually indistinguishable, but Seth seemed to be satisfied, for he used the end of his cane to rap on the door. "Miss Arielle Blaylock to see Miss Anna Louisa Fein."

No answer, and then an ancient old woman, so bent over she could barely walk, peeked out at them through a crack in the door. She looked ready to slam it in their faces, but when Arielle peered around Seth's bulk, a toothless grin lit up her wrinkled face. "Miss Arielle! So ye did come." She flung the door wide.

The bare interior was clean, and the strong scent of camphor leaves and other medicines drifted from the only other doorway. "Me daughter will be glad to see you."

Coughing sounded from the other room. Arielle shared a look with Seth that spoke of her concern, and then the old woman, whom Arielle very vaguely remembered as Miss Fein's mother, ushered them into a tiny bedchamber. It was barely large enough for the single bed with a single occupant and a battered nightstand that held a ewer of clean water and a towel speckled with blood.

Arielle stopped dead at sight of her old nanny's face. She had been plump and apple-cheeked, with twinkling blue eyes, the last time Arielle saw her. Now she was emaciated, with a sallow complexion, and even her eyes seemed gray in the dismal surroundings. But a glimmer returned as she struggled to sit up. Her mother helped her, propping two threadbare pillows leaking feathers behind her head.

She offered her hands to her old charge. The coachman and Seth both gave an uneasy look at the blood-speckled towel, but Arielle went straight to Miss Fein, took both hands, and kissed the sunken cheek. "Nana, it is wonderful to see you again."

"And you, kitten." She glanced at the two men, good manners obviously second nature to her. "I regret we do not have enough chairs, but would the three of you care for a spot of tea?"

"No, no, we are fine," Seth began, but Arielle gave him a shushing look.

"We should be delighted." She patted the withered hand and sat on the side of the bed to begin chatting about old times.

And so it was that when the old woman brought in four cups of weak tea in chipped teacups and some dry but edible scones, the strange gathering took on the air of a very odd afternoon tea. No gossip was exchanged, they had no butlers or maids in lacy aprons to serve them, but by the time they consumed the pitiful repast, the five of them all felt better about themselves and their mutual humanity.

Color had returned to Miss Fein's cheeks, a sparkle made her eyes blue again, and her mother moved more gracefully, her posture straighter. As they said their good-byes, Miss Fein clung a bit too long to her old charge, whispering, "I'm very proud of you, kitten, as your mother would be. Thank you so much for visiting me. I feel better than I have in an age. You got the things she left for you?"

"What things? All I have is one picture and an amulet that was . . . lost." Arielle frowned.

Miss Fein shook her head. "No, she left you her most treasured book and one of the costumes she used to wear when she communed with her ancestors."

"But . . . I've seen no sign of it. One time I even looked in the attic myself."

Miss Fein seemed sad. "Perhaps your father had them destroyed."

When he saw Arielle's expression, Seth took her arm gently. Then he looked out at the darkening sky. "We must go. It seems as if there's a storm brewing."

The coachman collected his blunderbuss and brought up the rear. All of them knew it was probably Arielle's last good-bye with her old nanny, but none of them remarked on it. Seth opened the door for Arielle. As she stepped out, her back to him, Seth slipped a bag full of rattling coins into the old woman's pocket. The old woman started to speak, but Seth held a finger to his lips.

Though Arielle was oblivious, the coachman was not. And beneath his cap the green eyes brightened with curiosity, but he looked quickly down at his feet when Seth glanced at him. As they exited, the tears sparkling in the old woman's eyes looked like diamonds in the reflected glow of the early fire, as if the bag she held gave her more than riches.

The three were quiet and mutually relieved

when they arrived back to find the carriage intact and their young guard still alert. Seth gave him another note for his trouble, and then they were off. Another carriage nosed into the flow of traffic behind them.

The inside of the carriage was quiet, and then Seth said, "I understand now why it was so important to you to visit her in her time of need. She has no one, does she, but that poor old woman?"

Arielle was staring out the window at the rapidly improving domiciles and did not answer. Above their heads, the panel opened again, and again the listening horn peeked inside.

Seth was too intent on Arielle to notice. "Arielle? As I was saying, she seems quite a charming, intelligent woman. Pity the consumption is so far along—"

Swinging away from the window, Arielle sobbed, "She was supposed to have a pension. Why did Father not check on her? Why did I not check on her?" Tears glistened on her face. "And my mother did leave me something. What else has he lied to me about?"

Seth reached toward her automatically and used a fingertip to brush the moisture away. "You went as soon as you heard she was ill, did you not?"

"Yes, but she'd been after me for an age to visit and I was always too busy. If I'd gone sooner, I could have helped her." Her voice broke again. She tried to turn aside, but then he was beside her on the seat, pulling her into his arms.

"Have your father send her some money."

"Too little, too late. Couldn't you see she's dying?" She struggled to pull away, but at his gentle but persistent hold, she finally collapsed against him, her breath coming in shaky little rasps as she fought her tears. "Besides, she would probably not accept."

"Why do you say that?"

She looked up at him seriously, her deep blue eyes midnight mysteries that, though she did not know it, were incredibly sensuous and inviting to a man like Seth, who was drawn to enigmas. "You should allow a woman some pride. We do have it, you know. Just like men."

An arrested look appeared in his eyes, and he looked at her as if he'd never seen her, really seen her, before now. "Actually, I do know that. I have observed it, especially in women of character." He held her a bit closer.

This time she didn't struggle to pull away. A little smile trembled on her lips. "Are you implying I'm one of them?"

"I'm implying nothing. I am stating that you, and apparently Miss Fein, are both women of strength and character." He dipped his head so low his breath tickled her ear. "Your heritage is in your face, Arielle, but it's also in your bones, your heart, and your mind. Be proud, my young lioness. Be bold, and taste of life with me." His words ended against her lips.

Arielle took a last shaky breath, and that was a mistake, for she inhaled the heady taste of him. A bit of cigar smoke, a bit of brandy, a few peppermints—

and all male. There was none of that exotic scent Luke favored to make her light-headed, but the weakness in her knees was so pronounced, she felt it even sitting down.

His lips moved gently and sweetly on hers, and his hold was so light that she could have pulled away at any moment.

She stayed still, feeling the quickening pace of his heartbeat against her breastbone, and the urgent answer of her own. That tingling began again in the vee of her legs, where no man had seen or touched. But when his kiss deepened, his mouth slanting sideways and opening as if he were famished for the taste of her, the urge to pull his hand there to that shocking place, to raise her skirts so she could feel the forbidden luxury of skin against skin, grew to an ache.

He didn't taste of Egyptian spices like cloves and nutmeg, but he didn't need to.

He tasted of man. A man who honored her, respected her, and wanted her, which accounted for his overprotectiveness. And everything feminine in her, including the strange powers that had been growing with every erotic dream, responded. It felt so right to be in his arms like this, as if here she belonged, and here she was meant to stay.

Sweet murmurings pleased her ears as his touch pleased her back, soothing her with light strokes, and the tip of his tongue teased her lips from corner to indented center to opposite corner, and back. "Thou art honey to my lips." And then he was speaking in that strange language, but the timbre of his voice told of the passion he uttered in the music of his mother's tongue.

Her hands cupped the back of his head, and his hat, already askew as he'd tilted his head, fell to the floor. His hair was thick and shiny, but somehow not soft to the touch, more wiry. He reminded her of those pictures of magnificent male lions, their manes black and bushy as their alert golden eyes watched over their pride. The image, so vivid against her closed eyes while he kissed her, aroused her further. She began kissing him back, using her own tongue and hands to good effect, or at least it seemed so based on his husky growls of pleasure.

Was this what she'd been avoiding in her virginal bed, this satisfying exchange of breaths, and touches, and tastes? Was this what her father shielded her from? What nonsense. It was she who unbuttoned Seth's jacket to pull urgently at his shirt so she could touch his bare, strong back, she who clasped his neck to pull him down atop her on the seat.

She felt him hesitate, and pull slightly away.

"Not here, Arielle. Not like this. You are too important to me."

"More." She said it like a child, but the look in her eyes was all woman, with the blood of her ancestors thrilling through her veins and flaring in her nostrils. Her eyes, though she did not know it, slitted like a cat's, and his own nostrils flared as if he scented her arousal.

With a guttural growl that sounded torn from him, he pressed her back into the seat and lowered himself upon her. The panel above their heads shoved open wider, and an inquisitive eye looked down. The panel was shoved open to its fullest extent as the dark, threatening clouds above broke in a torrent of rain.

Arielle was lost to her surroundings, lost even to herself. She knew only this man, this being who so reminded her of the dark lion-man of her dreams. His lips were surely human, yet he seemed, as he murmured strange love words, a being of another world where immortality was more than a legend, where good and evil were more than mere words.

The crack of thunder came while he kissed her, and somehow that felt appropriate, too. Light split the darkened sky and the carriage shook. Her eyes fluttered open, and she saw lightning fork above their heads just as cold moisture began to drip down upon them.

Seth felt it too, pulling away enough to turn and look up. The cold splats clearing their sexual haze, they both saw the open panel at the same time. They scrambled back to their former positions and straightened their clothes, unable to exchange glances in the aftermath of passion.

The coachman's voice came above the storm. "It's right disagreeable out here. Would ye have me stop or go on? We almost be home."

"Go on," Seth shouted back. "But close that blasted panel. We're getting wet."

"Can't. It's stuck." But the whip lashed and the carriage sped up. They managed to dodge the worst of the rain, and the boom of thunder precluded conversation until they finally drew up under the portico before the estate.

Arielle had her bonnet primly tied and her dress, which had opened at her bosom, demurely buttoned before she could regain her composure enough to speak. "Thank you for accompanying me."

"It was my pleasure." He lifted her hand and kissed it. "My honor."

Arielle stared down at his dark, wiry hair, feeling the strength and warmth of it against her fingertips like a tangible memory, wondering what she had begun.

His kiss had been even more enticing than Luke's. She felt his wish to give her pleasure, not just seduce her into his arms. But on a cool level, on the intellectual level that was a legacy of her father, she also knew that she did not trust either man.

They were both using her. For what, she did not know. But she must find out. And somehow she sensed that her mother's effects were the key to the mystery. She had to find them. . . .

Being alone with Seth proved how vulnerable she was to him. She had only one choice—she'd refuse to see him any more until she was certain what was going on.

Chapter Eleven

Seth had just taken his leave, and Arielle was trudging up to her room when the earl came into the hall from his study, his finger between the pages of a book. "Arielle, my dear. And how was our sweet Miss Fein?"

Arielle froze on the stairs, her back to him. "Very poorly." She climbed another step.

The earl frowned, staring up at his daughter. "And? Did something untoward happen?" He looked around. "Where is Seth?"

Ethan came into the foyer from the back of the house, shaking raindrops from his blond head. Shelly also entered from a side salon. They both paused, sensing the undercurrent of emotions between father and daughter as Arielle slowly turned.

She removed her bonnet. Perhaps it was the gloom outside, perhaps it was exhaustion, but this Arielle seemed very different from the naive young girl who limped and expected her father to protect her. This Arielle stood soberly on the doorstep of womanhood, coolly appraising her options. She could perhaps still be guided, but she could not be coerced.

"Your watchdog," she said, "has departed. Pray do not ask him to chaperone me again without my blessing."

"Why? What did he do?"

Wondering the same thing, Shelly looked at Ethan, but he was watching the confrontation.

"Nothing but boss me about, as if he had the right. Have you given him the right, Father?"

The poor earl, Shelly noted, looked as if he'd been set adrift on stormy seas without a compass or maps. "No, no, dash it, of course not, at least not in any meaningful way, that is—"

"Good. From now on I make my own decisions. And I have decided I do not wish to see him again." Arielle continued on her journey upstairs.

The book whammed against a hall table as her father climbed up after her to catch her arm. "What in blue blazes has your knickers in a twist?"

It was a measure of his frustration that he would speak to his daughter so coarsely, Shelly realized. She also realized, abruptly, that Arielle had more of her father in her than either of them knew.

Arielle turned on him, her wan face suddenly filled with glorious color. "You promised me you left Miss Fein a good pension. You promised me she was well. What other promises have you broken to me, and my mother before me? Was that why she really killed herself?"

He stumbled back, hooking his heel on a step and almost falling.

Ethan lunged forward, but the earl waved him back, catching himself on the balustrade. He looked pained as he stayed half bent over, as if his only child had just dealt him a low blow. "So this is what you really think of the father who has spoiled you from the moment you were born."

"Perhaps you are right. If you wish, I shall move out into a guesthouse on the grounds. But first I want you to bring me the box of things that my mother left for me." And she continued her martial march upstairs, no limp whatever in her gait, unaware or uncaring of the horrified look on her father's face.

Shelly noted that Arielle's feet scarcely made a sound on the steps, and this fact alarmed her more than anything else, including the girl's rancor.

The transformation was becoming more rapid. Arielle was reflecting not only the independence, curiosity, and fastidiousness of a cat, but also a ruthless propensity not to care about the feelings of others.

When her bedroom door closed behind her—quietly, indicating a measure of her new control—the earl's rigid posture collapsed. He looked, for once, his age as he grasped the railing for support and trudged back down to the foyer. Ethan moved to help him and was brushed aside for his pains.

"If you want to help me, assist Miss Holmes in

solving these murders," Rupert snapped. "I must know if Luke Simball is the killer. I can thank his pernicious influence for the poisoning of my daughter's mind against me, I make no doubt. We must have proof to take to the authorities and convince my daughter she is attracted to the wrong man." The earl moved toward the front door, but on the way he pointed at the book he'd left face-down on the hall table.

"Look at that book," he said tiredly. "It was one of my wife's favorites. I had the servants bring the last trunk of her belongings in from a hidden vault in the crypt, locked these many years since her death. Inside I found one of her outlandish costumes, a diary, and several books, the most ragged of which is this one. Now that I recollect, her strange dreams and night wanderings began after she became obsessed with reading it daily. Review it if you please, both of you, and see if you can find a clue to what is happening to Arielle. But please, no matter what, do not let her see the contents of that box. It is deposited with my housekeeper in the locked larder."

Somehow even the sound of his footsteps reminded Shelly of an old, old man as he went out the door. Just as it closed on him, he said, "I'll be at my club for some peace and quiet. No women allowed. Thank God."

When he was gone, they both scrambled, but Shelly picked up the tome ahead of Ethan and recited the title, *"Ancient Egyptian Rites and Beliefs of the Afterworld: With Excerpts from the Book of the Dead.*" She stuck it in her pocket, ignoring Ethan's glare, and walked up the stairs toward her rooms.

"I say, you have no right to abscond with the evidence. I'm assisting with this case, and Rupert gave me leave to—"

Shelly rounded on him. "Indeed, you are assisting. Perhaps that's why we're getting nowhere."

A wounded look flashed in those green eyes before they became expressionless. "Tell me, Miss Holmes. Is it me you fear or yourself?"

Shelly continued on upstairs, not dignifying his remark with a response. She forced herself to walk regally, head high, so he'd have no indication whatever that inside she was roiling with confused, ambivalent emotions. Half of her wanted—needed—not only to trust him but to depend on him; the other half warned her that, like everyone else she'd met since arriving in this benighted household, Ethan Perot was not what he seemed. He might have his own agenda, but to the end of Christendom, Shelly Holmes would not be on it.

And neither, while she had breath to fight, would Arielle. . . .

Inside her room behind a locked door, her windows barred again, Arielle sat in near darkness, oblivious to the battle brewing on her behalf, her eyes glowing. The visit with her old nanny had not only taxed her emotionally; it had opened her eyes to larger realities. She had heard the stories of women, even good women, in straitened circumstances forced into workhouses, or onto the streets to do what those poor women in Whitefriars were dressed to do.

The fact was, all her life Arielle had depended upon the largesse of a man, as her mother had before her. Her mother had received a small inheritance from her father, but the title and estates had gone through primogeniture, and Isis's Egyptian mother had been too scandalous to be accepted by the rigid social structure of the ton. She'd taken her daughter back to Egypt for a time, but returned when Isis was blooming into maturity, to try to find her a good husband who would not insist she wear robes or walk two steps behind. It was on that trip that Isis had met the Earl of Darby at a country party.

From the little she could discover, it seemed to Arielle that the match between her parents began with love and ended with hatred. Why? Had her mother also felt this nascent anger and frustration at being dependent on a man for the roof over her head and the food in her mouth?

Arielle went to the daguerreotype and picked it up, staring down at the vibrant face so like her own. "Mother, show me what to do," she whispered. Perhaps it was her imagination, but she thought she saw a wistful smile. But no answer came. Holding the picture to her bosom, she closed her eyes and tried again to walk in her mother's golden slippers.

Inchoate images flashed through her head, of strange vessels with pointy prows and enormous sails plying crowded, muddy waters lined with palm trees. She saw a black-haired little girl running and laughing under the most brilliant, burnished sun she'd ever imagined, and a huge white stone house with massive columns looming above the Nile on a steep hill.

But when she waited, breath held, for that little girl to turn to face her, she disappeared into the bowels of a mountainside. Darkness filled the world. Then a huge stone portal closed on the girl, now a shapely woman garbed in garments of gold, and royal blue, and carnelian. The woman wasn't laughing now, but she went to her destiny with her head high. The grating finality of that closing portal seemed to Arielle to be the loneliest sound she'd ever heard.

Was this to be her destiny too? A half-life, eternally alone, neither dead nor living because she chose the wrong man?

Arielle started awake from her half sleep, half vision, shivering, to find the amulet on her leg burning and the picture of her mother lying broken on the floor. Arielle reached down and picked out the glass, anguished to see the picture scratched, as if tangible proof of broken dreams.

And yet she also knew that she owed her mother a deeper debt than anything she owed to her father. From her mother came not only her looks, but the strength and passion to face all life had to offer and demand her portion. Cleopatra had for decades held a crumbling empire together against the might of Rome by seducing the ancient world's two most powerful men.

And she died of a self-inflicted asp wound when her empire crumbled, her father's practical half whispered, but Arielle chose to ignore that niggling little voice. She was convinced her mother was watching her from the afterlife, trying to guide her to a better fate than her own. At this point Arielle trusted her mother's love more than her father's edicts.

Setting the picture back in its place of prominence on the mantel, Arielle vowed it would be a reminder to her of the fate of every woman who depended upon a man for her entire existence. Nor did she wish to do what most young women of gentle birth did: switch one form of dependence for the still stronger bond of matrimony, tying herself to an even more arrogant man for the rest of her life.

Seth's face flashed in her head, stern and authoritative as he escorted her through the crowded streets of Whitefriars, and then came Luke's laughing face as he told her tales of the land of her mother's birth and shared with her, a cripple, the joy of dance. Each of them came to her in her dreams, seducing her in his own fashion, but she believed that only one of them was her destiny. If she could figure out which one, then she'd have an ally in her quest to understand her mother's fate and her own.

She knew of only two ways to learn more about her mother's strange warnings of danger: Madame

Aurora—she would hire her again, if need be in the privacy of the woman's rooms—and her mother's things. She knew her father had no intention of willingly sharing them with her, but before she raided the attics she'd see if Isis could guide her to them.

Arielle went to her dresser and removed the last of her monthly allowance, along with some of her grandmother's pearl jewelry. Then, folding her emerald cloak over her arm, she went to the door.

As she went out into the hallway, she heard a footman just around the corner complaining to another, "Fair gave me the shivers, it did, hauling that old trunk in from the crypt where his lordship sent it after she died."

Arielle shrank back against the wall, listening.

"What be in it?" asked the other, obviously younger footman. "Did ye see?"

"I had to help open it. Had some sort of heathen costume and an odd headpiece with a vulture and a cobra on it, just like them I seen on those etchings the *Times* put in the paper from that ancient tomb. But then the earl sent me off, right and tight, and that's all I saw."

"Ye think Miss Arielle knows that more of her mother's things survived than he tol' her?"

"I don't know. But I do know right and tight that if she finds out he's been hiding this stuff from her, there will be hell to pay." They moved off down the hall, their voices fading.

Tears gathered hotly behind Arielle's eyes as she listened, but she refused to shed them. Even the servants knew of the precious legacy her father had hidden from her. Her steps so light they scarcely made a sound on the oak treads, Arielle went the opposite way down the hall toward the servants' stairway and followed it down to the back of the house.

She must have slept longer than she'd realized, because it was dark. She hesitated, not wanting to fetch a carriage because she knew that would alert the household, but somewhat afraid of walking to the main road where she could catch a hansom cab. Then, her chin lifting, she took the shortcut through the woods of the estate, seeing the trees as bright as day despite the early evening gloom.

Just as Arielle was disappearing into the woods, Ethan and Shelly met in the upper study before a cozy fire. She held the battered tome that had been Isis's favorite book. It had been fascinating to read the English translation from the Arabic, but it was the passages about a lion-headed warrior god that most pertained to this case. The fact that the words were circled and the book fell open to the spot was proof enough that Isis, too, had been obsessed with cat-men.

Not bothering to sit down, Shelly related, "This legend says that the first Mihos was a warrior god who could transform himself into a great lion at will. But he strayed from the way of truth, drunk on power, and became a devourer of women."

Ethan's gaze fixed on her face. "Go on."

"When he died, despite his elaborate funerary

arrangements, the council of his elders condemned him to wander forever a twilight world, neither fully human nor fully feline, until he found his destiny in the loins of the descendant of Cleopatra."

They exchanged an even grimmer look. Ethan grabbed the book out of Shelly's unresisting hands to finish. "Once they united as one flesh, each feeding the power of the other, they would reign over the night, invincible, forever on the earthly vale, but the cost would be high: their *kas.*" Ethan scanned ahead, turned a page forward and back, and then he put the book aside with a sigh. "That's the only reference to him. This explains much, but opens a whole host of other questions. Namely, do Seth and Luke both consider themselves the reincarnation of this Mihos character? And if so, how do we stop them from turning Arielle to this dark fate, which will cause her to lose her *ka?*"

Shelly shuddered, knowing by now the Egyptian word for *soul.* "It's only a myth."

"The deaths of these women, the ability to change into cats—these we have seen for ourselves. Often myths have historical precedent."

Ethan set the book aside. Both of them were so embroiled in their argument, they didn't notice that the back pages of the volume, devoted to quotes from the Book of the Dead, were even more worn than the portion that recounted the myths.

"We may have to retain Madame Aurora again," Shelly reflected, staring into the fire. "I have a feeling only Isis can guide us through this mystery to the *maat,* or truth, as the Egyptians would say."

Shelly turned away, noticing for the first time the two brandy snifters, the tray of cheese and crackers, and the soft fur throw gleaming over a sofa. She took the tallest, primmest chair she could find.

Ethan patted the sofa beside him, his solemnity lightened by the little devils dancing in his green eyes. "I don't bite. Much. You, on the other hand, are welcome to do so."

She stayed put. Shelly wasn't sure quite what to make of that devilish smile, but she knew she didn't trust the emotions behind it, whatever they were. She couldn't shake the strange feeling that somehow he knew of her powers, and was trying to discombobulate her with his teasing. But that was nonsensical. He could not possibly know of her affliction from either direct observation or evidence. She'd been too careful.

"Let's stick to the facts, if you please. I'd like to know everything that happened this morning when the three of you went to Whitefriars. How did Seth behave?"

Ethan's open mouth closed. He stretched his long legs toward the fire and said bluntly, "He was flirting with her in a blatantly sexual manner."

Shelly frowned, unsurprised. "But he made no unseemly gestures?"

"Well, he kissed her. But she invited it. In fact, he declared his intentions as honorable in a roundabout way. And he did something even odder, something I certainly cannot equate with any creature who would kill as the cat creature has."

"And what is that?"

"A kindness. He left money for Miss Fein, and I would swear he did not want anyone to see, especially Arielle. It was as if he were determined to do the right thing, not to impress anyone, but because he wanted to reach out to someone he sympathized with. Human to human."

Shelly stared into the fire. This news was unexpected. The flirtation, yes, but sympathy for a poor ill woman, a total stranger? On the other hand, perhaps he fully intended for Arielle to discover his largesse and Ethan was mistaken.

"No, I'm not mistaken."

Shelly's eyes snapped to his face. "Did I say you were?"

"No, but you were thinking it."

No force in nature or civilization would make her admit that he had somehow read her mind, so she merely looked back at him stonily.

"Oh, very well, be difficult." Ethan put one ankle over his other knee, looking quite put-out. "You excel at it. Now, what else did you find out from the book that might be helpful in understanding the link between Mihos and Isis?"

Shelly let out a soundless sigh of relief. Finally, a safe subject. "How much do you know of Egyptian mythology?"

"The basics, certainly. Land and sea birthed the gods. Osiris and Seth were brothers, Isis their sister and also Osiris's consort. Indeed, intermarriage among Egyptian royals quite possibly led to the misshapen heads seen during the Akhenaton period, according to some of my archaeology brethren in the Royal Society."

Shelly's eyes kindled. "I suspected you knew much more of Egyptian history and rites than you let on." When it was his turn to stare back inflexibly, she decided he was an exhausting man and it was time to get to the point of her research. "Then you know that according to virtually every legend, Seth killed Osiris?"

"Hmmm. So it is written." He lifted his eyes piously to the ceiling.

"There is one picture of the god with the head of a lion." Shelly opened the book. "Mihos. The lion god of the pharaohs sent to smite his enemies. A fierce warrior." She flipped to an engraved foldout of a beautiful, hand-colored depiction of an Egyptian funerary scene.

Mihos was shown with the muscular body of a warrior clad only in a loincloth, but he had the head of a lion. He stood before the pharaoh Ramses the Great holding the head of an enemy as an offering. Beautiful young women bowed at his feet, worshiping, according to the historian, both Mihos and their pharaoh.

"Was Mihos friend or foe to Isis?"

"I cannot tell from the lore. So many of the stories vary according to the dynasty and the interpreter's motivation. However, I suspect he could be either friend or foe depending on who had his allegiance. And during the séance, you say Isis spoke of warring gods and then hailed Seth as a lion god?"

Ethan nodded.

Shelly looked troubled. "One of the most famous of the Egyptian myths is the story of the battle between the brothers Osiris and Seth, birthed by their parents the sky and the earth. In most of the accounts, the evil Seth overcomes the good Osiris by tricking him into a chest and tossing him into the Nile."

Ethan nodded. "Yes, I've heard that tale. And you think our Seth could be evil, too, and trying to lure Arielle to his way of life?"

"I do not know, but the parallels are troubling. To continue, in the myth it is Isis who saves Osiris not once, but twice, first by recovering the chest from a faraway land where it has drifted, and then, when Seth dismembers Osiris's body into fourteen pieces, by collecting them one by one, all except . . . except . . ."

Ethan's lazy smile replaced the studious light in his eyes with a twinkle. "Yes. Do be thorough, my very dear Miss Holmes."

"You know which part. As I was saying . . ."

"How would a woman go about replicating her husband's penis, do you suppose?" Ethan shuddered. "Poor chap. How he must have felt to awaken as lord of the underworld, sporting only a golden penis."

Shelly pretended not to feel the hot flush in her cheeks. "Must you reduce every scientific discussion to base matters?"

"Base?" Ethan sat up straighter, his outrage seemingly genuine. "A man does not consider that part of himself base, I can tell you."

"Indubitably. Instead you consider it divine."

Ethan chuckled. "Well, that's perhaps a slight exaggeration, but I do opine that most men like to have that part praised from time to time."

"Yes, well, as I was saying—"

"Do you know what your problem is, Miss Holmes?"

"Mihos was in service to the pharaoh in the myths, but—"

"You have not praised enough of these, uh, divine portions of a man's anatomy."

As she rose, Shelly whacked the book down on the table so hard that it pinched her thumb, still between the pages, but she was so flustered she scarcely felt it. "And I suppose you offer yourself to fill in the appalling gaps in my history." Shelly flushed a brighter hue as she realized the way her "fill in" remark could be interpreted, especially given the bawdy nature of their banter, but mercifully Ethan made no innuendo.

He said solemnly, the wicked smile at his mouth ruining his homily, "As you are so fond of pointing out, knowledge is kin to experience. Mere observation can take a scientist only so far. The more one, ah, empirically observes, the more one learns."

Hiding her fury and confusion, Shelly tapped her long fingertips on her chin. "Perhaps you are right. There is a particular footman who has been eyeing me in a most improper way. I shouldn't doubt that he will be happy to, ah, fill in those gaps in my experience." She turned to flounce out of the room, adding over her shoulder, "And when you are ready to give our investigation the weight it deserves instead of reducing it to frivolity, you may so inform me."

The speed with which he moved astonished her. One minute he was lounging at the library table, long legs spread before him and crossed at the ankles; the next he was pulling her away from the door and into his arms. "How is this for frivolity?" He put his mouth to her ear. He smelled of brandy and expensive cigars, and promised huskily, "If you go near another man when you have me veritably panting at your skirts, I shall paddle that enticing arse."

While Shelly gawked up at him, astounded, for never in all her life had any man dared so address her, he kissed her. She was so stunned at his effrontery that she was passive at first, even her instinctual predatory skills latent while she learned the first touch and taste of him. His kiss began hard, demanding, but when she was still, he lifted her unresisting arms about his neck and really bent to his art.

Once again, Ethan Perot did everything with both verve and passion, a true Renaissance man. That long mouth that was so fluent in verbiage displayed facility in "frivolous" matters as well.

His mouth was so soft, unlike the unexpected strength in his long, gangly body. He was pure muscle beneath the fine clothes, despite his slimness, but as she'd known since laying eyes on him for the first time, the true power of the most charismatic man she'd ever met came from his mind. He exhibited that charisma holding her in his arms, murmuring arousing love words in Latin and Arabic against her tingling mouth, urging her to open wider to him.

Meanwhile, his curious hands stroked her from back to hips, stopping just short of impropriety. His lips were so sweet, so soft and reverential on hers. She'd never been kissed like this, sensually, his mouth rubbing from side to side, yet with a promise of passion in the barest stroke of his tongue against the sensitive corners of her mouth. There was no other word for it: He wooed her. She could have shoved him away at any point, but perversely, his gentle control made her long to make him lose it.

He'd started this on his terms, but she'd end it on hers. Where was the harm in one kiss?

Opening her mouth, she teasingly traced the corners of his lips with her own tongue. His hands froze on her back. He stood still and let her take the lead. She used the very tips of her fingers to draw circles on the pleasing musculature of his back, testing his sensitivity by going progressively lower. When she reached the indentations at the top of his buttocks, he tensed those muscles, proving that even through the layers of clothing, he reveled in her touch.

With a shuddering breath, he broke the long, luxurious kiss and trailed a fiery path down the side of her neck. It was her turn to tense with pleasure. She arched into him, pressing her formidable bosom to his chest. He accepted the unspoken invitation, mirroring her actions by using the very tip of one finger to trace the areola hidden from him. So expertly he balanced the art of teasing with torment.

Her nipples hardened. He brushed one so gently she barely felt it, yet pleasure radiated from her greatest sexual organ—her brain—to the tips of her fingers and the ends of her toes.

She growled deep in her throat in pleasure.

Her eyes slitted open to find him watching her avidly.

"Your eyes are glowing, my very dear Miss Holmes. Now why would that be?"

Just like that, she shoved him away and fled across the room to the door, knowing she left him victorious in this battle of wills.

As the door slammed shut behind her, Ethan smiled—a smile she would have recognized, for it was often her own expression when, as a werewolf, she began the pleasure of the hunt. . . .

Naked, fresh from his bath, Luke Simball was prowling his apartment, feeling his fangs sprout with the need to feed, when an image flashed through his brain: Arielle, in her emerald cloak, a new determination in her glowing blue eyes as she daintily made her way through the woods outside her father's house. The same woods Luke had prowled before.

Finally it was time.

"Come to me, my love," he whispered. "I will be waiting."

Tonight would be the night. He'd prepared her carefully enough, with the wooing and kissing and catnip. Tonight Arielle would come to him as her true self and join him in the hunt. First he would initiate her into the ancient blood rites that were her birthright as well as his, and then he would initiate her into womanhood, sealing her fate and their bond, just as the legends foretold.

Dressing quickly, he called for his closed phaeton.

Chapter Twelve

In his own rooms, Seth shoved back his half-eaten dinner, his heart pounding with a sudden vision: Arielle, in a green cloak, sneaking through the estate grounds to the main road, where she hailed a closed hansom cab.

Next Seth saw Luke, his golden hair wet from a bath, indicating the haste with which he'd dressed, driving his horses around a bend. The phaeton almost tipped over before a skillful snap of the whip and adjustment of the steeds stabilized the vehicle again.

Seth leaped up so quickly he overturned the tray his manservant had prepared for him.

Arielle was alone and unprotected, and Luke was after her in a tearing hurry. Where were they going?

Seth called for his Arabian stallion, reaching out with his mind to Arielle as he hauled on a pair of boots and made sure he had his cane. *"Arielle, speak to me. . . ."*

At that exact moment, inside the hansom cab, Arielle sank back against the squabs, rubbing her throbbing temples on each side with two fingers. These probings into her heart and mind were powerful enough when she was asleep, but now, fully awake, she felt . . . invaded. Furthermore, she was pretty sure she knew who dared this psychic ravishment, demanding, *"Speak to me. . . ."* The presence trying to penetrate her mind was bold, arrogant, like Seth, and behind her closed eyes she caught a flashing glimpse of fierce golden orbs piercing into the most sacrosanct places of her heart and mind.

Just as fiercely she tried to block him out. She didn't want him to know where she was going. This was a journey she had to make alone, without his dubious protection or even Luke's laughing encouragement. If she were to become the true descendant of Cleopatra in name as well as deed, she had to learn, on her own terms, in her own way, what her mother was trying to warn her about. Only then could she figure out which of these men, if either, was her destiny.

And she'd brook no more interference from anyone in that quest, even Shelly.

Opening her eyes, lowering a mental curtain over her wayward thoughts, she picked up the travel book kept in the pocket of the carriage and read a boring account of the many picturesque sights around Bath.

When the presence still circled like a predatory cat, she began to read aloud, the same passage over and over, until she felt stupefied with boredom, her senses becoming slow and lethargic. Gradually the image of the golden eyes faded. She thought about putting the tome aside, but she didn't dare, so she continued to read all the way to her destination.

When she stepped down at the head of the alley that led to Madame Aurora's, misgivings struck her for the first time. It was almost ten o'clock, terribly late to come calling with no appointment. Yet the medium must be used to unconventional hours, for the lights in her small flat blazed.

Taking a deep breath, Arielle used the door knocker as loudly as she dared, letting the insistence of the sound speak for itself.

Luke reached the main post road long ahead of Seth, but even at this late hour it was crowded with partygoers, lured by the unusually fine fall weather, and cabs. They all looked the same, ugly black coaches, their occupants shielded behind drawn curtains.

Luke let his team slow to a trot, briefly closing his eyes as he tried to concentrate on Arielle, but though the image of her lovely face grew large in his mind, he couldn't sense where she was or what she observed. When she had been innocent of his powers, or while she slept, he'd been able to inveigle himself into her thoughts. But now it was as if she were alerted to his psychic ability and was resisting it—a development that actually gave him an advantage over Seth, because his brother's mental powers had always been greater than his own.

Though Luke knew her newfound strength made his task harder, it also pleased him, for she was becoming a fitting consort of Mihos before his very eyes. Her resistance whetted his appetites and made him more determined to dominate her and bend her to his will. Then, together, they would rule the night. Most important, his rival would be dead— after they combined their powers to defeat him. . . .

But first he had to find her, now, when she was alone and unguarded. It was finally time to complete the seduction he'd begun the other night in the woods. He slowed the pace still further, trying to peer inside the carriages, but it seemed hopeless, for he could make out only the barest glimpse of a lady's wide hat, or a man's beard. He pulled his carriage to the side, watching the stream of traffic, hoping for something alien to the feline world but very relevant to the hustle and bustle of London's ton: luck.

From the opposite direction, Seth also rode slowly up the main post road, eyeing hansom cabs with the same result. Short of rudely pulling aside each curtain, he didn't know how to find her. It was certain she was blocking him, for he'd caught the image of a book and then nothing but the Bath springs, steaming until he could visualize only the haze.

He rested his hands on the upper curve of his English saddle, contemplating the stream of carriages as he reappraised recent events. He would try some of Miss Shelly Holmes's logical tactics, which by all accounts seemed to be amazingly successful in deciphering puzzles at which others shook their heads.

One, he knew Arielle was quite upset, both with her father and with him. He'd considered reassuring her that he'd left the old woman a considerable sum to ensure better care for Miss Fein, but he needed Arielle to be powerfully drawn to him if she were to channel her powers to help him defeat Luke. On an instinctive level, she had to move as he moved, believe as he believed, and that type of bond came not from trust built through good deeds but from sheer animal attraction.

Two, he also knew Arielle's primary goal in life was to find out why her mother had killed herself and what Isis was trying to communicate to her daughter from the afterlife. So far, fragmented visions were Arielle's only link to her mother, but Madam Aurora had opened a powerful channel none of the rest of them could match.

Three, when Arielle was troubled, she always fingered her amulet or stared at her mother's picture. And four, the only other time Arielle had ventured out on an unescorted mission, she had gone to the medium.

Turning his black Arabian sharply, Seth cantered the animal in the opposite direction up the road, toward Madame Aurora's flat.

Arielle rapped the door knocker again, harder. This time shuffling footsteps approached. It opened a crack and a bleary eye peered out. The eye widened and the door opened slightly. "Miss Blaylock . . . this is a surprise."

"I apologize for troubling you so late, but I wonder if I might retain your services tonight? With a sizable bonus for the unconventional hour."

"I seldom do séances in my own domicile," the woman said dismissively, preparing to shove the door closed in Arielle's face.

With a strength and agility that surprised even herself, Arielle shoved the portal open, forcing the woman back into her tiny hallway. In the brightly lit vestibule, the medium looked old, most unexotic, and afraid. She wore an old dressing gown, and without the turban her hair looked thin and streaked with gray. With no paint on her face she was sallow, her face lined with too many years of unshed tears. Yet this woman of obvious questionable character but powerful psychic ability was Arielle's only true link with her mother.

Forcing a calm she did not feel, tamping down the strange urge to toy with the medium just so she could enjoy the fear in the woman's face, Arielle held out her grandmother's pearl necklace. "More than adequate recompense for your trouble, I believe."

"I can promise you nothing. I did my best at the séance, and the veils are much harder to lift without the channel to the departed that is provided by sitting in their chair, or using their things . . ." She trailed off as Arielle removed the amulet from her garter belt and let it dangle, glinting in the light with golden promise.

"There are powerful opposing forces trying to stop your mother from communicating with you," the medium insisted, refusing to take the amulet.

"I know that. The question is—from where are these forces coming?"

The woman shrugged.

"Please." Arielle stuck the pearl necklace and several pound notes in the woman's pocket. "I will give you more when I get my next allowance."

The medium's resolve was weakening as she fingered the pearls and bills in her pocket. "I can promise you nothing," she repeated grimly.

"Of course. But I suspect the psychic force shielding my mother's influence was sitting at that table with us, forcing her to speak in riddles. And . . . I was not ready. Now, alone with you, I have a much better chance of hearing her because I am more than ready to listen."

The medium looked from the golden amulet to Arielle's pleading expression.

"Something is happening to me I do not understand." Arielle pressed her advantage. "My mother experienced the same things, but my father has deliberately kept all information about her from me. I . . . don't remember anything of the séance."

She hesitated, but somehow putting the true reason for this visit into words made her feel better. "And I no longer trust either my father or Seth enough to believe all they tell me. I must see my mother for myself, speak to her myself. I do not care what it costs."

When the medium sighed heavily, still hesitating,

Arielle managed at last, "You're my only hope. Please."

Searching Arielle's gaze, the woman nodded begrudgingly. She escorted Arielle into a small adjacent salon that had a round table with chairs around it. She lit a brace of candles and set it in the middle of the table, turning down the gas sconces lining the walls until the room was dim. They both sat at the table. The woman held out her hand for Arielle's. Arielle clasped it, wondering if her own was as cold and clammy as the medium's felt. "You're afraid?"

"You know nothing of the murders all over the city?"

"Of course, but how are they related to us?"

The medium looked incredulous. "One or more great cats are stalking the streets of London. From events at the séance, I believe that cat wants you for his consort, and the strange dreams you're having, the feelings you do not comprehend, are preparing you for that transformation. Anyone who gets in that being's way is in peril. If I help you I'm in peril. If you have any sense, you will be afraid, too."

Arielle sank back against her chair in shock at the plain speaking.

"Do you still want me to do this? There was evil in that room, as well as good, and they both want you."

Arielle nodded. "I know. But I have to try. I cannot fight what I do not understand, nor separate evil from good without my mother's help."

The medium sighed reluctant agreement. Grabbing a turban from an adjacent commode, she stuck it on her head, shoving the thin wisps of graying hair under it. She looked silly in the ornate jeweled headpiece combined with her worn old dressing gown, but this time when she took Arielle's hand, her own did not tremble. Her eyes had begun to sparkle with that anticipation she'd exhibited at the séance. Some of the wrinkles seemed smoothed away, as if, with this sense of purpose for which she was born, she underwent the same rejuvenation she sometimes obtained for others.

Clasping the amulet in her free hand, she began a strange humming deep in her chest, her eyes closed, her expression beatific. The candle flames on the table began swaying with her, side to side in perfect tempo. Arielle blinked at this sure evidence that the medium had a strange energy that interacted with everything around her. It was almost as if the woman could not only feel the heat of the candles but could also control it.

Did she summon the spirit world as easily? Arielle truly remembered little of the séance, so, while her heart pounded a frantic tattoo of hope, she couldn't repress a bit of skepticism at the same time. What was her money really buying her? Even as she told herself that was her father speaking, the tablecloth began swaying, too, also in tempo with the back-and-forth movements of the medium's body.

The gas sconces joined in the dance. "Isisss . . ." hissed the woman. The candle flames all leaped in unison, also hissing, making Arielle jump. Perhaps it was a trick of the light, but the center jewel in her turban, cheap paste that it was, began to glow an eerie green. A thin beam of light pierced the darkness beyond the candle glow.

And then, as if called forth, two dim specks of green appeared at the table's edge. Eyes. Staring at her. Arielle reached out, her heart jumping as she felt a tender touch stroke back her hair. "Mother."

The specks danced back out of reach.

The medium suddenly went totally still with a great shudder. The wall sconces shuddered too, and then they were calm and steady, as were the ones on the table.

Arielle longed to leap up and approach what she now knew was the spirit of her mother, but she felt Madame Aurora's eerie stillness and stayed put. Whatever this connection was, it was tenuous. She could only draw a deep, shaky breath and force herself to wait.

As if in reward for her patience, the specks grew larger, brighter, and a shadow began growing on the wall next to Arielle. The shadow of a cat, a shape Arielle had known and loved all her life, for it was the same shape on the amulet clutched tightly in the medium's hand. The shadow grew deeper, more defined, and slowly began resolving itself into a colored image.

Bast appeared before Arielle, ancient Egyptian goddess of hearth and home, protectress of women and children. The black cat sat regally erect on her haunches, head high, ears pricked, a glowing carnelian necklace around her neck as she stared at Arielle with wise green eyes. Unable to help herself, Arielle reached out to what she knew was the living embodiment of all that made her mother good and vital.

"Mother . . ." Arielle whispered, almost afraid to breathe.

The brightly colored image faded as Arielle's hand appeared in its luminous circle of light. Arielle jerked back, and the image grew bright again, so alive it fairly made the air shimmer. Accepting the unspoken boundary her mother set between the living and the dead, Arielle sank back and reached out with her heart instead, ceding all rational thought. For a timeless moment she let her mother feel all the anguishes and losses of a lonely childhood, the pain of the accident that had left her lame, and lastly, her current state of fear and confusion.

The cat inclined its head. Finally Arielle heard her mother's voice, soft and lilting but speaking flawless English. "Daughter . . ." came the reply. "I have missed you. I am glad you honor your mother with this summons."

"I miss you, too. Every day of my life." Tears misted Arielle's eyes.

"I know why you have come, and you are wise. You fear them, do you not?"

Arielle took a deep, relieved breath that she didn't have to explain. "Yes. I sense somehow that Seth and Luke battle for my very soul. Help me understand. Why do they want me?"

"You are the daughter of Isis, both in name and in spirit. In our culture, Isis is goddess of wisdom and is the only being with power to resurrect life from death. Did you not study the book I left for you?"

"My father hid your things from me."

Bast gave a bleak little yowl. "Rupert," mourned a decidedly human voice with the remembrance of a human's pain. "Could you not have given our daughter this one gift from me?"

Arielle realized that the book must be with the costume her father had kept from her. "I'll find it, Mother. And read it cover to cover. But will it prepare me?"

"Only you can answer that, my daughter, by the choices you make." The glowing green eyes grew intense. "I see the change upon you, even earlier than it came upon me. But what will you do with that power?"

Arielle was puzzled at first, but then she followed Bast's stare to her hands. All ten fingers sprouted cat's claws, and when she turned her hands over, she saw pads forming on her palms. Arielle clenched her hands so hard that the claws pierced her flesh. The white-hot darts of pain made her gasp, and she was so horrified by this thing living within her that she felt a visceral reaction of revulsion. As they both watched, the claws receded and the pads faded, leaving her fully human again.

"You see," her mother said matter-of-factly. "You have the power to control your fate. But do you have the will?"

"Tell me what to do. . . ." She trailed off, for Bast was shaking her head before Arielle finished.

"Every *ka* must be balanced by the choices it

makes, Arielle, in this world and the next. I have given you all the tools for guidance that I could. It is up to you to learn to use them." The image began to fade.

"No, please, I must know. . . . Why did you kill yourself? Because you were so terribly unhappy with Father?"

The image stabilized as Bast's eyes grew bright, as if she suppressed tears. "I could not bear my. . . . becoming. My unhappiness with him made the lure of the night stronger, but it was not because of him."

Arielle understood, and a great sense of relief took her that at least her father was not directly responsible for her mother's suicide. "But cats are not inherently evil. Look at you now . . . you embody everything that is good."

"In this form, perhaps. There are others I took that . . ." If a cat could shudder, Bast shuddered. "The lure of the hunt is strongest of all in our kind, and the more we practice it, the stronger grows the urge to kill. Such was my fate, and my mother's fate, and Cleopatra's before her. That power has always been the source of the allure of the women in our bloodline. It is said only we descend directly from Isis and Osiris, giving us great influence over men. But the price we pay is costly indeed if we cede to the allure of the kill. We lose our humanity and our *kas*."

Arielle was confused. "Allure? For what?"

Bast sounded sad. "Immortality. Did you not know that if you embrace the cat's ways and unite with Mihos, you will live forever? But to live the forever half-life, you will become a thing of evil."

"How can I do such things? I'm just a girl, not even a woman grown."

"Yet . . ."

The bright image was fading again. "Be stronger than I was. Be guided by good, not evil, and you will live the long, happy life I could not. That is my wish for you. And that will be my rest, when you choose the right path. I have faith in your goodness, my daughter."

"No, wait!" Arielle reached out, forgetting the boundary, and the image dissipated into a shadow. Arielle cried, "Tell me, please, which of them is good, and which is evil?"

"That depends upon you . . . you . . . you."

Arielle shut her eyes, listening again with her heart, and thought she heard, "Study the Book, my daughter. It can save you. They are good words. Learn these words, for you shall have need of them."

One last time Bast was bright before her again, her cat face intense with passion. She recited, " 'No evil thing of any shape or kind shall spring up against me, and no baleful object, and no harmful thing, and no disastrous thing shall happen unto me. I open the door in heaven. I rule my throne. I open the way for the births which take place on this day. I am the child who traverseth the road of yesterday. I am today for untold nations and peoples. I am she who protecteth you for millions of years. Whether ye be denizens of heaven, or of the earth, or of the south, or of the north, or of the east, or of the west, the fear of me is in your bodies. I am she whose being hath been wrought in his eye. I shall die a peaceful death and walk the afterlife, not the half-life.' " Bast looked at her commandingly. "Say it with me: 'I am the child who traverseth the road of yesterday. I shall die a peaceful death and walk the afterlife, not the half-life.' "

Haltingly, Arielle said the words, once, twice, with Bast's urging. And then the lovely cat goddess purred, and a smile almost formed upon the slanted face. The green eyes seemed to twinkle their blessing. She faded into shadow, into a bare outline, and finally into smoke. Then even the smoke had evanesced into nothingness.

The candles flickered brightly, dancing again like normal flames. Madame Aurora blinked. The eerie glow from her jewel died to the dull glint of paste. With a shuddering breath, she stirred, looking exhausted. She rubbed her eyes once, twice, then focused on Arielle's tear-streaked face. She caught her shoulder. "I did not promise you would like what you heard."

She held out the amulet. Arielle took it. They both stared down at the woman's palm. A perfect imprint of Bast remained, hieroglyphics and all, burned into her flesh by the power of the vision for which she'd been the willing conduit.

"It doesn't sting," Madame Aurora said. "It will fade by tomorrow."

Arielle insisted on putting some salve on it before she left. Then, drained, she tied the amulet back onto her garter and shrugged into her cloak.

Madame Aurora was watching her worriedly. "You have a carriage?"

"I told the driver to return in an hour. He'll be waiting." Arielle held out her hand as Madame Aurora opened the door. "Thank you. You are a kind woman."

Madame Aurora ignored the outstretched hand and instead gave Arielle a brief, matronly hug. "Study, as your mother said, my dear. Somewhere in the things she left you are the answers you seek. They will guide you."

Arielle gave a hollow laugh. "To what? To become a toy for a cat's paw for all time . . . or to die because I refuse to live a half-life, like my mother, and must stop the madness overtaking me? What choice is this?" She exited, her bitter words ringing still after she left. Her gaze was blinded with tears, so she didn't see the glowing eyes watching her from an alcove.

As the hansom cab drew away, a horse tied to a hitching post shied aside.

It was a powerful black stallion of Arab blood.

A gold-headed lion's cane rapped on the medium's door.

Chapter Thirteen

An hour later Arielle was climbing into bed to stare dull-eyed into the darkness. The fact that she could see every object in the room as if it were daylight was no longer a mystery to her. The strange hunger she'd felt for cream, the allure of Luke's scent, which she now realized must have been catnip . . . all the signs of her "becoming," as her mother put it, had been there if she hadn't been too afraid to heed them. Now she was just exhausted, weary of looking for cures to an ailment no young woman should have to face.

She'd spent thirty minutes searching the larder for her mother's trunk, a box, anything, but she'd found no spell book, only a lovely costume of Egyptian glory. It was a diaphanous affair of golden fabric, finely pleated, that wrapped about the hips. Sandals inlaid with carnelian and lapis lazuli matched the beading on the gown. The almost bare bosom had an appurtenance that was unlike anything Arielle had ever seen. It was a breastplate of precious materials—gold, pearls, even a few unpolished diamonds—all inset into thin golden strands so finely woven that they would be flexible when worn.

And the diadem. She put it on, thrilled, wishing for a mirror. She recognized the ancient symbols of the pharaoh: the vulture and the hooded cobra, attached to the front of a crown that would leave the wearer's hair bare. For an instant an image of her mother wearing these garments flashed in her mind. Her father, much younger, coming into the room and yelling. Her mother, crying, folding the garments away into a trunk . . .

Arielle removed the diadem, feeling sad as she looked down at the very old but still lustrous garments. They didn't look old enough to have been Cleopatra's, surely, but if they were a legacy of her mother's mother, they were still precious. The mere fact that her father had not wanted her mother to wear them, and refused to give them to her daughter, spoke highly of their power to transform, and not just in image. Bundling them into a clean cloth, Arielle took them with her to her room and hid them in a box beneath several hats.

Then, exhausted, she'd changed and gotten into bed. Soon she'd demand the book from her father. Soon she'd look for the guidance both her mother and the medium promised. Now she needed only to rest and forget the trials and tribulations that lay ahead. Her head scarcely touched the pillow before she was asleep.

But it was not a dreamless sleep.

They were there. Both of them.

The one of brightness and the one of dark. As usual, she could not see their faces behind the lion-headed masks they wore, but she'd always thought the golden-haired one seemed the kinder of the two, for the man in the black-maned mask was rougher. He tormented her and teased her like the great cat he was, forcing her to taste her own blood and marking her with scratches as he learned her end to end. Yet strangely, the marks aroused rather than pained her, made her ache between the legs and reach back to him. But when she opened her eyes to see him better, a strange image stared back, a white leopard with spots and glowing blue eyes exactly the color of her own.

She knew she stared at herself, and what she would be soon enough. The lions and the snow leopard bounded off together into the darkness, roaring. Then came the sounds of tearing flesh and slurping, and she was drowning in the taste of blood . . .

She awoke drenched in sweat, her night rail sticking to her, so sick she had to rush to the ewer and vomit. As she straightened, wiping her mouth on a towel, she felt more than heard, *"Come to me, my love."*

She backed away from the window even as her heart surged in response.

"I will be waiting . . ." came the soft caress of verbal temptation. Smoke seeped through the closed shutters and barred windows of her room, filling her chamber with a scent she recognized, a manly scent counterbalanced by the spice of cloves and catnip.

The smoke began coalescing, glittering like gold dust, forming into a beautiful being. Luke stood before her, his chest broad and muscular, his legs lithe with controlled power. He wore only a simple sarong and sandals. He could have stepped down from an Egyptian relief, his face hidden behind a golden-headed lion's mask. But when he reached a hand toward her, the man's hand was tipped with powerful lion's claws.

Arielle shrank against the wall even as her nostrils flared at the luscious scents. He smelled so good, looked so magnificent. Exactly like her dreams.

But was he good or evil? The rogue thought came—*Does it matter? You are a superior being. Roam the night with him and become one with him.*

"Come, Arielle," Luke commanded. "It is time to seek your destiny."

Arielle forced words out past the lump in her throat. "No. Go away."

Luke stalked her as she sidled along the wall toward the hallway door. "You fear what you do not understand. Come with me, feel the wet grass soft on the pads of your feet, scent the night and let it fill you with its power. Such is your birthright. Why do you think your mother named you Arielle, lioness of God?"

Arielle dashed around the corner and put a table between them, struggling hard to remember the taste of the blood in her dream. "My mother now regrets what she became and wants me to be stronger. I am a Blaylock, too." Arielle took a deep, calming breath, trying to view the fantastic through her father's phlegmatic English eyes, but the inhalation made her dizzy with the promise of Egyptian magic.

Luke tossed the mask aside, revealing his handsome, frustrated face. "Every sinew and bone of you knows I speak the truth. All that makes you unique, all that makes you powerful, comes from your Egyptian blood. Embrace it. You are better than these weak humans. We can both live forever if you only accept your place by my side."

"And all that makes me human? You have no use for that, but it is very important to me."

Stubbornly, Arielle forced herself to stay put as Luke, with one swipe, knocked the table out of his way, leaving the glossy wood scratched with claw marks. Then he was on her, looking all male, but he had the acrid scent of an aroused cat. He touched her shoulder tenderly, with just a fingertip, and she realized he traced a scratch, one leftover from her dreams. "Do you resist me because of this? Seth did this to you. He likes it rough. He is not meant for you, Arielle."

He tasted of cloves and cinnamon and catnip, his lips so soft she barely felt them. But she felt his body well enough. His bare chest was warm and vital against her own almost bare bosom. She felt so . . . at one with him when he held her like this, gently, so that she could pull away whenever she pleased.

So very unlike Seth, who commanded, and lectured, and was often rough. Yet the mere thought of him brought that telltale wetness between her legs in a way Luke never had . . . No, she refused to think of him while she was in another man's arms. Rebelliously she told herself she had to give Luke a chance. Perhaps he was the good one, after all. The chosen one.

It was easier than she'd expected. That luscious scent invaded her nostrils as he kissed her more deeply, insinuating itself into her brain until she was filled with its promise of a better life. A life of forever, where she could cast off the infirmities and fears of her human half for the certainty of the hunt and the kill . . . Dimly she tried to latch onto her mother's face, but she saw only Bast, the cat.

"Be strong," Bast said.

She was strong. Had always been strong, never so much as now, in the arms of this being part man, part cat. Even more important, Luke filled her with joy, his tongue now gently assuaging the bitter, parched feel of her mouth, like the Nile blessing the sere Egyptian plains with life. He was right. Unlike Seth, he had never hurt her, either physically or emotionally. What else could she do but embrace him and the power he drew from her?

She kissed him back, fully and completely, her

acrid scent of feline arousal joining his own, hairs beginning to grow on the backs of her hands, claws peeking from the tips of her fingers.

Several miles away, in the alley leading to Madame Aurora's modest home, bobbies swarmed, blocking off the narrow path and keeping the curious at bay. Lights blazed from every room of the house, illuminating the interior in the predawn darkness. Inside, a physician could just be seen bent over something. The walls were spattered and streaked with what looked like dark red paint. A curious boy sidled under the rope blocking off the alley and dashed up to the window for a closer look.

He got a better one than he bargained for. He cried out, his dirty hand over his mouth to force back a gag. Inside the room a curtain was pulled shut, and then a bobby was jerking him away and shoving him back outside the rope. This time the boy went without protest. Some of his friends descended on him, whispering questions, but under the severe stare of several constables, the boy remained mum.

"Did anyone see anythin' hereabouts in the past hour or so?" demanded a tall, thin policeman. A portly man, in an apron streaked with flour, stepped forward.

"I was leavin' to deliver me bread when I saw this great black horse, and a man in a black cape standing quiet-like. In that alcove there." He pointed to a doorway directly across the street.

"Quiet-like? You mean like he didn't want to be seen?" demanded the bobby.

"Aye. He moved so quick and silent, like a dream almost, that he scared me so I near dropped me tray of johnnycakes and miner's pies. He looked in me direction once and I ducked behind a corner because somethin' about him . . . made me affrighted. But I couldn't hide there forever, and when I looked again I saw a girl come out, a girl in a green cloak, and I saw madam hug her good-bye. Neither one o' them saw the gent."

"You think he was a gent?"

"He had the dress and manner o' one, and a great gold-headed cane." The baker scratched his head, making his floppy hat even floppier. "I went on me way just as madam opened the door and let him in. Like she knew him."

"Can you describe him?" demanded the bobby, pencil poised over a notebook.

"It were dark and he moved so fast, and he wore a hat. But I saw that there cane clear enough in the light by the door."

"Gold, you said?"

"Aye." The baker swallowed as the door opened and a blood-spattered bobby staggered outside to retch against the wall. "It were in the shape of a lion: A roaring lion."

About the time Madame Aurora's mortal remains were wheeled away on a cart before a growing and frightened crowd of poor Londoners, the barred windows of Arielle's room burst free, taking a good chunk of wall with them, the racket bringing instant lights all over the mansion. As the wall continued to crumble, two magnificent felines followed the shutters and barred windows down, jumping the two stories as if they were two feet.

The larger of the two was a huge lion with a full golden mane and green eyes. The smaller, but no less imposing, was a snow leopard with enormous feet the size of small snowshoes. Her eyes were blue and she had a gorgeous white coat speckled with spots. They disappeared into the darkness just as several armed footmen, the earl in a cap and Shelly in a robe, appeared on the grounds.

They all stared from the debris on the cropped grass up at the gaping hole, then into the darkness. Shelly bent and tugged at something. It was the tip of a lethal claw stuck in a shutter, still curved and gleaming in the torchlight. They all stared at it. Without apology, Shelly grabbed a torch from a footman and pulled two long hairs off the side of the wall where they'd caught on a rough piece of stone. Turning them this way and that in the light, she said to herself, "Gold. Like a lion's mane."

The footmen and the earl all gasped.

Shelly went back inside without a word, pocketing the claw and hairs.

The earl collapsed where he stood. "Arielle," he whispered. And then, "Isis." He rocked himself back and forth, holding his head as if he could not bear the memories tormenting him.

The footmen exchanged a glance. His wife had died long before their employment, but they did not need to be told that the earl had seen this behavior before. He was so distraught that it took two of the footmen to help him inside. While they poured him a brandy, Shelly hurried downstairs dressed now in her breeches, a plain linen shirt, and a long peacoat.

"I shall do my best to follow them and bring her back," she said curtly.

The earl merely stared at a wall.

"Get him a doctor and tell Ethan Perot I have gone to Luke Simball's flat," she ordered the footmen and the butler, who had just come into the hallway, half-dressed.

The earl roused himself from his daze. "Simball? Why him?"

"Do you not know? *Simball* means *lion* in several African cultures. I have had colleagues investigate Luke Simball, and his whereabouts on the nights of the murders cannot be verified. Besides, I have other reasons to believe him dangerous." She grabbed a brace of pistols from a footman. "Something else I have recently discovered: Seth Taub is his half brother, and both of them had recently moved to England when their father was killed by cats. Seth is not what he seems and is not to be trusted with Arielle either." She slammed out the door, leaving the poor earl gaping.

The lioness of God had never felt freer or more alive. Luke was right: The plush, wet grass against the pads of her feet, the taste of the night on her tongue—these were the reasons she had been born. Why had she struggled against this becoming?

By the time the ground hit her feet outside, she

had only the vaguest realization that she now had four legs, not two. Her senses had never been so sharply acute, especially her vision and hearing. As she ran, she could feel her own muscles rippling, the whiskers making her nose unbearably sensitive.

And the small structures they passed with lights blazing inside . . . how confining they seemed. How pitiful, as pitiful as the creatures they sheltered. She looked at the being loping next to her and wondered if God had ever made anything more magnificent. Luke as a man was powerful enough, but as a lion, golden mane streaming in the night breeze, he was indomitable, a being born of bright things only kings could command.

And she knew, even without his saying so, that he wanted her for his consort. This was why he led her past the outskirts of London, avoiding the roads, deeper into the woods. This night would be her first test. Was she wild enough and strong enough to rule with him?

The dwindling human side of Arielle realized that for once her leg pained her not at all. She felt no unevenness in her gait nor awkwardness in her lope. She felt instead one with the night and the creature next to her who seemed to rule it.

She heard the rustle of wild things as they scrambled out of her path. With a lethal paw, Luke swatted at a pheasant without breaking stride and the bird collapsed in a bleeding pile of feathers, its head severed.

Arielle's nostrils flared at the scent of blood. She slowed, about to turn back, but Luke nudged her

Catspell

in the side, saying with words she heard only in her head, *"Not yet, my love. We feast soon on suitable prey. First you must learn."*

Reluctantly, her stomach growling, Arielle ran on, the woods so thick now that even her acute night vision was limited. Finally Luke stopped dead and crouched in the thick brush. Arielle dropped down beside him, peeking through the undergrowth to see what he stared at, his eyes glowing bright green in the fitful moonlight glinting between the thick tree branches.

Then she saw it. A buck. His magnificent antlered head was tilted warily, as if he picked up a strange scent. A doe and fawn fed next to him, attuned to his nervousness. Their tails began to twitch back and forth.

Arielle shifted her weight slightly, and a leaf, one only, rustled.

All three heads popped up to stare at the spot where they crouched. The three deer tensed to run away.

In a blur of motion, Luke burst free of the bushes in one giant leap, his claws dragging down the doe. He moved to bite the neck, but the buck bent his head and rammed Luke with all his might. Arielle ran out to help, but she shifted from foot to foot, unsure what to do.

Luke was hit directly in the head and blinked, dazed enough to allow the doe to struggle free. Her neck bleeding from the deep claw marks, she still ran fleetly, her fawn next to her, and disappeared. The buck blocked their escape for precious seconds. But when he turned to follow, Luke had recovered enough to hook his claws into the thick hide covering the rump. The buck kicked backward with his pointed hoof, but this time Luke was ready and merely used the opportunity to hook the leg with his other paw.

As if he swatted a gnat, Luke brought the buck down and bit casually into the neck, immobilizing the creature.

The scent of blood wafted to Arielle. Her deep blue eyes began to glow with icy desire. Without being told to, she joined Luke. Jaws gaping, she bent to nip at the neck, but Luke released his grip enough for the strangling buck to wheeze in air. Slashing the legs deeply, Luke held the buck in place and looked at Arielle, blood dripping from his mouth.

"I promised you play, dear one. He's all yours."

Arielle looked between the panic-stricken buck and Luke. Some weakening remnant of compassion made her hesitate. But Luke looked at her, his green eyes so magnetic and fierce with pride in her and the hunt that she could not disappoint him.

Minutes became hours of enjoyment as Arielle, the lioness of God, became Luke Simball's best pupil. Her first lesson opened new horizons of possibility, and for the first time she saw what Luke had known for two years: The joy of the hunt was almost as sweet as the taste of the kill.

As Arielle toyed with the dying creature, Luke watched like what he was—king of the pride, green eyes glowing with lust for this wild creature in all her forms.

* * *

Shelly looked up at Luke Simball's darkened rooms. She didn't think he'd be there, but she hoped a search would yield some clue as to where he'd spirited Arielle. She was about to slip around to the back of the flat when she noticed two things: Luke's dark glossy door was scratched with the deep imprint of a lion's claws. And to the side of the building stood a restive black Arabian Shelly recognized. Seth's horse.

A bundle was tied neatly over the saddle, and when she opened it a black cloak and black garments were revealed, wrapped neatly about Seth's magnificent lion-headed cane. When she shifted the bundle, however, her hand came away dotted with blood. She reared back, nostrils flaring at the familiar scent, but blood didn't carry the unique signature of a being as did skin, hair, and sweat.

He'd removed his clothes for the same reason she removed hers: to shape-shift. He was chasing Luke and Arielle. Shelly inhaled the familiar scent of Seth, and then she put the clothes back as she'd found them, wondering whom he'd injured, or perhaps killed, though there did not appear to be enough blood for murder.

Shelly moved warily closer to the scratched door, looking around for any threat, and then, using her powerful sense of smell, she sniffed the marks, not sure if she hoped the scent matched the clothes or did not, for this piece of evidence would be irrefutable. The one thing Seth could not hide no matter how skillful was his psychic abilities.

Every creature, whether man or beast, smelled slightly different. When she sniffed deeply of the claw marks, the scent was bold and dark, like the man who emitted it—Seth. Exactly the same scent was coming from the clothes. Shelly stumbled back at this proof that Seth was certainly a lion creature, perhaps Mihos himself reborn.

It was certain Seth had deliberately left his sign emblazoned on Luke's door, a blatant challenge. A battle was brewing. As she'd begun to suspect, there were two great cat-beasts wandering London, not one. And they were half brothers, both with Egyptian blood, who were also mortal enemies.

Most terrifying of all, Arielle was the prize they battled over . . .

Moving behind a huge pile of carpets at the back of a rug establishment, Shelly methodically removed her own clothes. Normally she'd never risk transformation in such a dense part of the city, but she had no choice. It would be easier to track the lions if she, too, were fleetly four-footed. She'd just have to try to avoid any innocent citizenry.

An alarm incited by cat creatures was bad enough.

A woman went behind the pile of rugs. A giant wolf came out, grayish-green eyes glowing with enjoyment of the hunt.

As Shelly slunk behind buildings and under bridges, sniffing a trail only she could have followed, she was too preoccupied to notice that she had been under stealthy observation as she entered the pile of rugs a woman and emerged a wolf. Smiling with a peculiar mix of admiration and rueful respect, as if he had no illusions about the power of the intellect he toyed with, Ethan Perot ducked out from under a wagon, where he'd hidden to observe her. He was dressed in rags, his face shielded by a muffler, but his green eyes were keen above the tattered wool.

His shoes were tied with rags to muffle their hard soles, and he followed her at a good distance as the cat tracks wove away from the streets, deeper into the countryside.

At Seth Taub's lodgings, his ancient manservant tottered to the door. "I'm comin'; no need to knock the damn door down!" He opened the door a crack, leaving the chain latched, to stare out with a watery eye. "What be the calamity?"

"We wish to speak with your master, my good man," said a bobby, his hand restive on his stick. He was backed up by several more bobbies, and behind them was a man in a suit and bowler hat.

"Do ye know what time it be?" the servant demanded.

"It's never too late to apprehend a murderer," the bobby retorted.

The manservant's eyes widened. "Mr. Taub is indisposed," came the cool response.

"Then we wish to search the premises. Does he own a gold lion-headed cane?"

The manservant hesitated. "Aye. But so do half the gents in London."

"Not like this one." A sketch was thrust through the door.

Dismay flickered in the rheumy eyes and was noticed by the silent, watching man in the background. He finally spoke. "I have verified Taub's use of that blasted sword in the cane. There's no need to lie and get yourself in trouble."

The manservant blinked out at the man. "And you be?"

"A member of his club. He attacked me with that sword cane once. He will not do so again." The gentleman looked at the bobbies. "I suggest we wait."

"Aye, your lordship. Excellent notion." The captain of the policemen motioned to his men, and they all piled across the street to sit on low walls and smoke.

Samuel Hathaway, Marquess of Brackton, Seth's onetime gaming opponent, pulled a file from his pocket and began to manicure his nails, looking forward to repaying a disservice with a greater disservice.

What could be more satisfying than to see that arrogant bastard jailed for murder? Whether he'd done it or not was immaterial to the marquess.

Chapter Fourteen

When, some thirty minutes later, she reached a small clearing in a dense woody copse not far from the main road into London, Shelly heard them long before she saw them. The smells that wafted to her on the breeze were both familiar and alarming: scents of blood and fear.

She crouched in the trees, looking into the clearing. Two great cats, one a golden-maned lion and the other a lovely, lethal snow leopard with blue eyes the exact shade of Arielle's, toyed with a buck. The victim lashed out with a hoof, striking the snow leopard in the jaw. Her head popped back at the blow. Then the glowing feline eyes, already slitted, narrowed.

As Shelly watched, the snow leopard sank her teeth deeply into a haunch. Blood spurted and dripped down the sides of her mouth.

Shelly couldn't bear to watch any longer. The

only way to save Arielle from the ruination of feline bloodlust was to kill the deer and stop the hunt. She looked coolly about the clearing, planning her attack—and saw a gun barrel poking out of a tree high above the ground.

Astounded, she looked up to meet Ethan Perot's eyes. He held a rifle in his capable hands, but he was not watching the grisly scene below. He was watching her. He stared at her with both fascination and . . . recognition. At that moment she knew beyond any doubt that he was aware of her were-wolf powers but had kept that knowledge to himself. To what purpose she could not say; nor did she have time to weigh the ramifications of this unwelcome revelation.

With one giant leap Shelly topped the bushes and landed lightly next to the dying deer, confronting both cats. Arielle was still mesmerized by the taste and smell of blood, but the lion stood to meet her, roaring. Wondering which of the two brothers she faced, Shelly braced herself, hackles raised, light on her feet. The minute he tensed to leap over the deer, she dodged in the other direction and knocked Arielle aside. With two swipes of her paw, it was done.

The poor stag lay eviscerated, dead within seconds. Shelly's nostrils flared at the scent, but she had more pressing priorities than feeding. Namely, defending herself. Furthermore, as she squared off with the lion, she knew she had two huge liabilities the cat-man didn't face: She dared not scratch or wound him lest werewolf skills be added to his own already formidable talent for killing; and she still had to find a way to protect Arielle and get her uncooperative charge away unscathed.

Perhaps it was fortunate Ethan had spied on her, after all.

The lion, with an enraged roar that virtually shook the treetops, attacked. The first swipe of his paw knocked Shelly off her feet sideways into a tree. She lay winded for a second, scratches in her side oozing blood, but she heard him coming and knew she had seconds to regroup. The report of a rifle shot echoed through the clearing.

The lion yowled in pain as an oozing hole appeared in his shoulder. He licked it.

Taking advantage of the distraction, Shelly staggered to her feet. As she watched, the hole in the cat-man's shoulder slowly closed, and the bullet popped free from the healed flesh. His regenerative powers were amazing, stronger even than her own. She barely had time to take cover behind the tree to avoid another blow. The claws slashed into tree bark instead. The creature tried to pull free, but his claws were hooked too deeply.

Shelly used the opportunity to try to hustle Arielle to safety, but she found herself facing a very angry snow leopard instead of the innocent young girl she'd been charged to protect. Arielle, in her feline form, was too new to her powers to be as dangerous as her companion, but she crouched on her haunches, long, magnificent tail switching, growling a warning. The lion struggled so hard to escape the tree's clutches that he ripped one of his claws loose. But the other four held.

And above their heads, the rifle moved between the two felines. Shelly gave Ethan a warning look and a shake of the head, but she didn't believe he'd ever shoot Arielle, even to protect her protectress.

Freezing so she would seem less of a threat to Arielle, Shelly said, "Arielle, I know you can hear me. Do you not see that this is exactly the sickness your mother warned you about?" Shelly inched closer as she spoke, but Arielle's only response was a vicious swipe of a heavily furred paw that still displayed lethal claws.

Shelly tried again. "The first time it will be a deer, but the next, he will seduce you into killing the ultimate prey—a human. And then it will be too late for you. You will forever rule the night, but at what price? I know something of the toll immortality takes on a human soul."

Arielle's switching tail slowed. The bloodlust in her blue eyes began to dim.

And above, Ethan was riveted on Shelly.

The lion struggled harder at the tree, growling in frustration, but his claws remained embedded. His voice was unrecognizable, interspersed with hisses, as he said, "Arielle, your mother was not strong enough to survive the change and turn it to the good it can serve. This shape-shifter stinks of the jackal and is not to be trusted—"

Shelly seized the opportunity her new knowledge of Egyptian mythology granted her. "Yes,

Catspell

Arielle, I am related to the jackal. I serve Anubis, god of the underworld. Heed me and you heed him. He dwells with your mother—"

So stealthily had the cat-man worked his claws free that Shelly scarcely had time to react before he was upon her. She moved slightly aside as she felt the movement behind her, and the killing slash of lethal paws that would have taken off her head landed on her shoulder instead. She felt the strike pass deeply through flesh to bone.

Yelping, she reacted instinctively, turning on him with her teeth bared in a grimace partly of pain and partly of determination. With all her might she latched onto one of the paws lashing at her, her jaw clamping down as she tried to drag him away from Arielle. It was a delicate balance, for she had to be careful not to bite hard enough to bring blood.

The lion didn't try to pull away. Like the vicious killer he was, he turned her attack to his advantage and used their close proximity to sink his fangs into her neck. He didn't struggle to pull his paw away. He let her bite.

Through the searing pain, Shelly heard the rifle shots in rapid succession, so close that she smelled the singe of hair and didn't know if it were the lion's or her own. But she also knew the puny rounds would scarcely slow the creature down, even if Ethan could hit him in the darkness from a perch high above.

If he hit the cat-man, the shots did no good, for she felt her lungs emptying of air as he bit harder. Blood began to seep from the wound, and she

257

knew he was near her carotid artery. In reflexive self-defense, she bit down too, hard enough to bring the taste of blood.

Despite the dangers of turning him into her kind, she had little choice but to try to hurt him enough to make him slink away. He could not kill her like this, but he could incapacitate her and make off with Arielle. Shelley's fierce will began to waver as her sight grew dim. She clamped down viciously, hearing bone crack. Still the lion didn't struggle, biting harder at her neck in their obscene embrace.

For now, he won. Her jaws relaxed automatically as her consciousness began to fade. He pulled his paw free even as he bit harder, trying to suffocate her in the way of his kind.

Shelly went limp, her breath stolen, her neck bleeding.

The cat-man released her and watched her fall to the ground. Almost lazily, he licked at the paw that was now only half-connected to his leg by a few frayed tendons.

The paw began to reform. The lion looked over at Arielle. She stared at Shelly's limp form, then back at him. He began to approach her, his eyes never leaving hers, limping on the bad paw that was still re-forming.

Above, Ethan rapidly reloaded, but the frustration in his face was a testament to his sense of futility. Worriedly he glanced between the lion's wound and Shelly's still form.

The cat-man nudged the dead deer with his nose,

shoving it toward Arielle. "Feast, my love. You have earned the taste." Arielle looked first at Shelly, then back down at the deer. Her nostrils flared. She delicately licked the side of her mouth, still flecked with blood. The fear and confusion in her gaze began to fade again behind the glow.

"Feed, Arielle," coaxed the cat-man. "It is your birthright. Join me and we will both live forever."

The gun wavered in Ethan's hand. He pointed the barrel at the lion, then moved it toward Arielle. One shot in the chest. She probably had no regenerative powers yet, since the transformation was not complete, but her mother would not want her to live as Luke's consort, a ruthless feline without morals or conscience, preying on mortals for all eternity.

Just as his finger tightened on the trigger, tears glazing his eyes at what he had to do, an enormous figure leaped into the clearing, a lion with a black mane and glowing golden eyes. With the distinctive, rasping cough of a feline challenge, he stared directly into the other lion's green eyes.

"Luke, you will not do this. If you insist on turning her to evil merely so you can achieve immortality, you leave me no choice but to kill you to stop it."

Ethan almost fell out of the tree as he leaned forward to watch in astonishment. He had to catch himself. The gun went flying. All he could do now was observe.

The first lion, which Ethan now presumed to be Luke Simball, glanced at Shelley, giving a scoffing cough. "She tried. I shall be happy to teach you the same lesson: that I cannot be killed easily."

Seth looked at Shelly's still lupine form, and when he stared at his brother his pupils had grown narrow, black and menacing, stark against the golden irises. "I'll kill Arielle myself before I'll let you steal what humanity she has left."

Oblivious to the battle for her soul, Arielle had begun to feed again.

"Too late," Luke said tauntingly as Arielle bit deeply into the buck's still heart.

Seth tensed and leaped right over Luke to tackle Arielle and force her away from the deer. She snarled at him, swatting. He swatted back gently, but the force was enough to roll her across the clearing into a tree. She whacked her head against the huge bore of the oak and collapsed, unconscious.

His maneuver gave Luke time to attack. Seth barely had time to turn to meet him, and Luke's first strike caught him squarely in the chest. Claw marks slashed into his breastbone, but he struck back with a vicious slash of teeth and claw that brought great gashes into Luke's side and neck. Luke tried to counter with more bites and blows of his front paws, but Seth was, for once, the one who seemed possessed.

The two lions reared back on their haunches, slashing with front paws and biting. The clearing rang with their roars, and blood soon dotted the leaves beneath their great paws. But while Luke soon grew weak, already exhausted by his battle with Shelly, Seth seemed immune to the wounds he received. Every attack Luke made was met with more vicious parries. Seth was slightly larger and obviously stronger, and his superior ability soon made the difference.

"You're not immortal yet," Seth purred, using his head to butt Luke halfway across the clearing. The sound of cracking ribs preceded a grunt of pain.

Taking advantage of the distance between them, Luke slunk into the darkness, bleeding from numerous wounds and limping. Seth stared after him, breathing hard, and then he went to awaken Arielle. He licked her cheek gently, and then turned the same tender attention to her mouth. She began to stir, and when her eyes flicked open she looked dazed and bewildered. The woman looked out at them through the cat's eyes, and immediately she began to transform. Sitting back on his haunches, Seth watched, giving a great cat's purr of contentment.

But when her limbs formed into supple female thighs and calves, and the powerful rib cage became an indented feminine waist and pretty breasts, his feral gleam changed to male appreciation. He, too, began to transform. Soon enough two naked people stared at each other. Seth's body was streaked with wounds, but as Arielle stared at his powerful angles and planes, so in opposition to her own curves and valleys, Seth's wounds began to scab over and heal.

Ethan clambered down from the tree, but took care to retrieve his weapon and stand over Shelly before facing Seth, who stood over Arielle.

The man of science and the being not quite human, not quite feline, stared each other down. Ethan's mouth curved. "Somehow challenging you to a duel to protect Arielle's virtue seems pointless just now. Not to mention suicidal."

"Then move aside. Arielle's beauty is for my eyes alone." He ripped the long coat off Ethan's shoulders and carefully wrapped Arielle in it.

She looked from the dead deer to the blood spatters in the clearing to the wounds still healing on Seth's chest. Her gaze compulsively moved down his form, then skittered away as her eyes reached his waist. "What happened?"

Seth took the muffler Ethan offered and wrapped it about his loins. When he was finished, he looked exactly like the powerful Mihos warrior god in the drawings in the earl's study, a loincloth his only ornament. Even his hair was coarse and wiry, like a lion's mane.

"Luke tried to get you to join him in his killing sprees," Seth answered baldly. "I stopped him."

"Why?"

Seth stared at her, that arrogant smile that had so maddened her playing about his lips. "Do you not know? The instincts of both cat and woman should tell you true. If you're brave enough to listen."

Arielle looked away as if she could not bear any more truth, at least not at this moment. Instead she let him help her into Ethan's long coat. But when he tugged her toward the darkness, she resisted, looking back at Ethan and the great wolf still on the ground.

"Shelly . . . why do I sense she was here? And who hurt that wolf? I've never seen one so enormous . . ."

Seth and Ethan exchanged a look, but Seth only tugged on Arielle's arm. "Come. We must go now. He'll be back. Stronger."

"And we'll stop him. Again," Ethan said. "Is there no way to end his bewitchment without killing him?"

"No. Why do you think I've tried to avoid this night? I do not want to kill my own brother, whether we were ever close or not." Seth's gaze turned bleak as he stared at the place where Luke had slunk away into the night.

Ethan sighed heavily. "You may have no choice. He's doing all he can to implicate you in the murders he's committed. Do not go back to your flat. The police are waiting. There are witnesses who placed you at Madame Aurora's shortly before she was killed."

Arielle's eyes widened with fear. "What? But how? Who killed her?" Tears misted her eyes.

"Luke," Seth said grimly. "Probably right after I left her to find out what had happened during your séance with Bast. To stop your ability to commune with your mother, and to implicate me. Let me worry about that, Arielle." He pulled her under his strong arm and looked back at Ethan. "For now, take your woman and see to her. Give her my thanks for risking her hide to save Arielle." And with that, Seth lifted a protesting Arielle into his arms.

All mirth fading from his green eyes, Ethan

blocked Seth's path. "I cannot let you do this. How do I know you won't also try to turn Arielle? You obviously enjoy being a cat, too."

Seth looked down at Arielle, his eyes glowing again, but now with a very different—and very human—emotion. Ethan thought it must be the same look he wore when he stared at Shelly's cleavage. Desire.

"Because there is one very great difference between me and my brother," Seth murmured, his strong face transformed. "I don't want to turn Arielle into a soulless shape-shifter doomed to hunt the night for eternity. I want her for but one lifetime of passion. Passion enough to fill nine lives. When she understands what it means to be a woman, the lure of the cat will fade."

Arielle stopped her struggling and caught her breath. The last of the crazed obsession faded from her eyes as she stared up at his face, as if finally she recognized it, saw it fully and opened herself to its appeal. For the first time that most powerful of emotions between man and woman appeared in her eyes, a pearly glimmer of a beginning: trust.

Seth shifted her more comfortably in his arms and said softly, as if talking to Ethan still, but staring at Arielle all the while, "This is the gift Isis wants me to bestow on her, and bestow it I shall. I suggest you do the same with Shelly."

And thus Seth Taub carried his burden and his treasure into the night.

Like the honorable man he was, Ethan stood aside and let him carry her off. Arielle either went

264

to her salvation or her ruin, but he was fatalist enough to know this moment had been inevitable from the day Arielle was born. No one could deny his heritage or his destiny, and Arielle had to choose between her human half and her feline instincts.

He stared down at the still figure on the ground, his thoughts now finding voice. "Not even you, my very dear Miss Shelly Holmes, can deny the destiny that brought us together." And then, after trotting to the road to hire a cab, Ethan hurried back with a carriage blanket, pulling a pouch from his pocket as he ran back to his werewoman.

Whatever this night brought, whether his own death or their mutual fulfillment, Ethan knew he'd never get another opportunity like this one. It was a moment for which he'd prepared himself for some time. He had to take it, or she'd continue to hold him—and her own emotions—at arm's length. Now, while she couldn't protest, was his only chance to whisk her off to his lair. There he'd imprint himself upon her in both the way of the man and the wolf.

A smile playing about his uncommonly wide, flexible mouth, Ethan sprinkled the wolfsbane on a kerchief and held it to the werewolf muzzle, anticipating the titanic battle of wills to come.

A mere half mile away, Luke's wounds throbbed as he huddled beneath a weeping willow, so weak that he was having a hard time maintaining the transformation. He'd licked the great slashes Seth had left on his shoulders and legs, and those had begun to heal, but he couldn't reach his back and the upper part of his chest. Those wounds bled profusely, weakening him.

The blood loss was accelerated by the fierce thumping of hatred in his heart. Seth, his brother. Seth, who had always been bigger, stronger, smarter. But the frequent use of his own powers in the hunt had strengthened him just as he'd hoped. He might even have been able to defeat Seth tonight if the earlier battle with that were creature had not tired him. And Arielle had been so close to turning to him, so enthralled by the scent and taste of death. . . .

Luke looked down and saw that one of his appendages was feline, and the other fully human. If he'd had a mirror, he knew he would be shocked at the pathetic figure he made, a weak man aspiring to a god's immortality. An immortality he would have already achieved, his consort by his side, if not for Seth.

Seth . . .

Fury strengthened him. With a great arching of his back, he roared, feeling strength returning to him. The ugly human hand grew sleek and feline again, tipped with murderous claws.

The unearthly sound carried over the hillside to the cottages with cheery, blazing windows. At more than one table, mother and father hurried to comfort crying children, their own hands trembling as the hideous sound of despair and fury came again, louder.

The priest in the village crossed himself and fell to his knees.

The magistrate grabbed his gun and ran outside, looking around wildly.

He never saw the great cat that leaped at him out of the darkness. He knew the shotgun was ripped from his grasp, felt the heavy weight on his back. Then, with one instant of searing recognition and pain, his last thought was that he'd be the latest victim of the cat creature.

He heard strange words, guttural hissing words, as if the thing that uttered them were not human. " 'The slaughter block is made ready as thou knowest, and thou hast come to destruction. I am Mihos, who stablisheth those who praise him. I am the Knot of the god in the Aser tree, the twice beautiful one, who is more splendid to-day than yesterday.' "

Then the magistrate knew nothing, for his heart was ripped from his chest.

And the thing that had been Luke Simball, brother to Seth, son of Fatima, fed and grew stronger. Though he did not see it, brown tufts of werewolf fur had begun to grow along the ridge of his back and between his paws, and his acute hearing was now so sensitive it was almost painful.

And overhead the full moon glowed, beaming down a malevolent smile on Luke's new becoming.

Chapter Fifteen

Arielle awoke feeling very odd. Ethan's long coat was wool and lined with fleece, so it was uncommonly warm, but the wind had become blustery in the open carriage. She should be freezing, naked as she was beneath the coat.

Instead she felt heated from head to toe, even her exposed feet. Every sense was alive to the man and the moment. She tried to keep her gaze away from his all but naked body, clad only in a wool loincloth, but she found him fascinating in the fitful carriage lantern light. He had always looked sleek in his somber clothes, but without his shirt, the curvature of his muscles, limned in golden hues from the lantern, was mesmerizing. He truly did look as if he'd stepped down from the wall of an Egyptian tomb, lacking only the magnificent golden lion's mask.

Even the long scratches and bite marks that were fading rapidly from his muscled flesh added to his allure, for they were visible signs of how much he wanted her, of how determined he was to protect her.

This being, part man, part beast, had just risked his life for her. She had only disjointed memories of the night's events, but she had inchoate images of two great lions fighting, one with a golden mane and green eyes, the other with a black mane and golden eyes.

Luke and Seth. She knew finally that her tormenting dreams had been prognosticators of the choice facing her now. One of the dark, one of the light. She'd believed Luke to be the one of the light, the kind one, and Seth the dark, arrogant one, but she remembered enough of the night's events to comprehend now that it was Luke who had seduced her into killing. And Seth who'd risked his life to pull her away from a feast of blood and death that would have condemned her to her mother's brutal choices . . .

He'd wrapped her in Ethan's coat even as he held her with a predatory hunger that somehow did not frighten her anymore. Still, with a newfound strength whose source she was too nervous to explore, she drew the coat down over the exposed legs that he found of entirely too much interest. "You're taking me home, yes?"

"No." He continued to appraise her as if trying to decide which body part were tastiest. However, this particular expression was purely male, and purely human, and it inspired a like reaction in her femininity.

From somewhere she mustered resistance, not at all sure she was ready to be swept away by this man, whether he'd risked his life for her or not. How did she know he didn't want her for his consort, too, and was manipulating her now, just as Luke had done? She narrowed her eyes at him. "I demand you take me home. My father will be worried."

"Ethan will tell him you're with me."

"Indeed. I fear that may be the case." Her father had already made his approval of Seth clear. He'd probably be delighted if she were forced into marriage after . . . after . . . She had to look away from those glowing golden eyes that were evocative of her past—and the present and future that could be hers if she were bold enough to follow that alluring golden promise.

While she was still grappling with confusion and temptation, an even more troubling thought came. Which of them, in her dreams, had inspired ecstasy with his rough caresses, even bringing blood and forcing her to lick? Her heart skipped a beat as she remembered the powerful sensations inspired by those tiny scratches. They had not hurt at the time, quite the contrary. The telltale wetness between her legs was testament enough to her reaction.

Then and now.

She squirmed, trying to calm the surging in her blood, but her resistance was wavering. He looked too good, smelled too wonderful. Even his sweat appealed to her on some instinctive level. Deep inside, she knew it was too late for the innocent girl who had been Lady Arielle Blaylock.

She was becoming, as her mother had become. But unlike her mother, would she be able to master these atavistic, primitive urges and rule them with her will, or would she become a servant to their dark power, unable to control the need to kill and feed?

Fear leaped in her stomach like a live thing, and suddenly the inevitability of her fate was too much. Nausea built in her stomach and she had to hold her hand to her mouth and swallow back the tastes of blood and raw meat.

"Arielle," Seth said soothingly, taking one hand from the reins to draw her near. "This is the hardest part of the transformation. This battle between your civilized code of behavior and the urges of the cat is quite normal. The trick is to allow the power of your human intellect to control the baser instincts. Shelly has obviously accomplished this. I went through it, too, and so can you."

"You're stronger than I am."

"No, I'm not. Not mentally, not emotionally. Why do you think Luke has tried so hard to seduce you into his twisted ways? He needs you and the power you'd bring to him as his consort. You've just been so sheltered and smothered by your father that you've never had a chance to be who you really are: the last direct descendant of Cleopatra, the daughter of Bast."

"And what curse is this? Dear God, what if I can't control it? My mother couldn't."

"You're stronger than your mother." He rubbed her soothingly on the back as he spoke. "You must read the history of Cleopatra again. She changed the face of the globe with nothing but her feminine wiles and her will."

"My father tried to keep me away from all things Egyptian."

He turned to frown at her. "You never even read Shakespeare's *Antony and Cleopatra?*"

She shook her head.

"Pity. I think the Bard captured her better than any of the many playwrights who have been infatuated by her beauty and power."

"I have heard that she was not beautiful at all." She peered up at him, and that arrogant little smile playing about his lips that had so infuriated her was now comforting. The nausea had faded in the warmth of his embrace. How could something that felt so right be wrong?

She was past struggling against him, even though she felt the bare brush of his leg against hers. It was a strange feeling, the hairs on his leg rough and pleasurable, stroking against her. He bent his head to her like a great cat inviting her petting.

Her fingers curled with the need to respond.

A soft purr emanated from his lips, and he finished a breath away from kissing the side of her neck, "Shakespeare said of his queen of the Nile: 'Age cannot wither her, nor custom stale her infinite variety; other women cloy the appetites they feed, but she makes hungry where most she satisfies.'" His warm breath was the precursor to the kiss on the side of her neck. "Satisfy us both, Arielle. You know you want to."

She shivered, thrills running down her spine as he nuzzled her hungrily with nose and lips and finally with the graze of gentle teeth. He said between kisses, "He might have been writing about you. It's time you stopped struggling against your birthright. Cleopatra toppled two dynasties because she lived life to the fullest, with passion and a refusal to be conquered."

"And men died because of her," she managed over the thumping of her heart. The queer feeling that had assailed her since she awoke in his arms was growing stronger. She looked up at him, her mouth parted with her quick breathing, hoping he'd take the choice away from her and kiss her senseless.

But he pulled back, drawing on the reins and saying only, "True. But a new, better world grew from the ashes of their defeat. Join me, Arielle. Together we can defeat Luke and stop these senseless killings. But first you have to be mine."

Only then did Arielle realize the carriage had rolled to a stop. They had been traveling for hours, and she had no idea where they were. Seth jumped down, and she saw they were in a small clearing that held a thatched cottage. Behind it was a bubbling spring, steaming in the grayish hue of incipient dawn. She recognized the mineral smell emanating from the steam.

273

They were near Bath and the hot springs. Another dream come true.

He had brought her here for one reason.

But just when she was so close to accepting her destiny at his side—for she was certain now he was the good one, the one of brightness despite his dark hair—he'd withdrawn his mesmerizing kisses and tempting warmth. She looked from his somber expression and outheld hand to the windows glowing with welcome. He had planned this, obviously. Just as obviously, he was offering her a choice. A conscious choice.

His hand began to tremble a bit, and she sensed the power of his need for her, a need that went beyond desire to a deeper level, as if she were his only hope of an earthly soul mate.

"I see the conflict in your eyes, my love. Indeed, how could you know that I am very different from my brother? I don't want you a slave to me, like Luke wants you, as my entry to eternity. I want you today, tonight, tomorrow, a woman to walk beside me as we rule the march of one lifetime together. I think you know this night was meant to be, down through the aeons back to the birth of Osiris."

"You don't wish to live forever?" she asked skeptically.

"Not at the cost of my soul. The cat is a wonderful creature, agile, brave, independent, and affectionate when it pleases. But it has no moral center. Luke is an example of what you will become if you allow the temptation of your feline side to rule you. I want better for you. Your mother wanted better for you."

Arielle could no longer sustain the intensity of his stare. She looked away, nibbling at her lip, hearing the ring of truth in his words. When his gaze fastened on her mouth, she felt his hunger, a tangible thing, reaching out to her. But he only straightened, releasing her hand, as if he knew she had to make this choice willingly, with clear logic, not sexual temptation.

"I will not tempt you further, though I suspect I could sweep you away with little effort. Think only of this before you decide . . . Luke wants the power you give him," Seth said softly. "I want you. The woman, not the cat."

He didn't smell of catnip, he didn't tempt her with the taste of fear and blood, and he didn't promise her forever.

The conflicting feelings that had almost torn her apart faded. For once she squelched the lecture of her rational half, the legacy of her father, listening instead to passion, like a true descendant of Cleopatra. She wanted him, had been incredibly drawn to him, which was precisely why she'd fought so hard against this moment. But somehow she knew that both Isis and Osiris were smiling as she stepped down.

Like the woman she was about to become, she let him kiss her hand and lead her into the cottage.

In a very different place, two very different people were embroiled in a similar battle of wills. Ethan had struggled inside his London flat, remote at the end of a cul-de-sac, with his sleeping burden, muttering down to her, "My sweet, you are a hefty woman in more ways than one." With a nod, he indicated to his manservant that they should be left alone. He staggered down the stairs to his laboratory as his doubtful valet, with a last look at the still woman in Ethan's arms, departed as ordered, leaving the two of them alone in his large flat.

Ethan set Shelly, now fully human and clothed only in the carriage blanket, down in a wide wing chair. He locked the steel-reinforcement door and pocketed the key. Then he waved smelling salts under her nose. Her nostrils flared and her head turned slightly away, but she moved as if every motion were an effort.

When her eyes flickered open, Shelly looked around groggily. She shifted her feet, the tiniest movement, before horror flared in her eyes. She was held immobile, awake but helpless, by the powdered wolfsbane and silver leaves Ethan had tied in pouches around her neck, wrists, and ankles. She had only two weapons available: her eyes and her voice.

Both were formidable. "You unregenerate scoundrel. Do you think incapacitating me like this will get you what you want?"

"And what is that?" Ethan asked with the mildest interest.

As she watched, he busied himself moving the beakers, burners, microscopes and other scientific equipment littering the long table in the middle of the room to an empty cabinet, which he locked.

Her forebodings increased. It looked as if he were preparing for a war. "My . . . my person."

"For an extremely intelligent woman, my very dear Miss Shelly Holmes, you are amazingly obtuse. Do you think I intend to have my wicked way with you against your will?" He laughed. That rich male amusement, so tempting in tone and so appealing in the animation it gave to his face, angered her even more.

"Why else would you immobilize me and lock me in your private quarters?" she spit back.

"I saw opportunity, and I took it." While she stared at him, totally confused, he locked away the last of his implements, leaving the laboratory all but bare. It held now only a long couch, the chair she sat in, and the long table and cabinets, all locked. As he worked, he explained helpfully, as if she were indeed obtuse, "We have been at cross purposes long enough. Luke is growing stronger, and only our united efforts will stop him. If you had not tired him before Seth arrived, I think Arielle could well be his slave by now. And since you, ah, had to defend yourself, what if he begins evincing lupine tendencies as well?"

"So it was Luke I was fighting. I thought it must be," Shelly mused, sick at the thought. It was the time of the full moon, so it was quite likely Luke was already beginning the change, adding her own skills to his arsenal of killing abilities. She continued, "If your motives are to help protect Arielle, why am I naked beneath this blanket and alone with you at your mercy?"

He made a rude sound, pulling a ladder-backed chair in front of her. "You are never at anyone's mercy, save your own. Sometimes I wonder if you self-flagellate or wear hair shirts." He sat down backward, legs spread, crossing his arms on the top of the chair. She avoided looking at his lower body, but that merely forced her to meet his thoughtful gaze.

He continued in that reasonable, nonthreatening tone that grated on her like sandpaper, "You were not exactly overdressed in your prior persona. The blanket was all I could find to clothe you in. I have not peeked, I assure you." A wicked smile played about his lips, lightening his solemnity. "But neither am I blind. I did have to wrap you in the blanket. I was aware you were well-endowed with brain capacity, but your other endowments are, shall we say, equally impressive. Why do you try so hard to hide them?"

Shelly hoped he couldn't see the reddening of her cheeks. "Because they are inconvenient symbols of my weakness." She bit her lip, regretting her frankness.

What might have been a wisp of sadness appeared in his darkening green gaze. "What was it in your past that made you detest your own femininity? Sad, that. Your uniqueness as a detective comes not from your male traits, but from your feminine intuition and your compassion."

He shoved the chair aside and knelt in front of her. This time she could hardly avert her gaze from the prominent area at the apex of his rough breeches. No matter his protestations that he'd

278

not take advantage of her, it was very clear this man wanted her. That damned tingling he always aroused, even when she was angry with him—like now—returned to plague her.

She would have reared back—afraid of him, but more afraid of herself, exactly as he'd said—if she'd been able. But she couldn't. Her world was filled with Ethan's face, her nostrils invaded by the scents of sweat, and man, and yes, of arousal. Her acute hearing detected the quickening beat of his strong heart. He, too, was more affected by this battle of wills than he'd admit, but for the moment he literally had the upper hand.

She had to sit still as, very gently, as if he feared pushing her too far, he cupped his hands beneath her tousled hair and cradled her skull. "Yes, I want you, Miss Shelly Holmes. Your body. Your heart. Your soul. But I want to receive, not take. To cherish. Not dominate."

Shelly's heart leaped like a wild thing in her breast. With a mighty effort she managed to scoot her chair back a half inch. It wasn't enough. Half the world away would still not be enough to make her forget this man and what he did to her. Still, she pretended, as much for herself as for him. "I give no one that degree of power over me."

"Yet." He came closer, until his dark green eyes poured his indomitable spirit into hers, as if he would sap her will as he'd sapped her energy with his wiles. He gently rubbed her skull. "There is only one way to conquer you. It lies not through your womanhood, but through this. . . ." So softly, so tenderly, he kissed her wide brow. "This is the pathway to your heart and body. This is what I covet. For when I'm in your brain, I will be well on my way to possessing your heart."

Damn his penetrating eyes and wisdom! How could he, alone of all the men she'd ever met, understand her so well when she'd done all she could to keep him at bay? Mesmerized, she let him delve deep into her eyes, deeper than she'd ever allowed another soul. She was so rapt she barely felt his light touch at wrists, ankles, and finally her neck. The overpowering scents of wolfsbane and silver leaves that had kept her immobile were gone as he flung the pouches across the room.

He leaned back as she stirred, but stayed there on his knees before her, well within striking range. As power flowed back into her body, he said softly, "Your *ka* is a lovely thing, dearest. But it is wounded and has been solitary far too long. Let me in. Let this powerful feeling neither of us can deny heal us both. Or do with me as you please. For if I have to survive one more night without knowing you, mentally, emotionally, and yes, physically, I'm not certain I wish to survive at all."

Shelly's eyes teared up. Precisely because she hungered so much to respond to his moving overture, she leaped to her feet and ran in the opposite direction, the blanket catching on a table leg and dropping to the floor.

She tugged furiously but found the door locked. Her wild eyes noted the high, narrow windows in this basement lair; there was no other egress. She was trapped. She turned back to face him as he rose slowly. He eyed her warily, obviously aware he'd pushed her as far as he could.

Just as he said, he was inside her head. He knew her.

He knew her ailment, knew she could turn vicious at will, so he'd immobilized her just long enough to get her here, trapped with him, to force her to listen. His gaze caressed her exposed body as if he indeed shared her hunger for flesh, but in a very basic male way. "Kiss or kill? An interesting choice, even for you, my very dear detective. I await your decision."

Her nipples surged their response, and she was so overcome by the need to fly into his arms that she stoked fear and confusion into rage. She crossed her arms over her chest to hide her reaction to him.

How dared he play his little mind games with a werewoman? Did he really expect his blandishments to seduce her into his arms when she'd never trusted anyone? And he'd given her every reason to distrust him: His motivations in helping with Arielle were suspect, his former relationship with Isis quite likely scandalous, even his scientific knowledge used as much against her as for their mutual benefit in this investigation. He'd had meetings behind her back, spied on her when she didn't know it, and now he'd capped all that dastardly activity by kidnapping her.

It was time he learned she would not be toyed

with. Closing her eyes, Shelly began the transformation. So quickly could she master it now: the elongation of jaw into a snout, the lengthening of her ears into pricked-forward triangles, the strengthening of rib cage and the bending of her appendages into paws, tipped by lethal claws. As quickly as that, the imposing, full-figured woman became an enormous wolf.

When she looked at him with a feral gleam, her eyes glowing greenish gray in the dim room, he sighed. "It's a good thing I removed all the breakables."

And he crossed his arms over his chest, watching the were-creature stalk him. For the first time a bit of fear blended with the fascination in his eyes.

Luke Simball stepped out of the bath, flexing his muscles in front of a mirror. The last feeding had accelerated his regeneration. The huge wound on his shoulder with the hanging flap of flesh had almost totally healed, and the less serious scratches were gone.

As he reached for a towel, he accidentally brushed against the curtain blocking the window. The moon winked through the gap. He paused to look up at it, curiously drawn to it. He moved the curtain aside even more, somehow feeling empowered by the golden glow. He felt the change before he saw it, the hairy tufts appearing at his ears, the heightening of his sense of hearing, the acuteness of an even more sensitive than usual sense of smell.

Curious, he looked in the mirror, standing in the bright glow of moonlight, and the truth hit him like a slap. The being that stared back at him was not man, not lion, and not wolf. It was a combination of the three, standing erect like a man. The brown hairs of the wolf interspersed with the lion's golden fur, and his full mane now had a canine ruff. When he bared his teeth, his fangs were even longer and more formidable. All his senses now were unbearably acute, for he had the skills of scent and hearing of the canine and the sight of the feline. He blew out the gas lamps and saw as if it were daylight. When he looked down at his paws, they had the power of the lion's and the strength and agility of the wolf's. He flexed them.

"Thank you, Miss Holmes," Luke whispered, his eyes glowing greenish gray now instead of bright green.

Then, whisking the curtain closed, Luke looked at the clock and calculated the time he'd have to wait for daylight. With an effort of will that was becoming easier all the time, he closed his eyes and visualized himself as a man. Soon the hairs faded, the teeth became blunted, and when he looked in the mirror a few minutes later, he saw the handsome face of Luke Simball, the man.

Mihos would have to wait one more night for his due.

His alter ego had an early appointment to keep—with a certain lord who was known to detest Seth. After that, Mihos could visit Arielle in all his glory.

Fully human again, Luke began to dress. For the first time since the humiliating rout in the clearing, confidence flowed back into him. One way or another, Seth would soon be an afterthought, fodder for Arielle's new destiny as Mihos's consort.

Chapter Sixteen

Inside the tidy cottage, Seth knelt and stirred to life the slumbering embers. Arielle's heart pounded in her chest, as she could not help recognizing the symbolism of his action. Indeed, when he turned to her, she felt as if she'd been sleeping all her life and only now knew the joy of awakening . . . But to what? And what would she become after tonight?

He came to her, his movements as always silent and sinuous, but gentleness transformed his usual arrogance as he rubbed a fingertip beneath her eye. "Why the tears, my love?"

Wet lashes lowered over her azure eyes before she realized she was crying. Still, even knowing that before she left this cottage she would be fully his woman, she kept silent. When he tried to lift her chin up, she buried her face in his chest. Her emotions had been volatile of late, but nothing had brought home to her what she was about to do like the simple act of his stirring a fire to life. She knew that once the fire in her was lit, it would never go out. Was she ready to give so much of herself to any man, even one the gods had decreed would be her consort?

He must have sensed her ambivalence, for he brooked no opposition this time as he forced her chin up so he could see her face. Stubbornly she kept her eyes downcast, but a gentle fingertip traced the mulish set of her mouth. The friction of his simple touch warmed her even more than the now roaring blaze. She was still clad in Ethan's coat, but it was slipping from her shoulders, and she wanted nothing more than to fling it on the flames like the encumbrance it was.

But that rebellious urge kept her still.

The amusement in his voice was like a golden thread, binding them together. "Ah, I see. How obtuse of me. Now that I've shed my blood to defeat my rival in your affections, you want me to win you in a dance of desire and dominance, my little cat."

He had expressed her feelings better than she'd understood them herself. She was so shocked that she looked up and let herself be captured in the glowing amber of his eyes. As their gazes held and tugged, each striving for dominance, his pupils narrowed to diamonds. She sensed hers were doing likewise.

And she knew, finally, with utter certainty, that these were the same eyes that had tormented her in her dreams. This was the being of bright boldness . . . and the dark man-beast who had marked her and taught her to revel in the power of passion. Unlike Luke, he didn't offer her immortality, or subjugation of the human heart to the amorality of the feline.

But he did offer something far more attractive to her: a dominant male spirit that, like her, thrived on challenge. He would be satisfied with nothing less than a total melding of both their human and their feline worlds. When he took her body, there would be no going back. She'd be his consort in this world and the next. But she would sacrifice neither her humanity nor her *ka* in the process.

Also unlike Luke, he offered her a relationship based on mutual respect—and mutual enjoyment. Her nostrils flared as the scent of him made her so hot she felt as if she had a fever. The urge to cast off the last of her inhibitions with the coat almost overcame her. She wanted to pounce on him and roll over and over on the floor, kissing, biting, scratching . . .

Seth's smile grew knowing, revealing sharpening incisors, and heat flooded her cheeks as she realized he'd read her mind. Sounding like a great, contented cat, Seth purred, "I am yours to do with as you please, mistress." And he unwrapped his loincloth and let it fall.

He was burnished gold in the firelight, his musculature long and lean, but so pure of form that indeed, he could be only the lion god come to claim his due. Finally she could see him clearly, and reality was far more arousing than any of her erotic dreams. The heir of Mihos had a chest bare of hair, in the Egyptian style, but broad shoulders tapered into his indented waist, then tapered again into male hips and long, muscular legs: and all this beautiful form was a befitting frame for its most basic function.

Unable to stop herself, she looked at the center of his body. She had expected to be wary of the size and length formed to fill the void even now aching to receive him. But virginal fear had been cast aside with the old frailties of her limp and shyness.

This was the essence of his manhood, the part girls giggled about, obsessed over, and both feared and longed to see. He was, she suspected, though she had no personal experience with such things, fully erect for her. And he was beautiful, so hungry for their bonding that the burning she felt grew to a conflagration. Even more arousing, despite his obvious need, was that he stayed still and let her look at him, one foot slightly forward, hands on his hips, as if he were ready to meet and match her first step toward him.

But she had to choose that first step.

Gladly she took it, letting the sagging coat drop to her feet. It was her turn to stand still and let him admire her nakedness. Such was his due; he'd fought, literally tooth and nail, to gain it.

The impossibly long length grew, preening under her gaze. His breathing quickened, and he clenched his hands with the effort, but he stayed put. She realized, abruptly, just as he'd said, that all this indomitable masculinity was hers to toy with at her will. For this he had taunted and challenged her. For this she had been born.

That second step to a new beginning was incredibly easy after all.

Purely on instinct she began to stalk him, her movements sinuous. Her long black hair shielded and revealed the milk-white breasts crowned with pink areolae. Her incisors, too, were pointed. Never had the blood of Cleopatra surged harder through her veins than now.

She was close enough to touch that tempting flesh when . . . he darted sideways.

She whirled, only to find him behind her. A teasing fingertip traced the graceful curve of her spine down to her buttocks, but when she tried to catch that hand on her hip, it was gone.

She spun again, and then they were circling each other, their feet soundless on the creaky wood floor of the cottage—like cats. Battling for dominance until the very air between them sizzled.

Seth lunged toward her and nipped her shoulder. The tiny dart of pain sent a thrill of pleasure through her that centered below her waist. Instinctively she bit back, sinking her incisors into the throbbing pulse in his throat, feeling the beat of his life essence against her tongue as if she needed it to survive. She felt the powerful urge to bite down, just enough to draw blood . . .

He gave a little grunt of pure pleasure, then rasped, "Bite me. Taste of me and give it back to me on your tongue."

Her eyes widened, the diamond-shaped pupils

rounding again as she realized what she was doing. She backed away, her hands coming up, not to ward him off, but to control her own wild urges. The primitive need to attack him, scratching, biting, was about to overcome her, and she was overwhelmed with the power of the urges he'd inspired first in dreams and now in truth.

"You want it." He approached her, one step.

Again, he'd read her mind. She backed away, one step. "No, I don't. I'm a woman, not some amoral feline in heat."

He looked down at her breasts. She followed his gaze. Her nipples were hard despite the warmth of the cabin.

Instinctively she covered her breasts with her hands, but it was too late for false modesty.

"Join me in the best of both worlds, Arielle. We can mate, rolling around on the ground like great cats hissing and scratching for dominance. And we can make love, caressing and kissing the night away in a proper marriage bed. The choice is ours, because we control the change. What is more liberating than power one can control? Pity Luke has never figured that out. You have but to master the urges, instead of letting them master you. Shelly has done it. I have done it. So can you. This is your first lesson. You are built for passion." His eyes were slanted now, his incisors elongating into fangs. Grabbing her shoulders, he brought her to his chest and kissed her.

Full bore, his mouth slanted over hers as his powerful arms bent her back so far her feet almost left the floor. This was what she had feared, and this was what she had wanted.

Passion given like a gift so powerful that it hurt . . . even as it pleased. She pulled away, glaring up at him like a snow leopard in heat. When his lip curled as he grimaced back at her, she recognized his expression as a reflection of her own.

The shock had less impact the second time, wrapped as she was in his arms. He didn't give her time to pull away, holding her tightly to him with one hand, and with the other learning the soft curve of her buttocks and upper thighs. His large, warm hand was fully human, but when he bent his head to the sweet arch of her neck, he followed the path with tiny stabs of his tongue interspersed with nips that twinged but did not draw blood . . . and his tongue was rough.

It was as if, even as humans knowing their first coupling, the power of their bond was made stronger by the urges of the cat . . .

Pleasure thrilled through her from head to toe. Her urge to bite back returned more powerfully. Her fingers curled into his shoulders; then she trailed them down his strong spine. Only when he gasped into her neck did she realize she'd scratched him.

The second realization was even more powerful: His gasp was not one of pain.

Growling deep in his throat, he bent her back over his arm and lavished attention on her breasts, suckling, licking around each pale areola, not quite touching the nipple. She squirmed in his hold, catching his hand, trying to bring that tormenting caress to the place no man had ever touched. She felt the quickening of his breath, the strong heartbeat throbbing against her, and knew she pleased him, too. For the first time in her life she felt beautiful.

And strong. And bold. Grasping his thick, wiry hair, she hauled his mouth to where she most needed it. He licked her, his touch on her nipple at first gentle. But his tongue grew rougher in texture as his arousal increased. She felt him stabbing urgently into her hip and had to know him in return, to pleasure him in kind.

Tentatively she palmed him, sucking in her breath in shock at the length and width overflowing her hand, throbbing with the need she inspired. She felt the graze of sharp teeth over her nipple as his caress at her breast grew more demanding. The pleasure-pain made her hand contract. Her moan was drowned out by his, and then his lips had taken the sweet sound of wild need and given it back to her with a deep thrust of his tongue into her mouth. Since her touch obviously pleased him, she did it again, setting up a rhythm of squeeze and release that both fed their hunger and increased their need for more.

The primitive urge to possess him, to mark him as her consort, grew uncontrollable.

She slanted her head to the side to kiss him as deeply as nature allowed, learning the sweet nectar of his mouth with the tip of her tongue. He quested deeply in return, stabbing back with a full length she knew instinctively was evocative of the other length to come. Their labored breaths became one. Suddenly she wrenched her mouth away and bit deeply into his shoulder, finding the taste of his blood an aphrodisiac, then danced out of his reach.

Daring him. She stood, legs spread, long black hair flipping about her shoulders as she tossed her head in defiance. Her blue eyes had darkened to the twilight of dreams, where she'd first met him, but there was no fear in the dilated, diamond-shaped pupils. Her nostrils flared as she scented him.

His nostrils flared in response. He touched the place where her sharp incisors had marked his shoulder with two bright red dots. He brought his hand away and stared at the smear of blood.

"Drink. Taste the essence that belongs to me, blood of my blood," she purred.

His dilated eyes snapped back to her face, and he obviously recognized the words as ones he'd spoken to her in her dreams. If she'd put a collar about his neck, she could not have more thoroughly declared her ownership.

The way of the cat. And of the woman he'd helped her become.

Holding her eyes, he touched his own blood again and then delicately, tongue curled, licked the taste from his fingers.

For a timeless moment they stared at each other across the width of the fur rug he'd spread on the floor. Then, their arms spread, they began to circle each other in that ageless dance of dominance, the circles becoming narrower and narrower until, with his greater reach, he could snatch her to him.

This time, when he kissed her deeply, he let his passions rule. Tongue, teeth, hands all explored her at the same time, plundering the abundant treasures hoarded just for him. But it was she who hooked her foot behind his ankles, pulling him off balance.

He crashed to the rug, pulling her atop him as he went. Then, as in her most erotic dreams, they were rolling across the floor, biting, licking, scratching, hissing deep breaths of arousal. They landed back on the rug again, him on top, his knees spreading her unresisting legs apart. Holding her gaze with his, he connected the head of his sex to the softness that had hungered for him day and night.

He was about to plunge home, and she was spread for him, quiescent. He paused, barely connected, the possessive fire in his eyes muted. His voice was so hoarse it was scarcely recognizable, and later she could not say whether she heard it in her head or her ears. "No. You do it. Mark me."

Her eyes had fluttered closed as she awaited him, and they flew open in shock. To her dismay, he withdrew that tantalizing warmth and sat back on his heels, eyeing her with an expression so arrogant she wanted to smack him. His need for her was blatant, but he merely sat there, waiting for her reaction. He didn't want her surrender. He wanted her participation.

She swallowed, licking her dry lips. His gaze latched onto her mouth, and its muted golden glow turned luminous again, but still he waited.

"I . . . don't know what you want me to do."

"Yes, you do. Follow your instincts. You have to choose this, too."

Follow her instincts? She'd attack him, consume him, make him hers forever . . . Somehow with the thought the action came naturally. She leaped on him, spreading her legs about his waist, wrapping her arms tightly about his shoulders as she sat on his upper thighs and squirmed to get the hard head in the right place. *Ah, there.* She knew it, as she knew this moment would alter them both forever after in a form of immortality Luke Simball would never know.

Her eyes drifted closed again, so pleasurable was the feel of that velvet iron at the opening to her body. She squirmed on him, placing him where she needed his hardness most, but he wouldn't allow her even that much privacy.

"Open your eyes," he commanded with a growl.

Obediently she opened her eyes. His eyes were slanted, flaming with the power of this joining, and when she lifted slightly to give herself better leverage, he was there to meet her.

As she pushed down, he pushed up, no gentleness offered or demanded. His mouth was on hers, ready to take that first sweet cry. He sundered the last barrier to her becoming, his full length entering her to the hilt even as she opened to accommodate him. It felt as if a knife severed her, and he swallowed her sweet cry even as she bit him in retaliation, drawing her life force from his. She was his, but he was hers, too, and nothing in her life had ever been more liberating than the sundering of her most intimate flesh at her own command.

Just as he'd promised in her dreams, when he took her blood, she took his, too.

Gasping against their locked mouths, they luxuriated in the intimacy of the moment, his throbbing possessiveness opening the way for their bonding of spirit and body. The second thrust hurt less than the first, the third not at all. When he felt her relax as the stabbing pain faded, he lifted her gently at the waist and as gently pushed her back down. Full, empty, full, empty—the movements grew wilder in tempo as the sounds of moans, both male and female, crowded out the roaring of the fire.

That fire was building between her legs, reaching higher and higher, as he was, for the essence of her feminine power. Then she was flat on her back and he was pounding into her, deeper but never deep enough. She locked her legs about his waist then higher, about his neck, the plunge and retreat ringing in the room as their bodies slapped together, but she felt no pain.

Only ecstasy. The pressure built in her uncontrollably—there, almost there. She arched against him, crying out as the fire exploded within her, radiating to her fingertips and the follicles of her hair. Flying apart, she gripped his thighs hard, feeling the clench and release of his own fruition in her womb. The intimate splashes made her spasm again, and again she clenched his thighs with her nails, digging deeply.

From somewhere she heard a hiss of pain mixed with delight, and then, slowly, she collapsed, her heart pounding a paean of thankfulness to her ancestors for granting her the power of passion that could revel in such a moment. For this she was born. And from this becoming she could never return. But for the first time in her life she knew who she was, and was serene in the knowing.

Slowly she grew aware of earthly things. The dying fire, logs falling in a shower of sparks. The heavy weight of the man against her, kissing her with joy, Egyptian love words mixed with English, all filled with praise and tenderness.

She caressed his back. When she held her hand out, she saw claws peeking from the ends of her fingers, and surprisingly she was not horrified at the sight. She turned them curiously, examining them as pads began to grow on her palm. She imagined her hand as fully human again, and the pads faded, the claws receding.

She looked up to find Seth smiling at her. "See, it's not so terrible, is it? You can control it, just as I said." He lifted her to a sitting position, and it was then that she saw the deep scratches in his upper thighs.

She gasped, running a fingertip apologetically over the claw marks. "I'm sorry."

He brought her hand to his mouth and kissed it, fingertip to fingertip, and then he led her before a full-length mirror, pulling her against him. The shock of what the passion had brought them to was both frightening and arousing. She had bruises on her collarbones where he'd sucked too hard, and love bites on the top of each breast. He had scratches on his back, waist, and thighs, and the clear imprint of sharp incisors on both sides of his neck.

She was brought back to herself when he knelt in front of the mirror, so she could still see, and bent his head in homage to her femininity. As if in reward for her bravery, for an instant she felt his tongue grow rough in texture as he lapped at her in the aftermath. The fingers gripping her thighs to hold her wide began to dig into her skin, and when she looked down she saw claws tipping them. But even as her heart surged and she felt her own claws growing, he sighed, rubbing his cheek against her femininity, and his claws receded. So did hers. And the next time he kissed her she felt only the silky glide of his tongue.

"Do you see now?" he murmured into her heated skin. "No one can doubt we belong together. We are two of a kind, my lioness. But you've known passion. Now feel tenderness." And he led her to the hot springs just outside, laying her on a long, shallow ledge. He bathed her in the soothing warmth, end to end, the cloth first a cleansing tool, but soon a temptation.

The soft cotton barely brushed between her thighs, cleansing her of any remnant of the virgin, leaving only the woman grown. And the man drew her to the soft, mossy bank, spread her wide, and dipped his head between her thighs. Before he was done, Arielle had her second lesson: Love took many forms, and they were all available to those bold enough to try them.

And it was still good to be fully human, too. This time, when she returned to herself, he had his hand outstretched.

"Come. We must rest." Still naked, he led her back to the cottage. They curled up together on the bed, utterly replete.

Arielle's last thought as she drifted off to sleep was that somewhere her mother rejoiced to see her daughter find joy, both as a cat and a woman.

Many miles away, in a genteel, proper part of London, most uncivilized and improper events were also occurring. Perhaps it was the full moon . . .

Ethan Perot, peer of the realm, scientist and arbiter of taste, had just performed his most daring experiment ever. From the satisfied look on his face, he'd both expected and longed for the outcome that faced him now.

An enormous wolf approached him, her grayish-green eyes luminous in the dim light of the overhead gas lamps. Her fangs were bared, and a deep growl emerged from her powerful rib cage. Even with her standing on all fours, her head came almost to his shoulder. As she approached her shadow grew larger, obscuring his feet, his legs, and finally his upper torso, until only his eyes caught the light. They remained that brilliant, fascinated green.

Frustrated, Shelly gave a louder growl, allowing a few drips of saliva to decorate her snarl. She was determined to frighten him.

She failed. When she grew close enough to lunge, to her utter shock it was he who bridged the last gap between them. He raised his hand to pet her great head. The touch sent a thrill of pleasure through her. "You are an amazing creature. What is it like to have such power?"

Inside the fearsome wolf, the woman understood, finally, why he had such allure for her. They were kindred spirits in their thinking, and in their curiosity about life. Like her, he'd risk his life for the sheer glory of new experience. And she was currently his favorite subject.

She reared away, snarling. She snapped at him, her powerful jaws coming together with a clang. But she'd taken care not to graze him, and he knew it, curse him, by the little smile on his face.

She lunged at him on her hind legs, glaring down. Now, her paws resting on his shoulders, she was taller. Now he'd be afraid and back off, let her out of here, never to trouble her again.

As usual she underestimated both his nerve and his verve. He staggered a bit under her weight on his shoulders, but put both hands over her paws and rubbed, as if even this contact were pleasurable for him. How could he dare toy with her when she was in this form?

"Your eyes betray you. I dare such things because, my dearest Miss Holmes, you are as uncommon a werewolf as you are a female," Ethan said softly. Shelly's bared fangs were inches from his throat. "Above all things you relish control and your freedom. If you so forget yourself as to tear

300

me limb from limb in this laboratory, you will have to deal with untidy matters even your formidable powers of logic and prevarication cannot explain. My experiments are so volatile—never more than this one, I might point out—that I had this entire laboratory reinforced in case of an explosion. Even you cannot knock down a steel door, and my manservant will return by morning."

To Shelly's astonishment, he even went so far as to stroke the ruff of fur over her ear, though he could barely reach it, so tall was she on her hindquarters. "I am thus free to irritate you at my whim."

While she stared down at him, her jaw growing slack at his temerity, he leaned closer still, until his breath stirred the fine hairs at her ear. "And above all things in life, it is my goal to see you lose that control when you are beneath me writhing in pleasure. You must, in truth, be a wild woman."

Even in her lupine form, Shelly felt a responsive thrill of pleasure in her female parts. She felt herself starting to change back into a woman simply from the longing he inspired. Leaping down, she backed away two steps. He spanned the gap in one stride, the stalked becoming the stalker.

"Come to me, Shelly Holmes. Let us find rest in each other. We will work together much better in our investigations as a team."

Shelly's desperate gaze went between the hunter and the door. It did indeed look like reinforced steel, and the only windows were tiny affairs, far too narrow for her to slip through even if she could reach them.

To win this battle, she didn't need the skills of a werewolf. She needed the skills of a woman . . . rusty as they might be.

As she closed her eyes and allowed the womanly urges to grow, she noted that the sky was lightening outside.

Dawn approached. The first dawn after a full moon. She had to get out of here and check to see what Luke Simball had done after his humiliating defeat, and what he had become.

Instinctively, Shelly knew they would all too soon face a creature part lion, part werewolf.

And in that final battle, if she rejected him yet again, would Ethan Perot be friend or foe?

Chapter Seventeen

The door suddenly seemed very far away, for Ethan blocked it. Even if she somehow found the key, it was too late to run. He knew. He knew she was a werewolf; even worse, he knew she was more strongly attracted to him than to any man she'd ever known. This confrontation had been brewing between them since the first time they met, appropriately enough in a crypt, and she was tired of avoiding it. As he said, they needed to get it out of the way so they could both concentrate fully on the titanic battle to come for Arielle's soul.

If the werewolf couldn't cow him, perhaps the woman would.

Indeed, his hands were loose at his sides, and he watched her change with utter fascination—and absolutely no trace of fear.

She made no attempt to hide her transformation, flaunting the power of the wolf that somehow enhanced both the power and stature of the woman. Her back arched as she stood on her hind legs, the front paws changing into long, graceful arms, the muscular rib cage softening into the curvy bosom of a woman boasting a long, indented waist. Her hind legs straightened and grew shapely, the calves lean and long and muscular, the fit female form made sleek by the strength of her alter ego.

And when Shelly Holmes stood before him, the residual stare of the wolf—direct, hungry and without pity—still glowed from her greenish-gray eyes. "Come near me at your peril," she warned.

At first he seemed to heed her. He stayed put and feasted his fill of her from the top of her thick brown hair to the tips of her pink toes, lingering on points in between.

Legs spread, arms loose at her sides, she let him look. Her gaze strayed up and down, too, with its own primitive brand of hunger. She eyed the apex of his thighs, where his proper breeches displayed a most improper protuberance. She hesitated, for she still didn't want him to know how much he, too, fascinated her, but the question came of its own accord. "I do not frighten you?"

A sound that was a strange mixture of pain and delight came from his lips. One minute he was halfway across the room; the next he was there, holding her hand to the front of his pants. When she froze, afraid to touch, afraid not to, he nuzzled the hair away from her ear, whispering into it, "Yes, you frighten me. You arouse me so much I feel like a lad again. You make me wonder and care and hope again, for in you I see the possibilities of life and love. Dangerous emotions for a man my age. And I know you reciprocate, Shelly Holmes. I feel it here." A hand cupped her breast right over the pounding of her yearning heart. "And here." The hand had the temerity to tenderly rub the moisture between her legs. "Quit fighting yourself."

Shelly arched her back, feeling the same strange mixture of pain and delight. Delight radiated from his touch, making her very glad she was a woman, but pain also assailed her at the same time, for unlike him, she knew there was no future in this joy. She was a lone wolf long before she was subject to the lupine madness, and there would be no life mate for her. Aside from the fact that she was a werewolf with a very long life span, inside she was still a woman of intellect and reason, whose passions were held firmly in check.

Neither persona was suited to fidelity or infatuation, and both were equally wary of the depth of feeling this man inspired.

He saw her thoughts in her eyes even as they touched the most intimate parts of each other. She might as well have stated, *You frighten me, too,* for that was the truth of the matter. Still, when his gentle finger probed a bit higher, finding the bud of her womanhood and bringing it to full bloom, even a lifetime's worth of discipline could not block him or the way he made her feel. He bent his head to sip at the hollow of her neck, as if only there could he find sustenance, his lips warm and vital and male.

But all along his movements were gentle and tentative, as if he knew he played with a combustible chemistry. And then the elements flaming between them since their first meeting burst into roaring life . . . Groaning a sound very like the one he'd made, she hauled his head up and latched her lips onto his.

In the stoic march of days, this was only their second kiss chronologically. But in the timeless communion of bodies and minds only lovers know, they fit together, two halves of one whole, in that ineffable connection that had forged dynasties and changed the course of history. The tenuous link between two like minds was now strengthened by two healthy bodies. The kiss was desperate, famished, as if they both keenly knew time marched against them. If this would be their only interval together, they would mark it well.

Her mouth moving urgently under his, Shelly tugged desperately at his breeches. He helped her, his mouth still locked on hers, drinking a man's most basic nourishment from her lips, her tongue, even running his own tongue over her teeth.

His wild need called forth her own. His breeches were off, his shirt half-unbuttoned before she realized she'd ripped them.

He laughed into her mouth. "Totally unfair, madam. You have no clothes on for me to rip." And then, to her utter shock, he scraped his fingernails delicately from her nape to the curve of her buttocks, hard enough to redden her skin. But a thrill of pleasure coursed through her so strongly that her knees quivered. "But you like it better like this. What a passionate creature you are. It's criminal that you hide it so well."

How did he know this of her? He touched so easily this wild streak that had been part of her even before she became a werewolf, yet no other man had ever mined so deeply into her most private fantasies. Most men were intimidated by her, even in this basic act of copulation.

And then . . . he turned her around and ran his tongue over the same path, tenderness more blistering to her skin than the scrape had been. This time her knees did buckle, and he caught her in his arms. He lifted her and rested her gently against the edge of the long scientific table, conveniently bare of breakables.

Her eyes flamed now, all the wildness of the wolf and the woman bare for him to see. "You planned this."

"Is there a more appropriate place to experiment with such a volatile mixture as the two of us? We are both scientists." Gently he nudged her legs apart. "I hoped you would reciprocate in this most personal exploration."

What was he yammering about? Why didn't he just get on with it? She measured his fullness in her hand, admiring. "I knew you were well-endowed."

He leaped to her touch, sighing his own delight. "And you are a wicked woman, teasing me so until you got me to this state."

"As I recall, you suggested I needed to . . . ah, what was it? Ah, yes, praise this part of a man's anatomy more." And suiting action to words, she bent and took him tenderly into her mouth.

It was his turn to grind his teeth as he'd made her do so often. He rose still more to her homage, and then, with a hoarse groan, he lifted her so she was lying back on the table and stepped forward into the vee of her legs. He nudged her that first tantalizing bit, but he stopped at the moist gate to her body. He caught her head in his hands and said through his teeth, "Look at me. I want you to know whom you belong to. By your own choice."

She shook her head, closing her eyes, telling herself she was lost to the moment and that although she'd regret it later, she wanted it now. That was all it was, all it could ever be: one moment.

He shook her shoulders slightly, pulling away still farther until the warm contact was broken. "Look at me, damn you! Say my name. Say, 'Ethan, I want you.'"

She turned her face away, eyes still closed.

A vicious curse was her only reward.

He pulled away and stomped to his pants. She opened her eyes, astounded. He had stopped, though he obviously wanted her at least as much as she wanted him. For such a foolish reason? She sat up, watching him put a leg into pants that were backward, curse even more viciously, and then turn them around correctly.

When he was somewhat dressed, his ripped pants held up by his belt, he turned to look at her coldly. His hand went to his shirt pocket and removed the key, which he dangled before her. "Odd place to look, what? Even odder that you didn't try. Think on this, my stubborn darling: While you'll allow yourself to be swept away to passion so you can curse me later, that is not what I want from you. And this night is not the only time we'll ever have. I'll chase you past hell's minions to the gates of heaven if need be, but you will not escape either me or yourself. This taste of passion is but the beginning. But . . . you have to reach out to me before I'll go further. Otherwise I leave you to burn in the hell of your own unfullfilment."

He stalked to the door. She slipped down from the table, feeling totally naked and exposed, and not just physically. She looked about for the blanket. She'd wrapped it about herself when they both heard the noise at the door.

A scraping, then a grinding of metal. As Ethan inserted the key in the complex lock, the mechanism began to twist before their astounded gazes.

Shelly rushed to the door, stuck her nose to the crack, and smelled. "It's Luke!"

She and Ethan both tried to catch the inside of the latch to stop it from twisting further, but with a hideous grinding noise, it turned under their fingers into a twisted wreck of metal.

Footsteps receded.

Shelly and Ethan looked from the inoperable door to the tiny windows in the foot-thick walls of the basement.

When she looked back at him, he winced.

"This is why I choose to remain alone. And I will never forgive you for trying to seduce me out of my resolve, especially if Arielle pays the price for your egotism."

And she began stalking around the perimeter of the room, looking for egress where there was none, somehow regal even in the tattered blanket.

Luke Simball drove away from Ethan's laboratory, confident he'd twisted the complex locking mechanism enough to stop it from opening, even under the great pressure a werewolf could apply. How fortunate that Perot had whisked the nosy bitch to his impenetrable lair, not realizing that Luke, far from cowed, had trailed them with his newly enhanced olfactory abilities. Shelly's smell was unique, part woman, part wolf, and after he'd cleaned himself at his rooms, his strength far greater than ever before, it had not been difficult to retrace his steps to the woods and then follow the scent she'd left behind to the road, where Ethan's heavily indented boot tracks disappeared into the rut of a carriage's wheels. Since Luke had already discovered where Ethan lived, it had been easy enough to find them at his flat . . . and lock them in.

As he got back into his carriage to begin the final journey to complete his powers, he enjoyed the varied scents he could detect on the breeze. Now he had the keen sight of the feline and the keen sense of smell of the canine. He felt indomitable, unconquerable. Once Seth was dead, and Arielle's link with her mother was forever severed, he'd take his rightful place in eternity as Mihos, with the descendant of Isis and Cleopatra at his side, just as the legend foretold.

His thoughts were pleasant company, and he arrived quickly at his destination. It was still early, and he knew Arielle had not yet returned, but that suited his purposes. He knocked twice on the door of Hafford Place, eyeing the dawn light tingeing the sky. When the butler answered after the fourth knock, Luke used his most cultured tone. "Forgive the earliness of this intrusion, but I wonder if I might have a word with his lordship?"

The sleepy butler rubbed his thinning hair beneath his nightcap, fumbling for his spectacles in his robe pocket and obviously not finding them. He squinted into the dimness. "I don't know, sir. May I say who is calling?" *At this ungodly hour,* added his tone.

Taking care to stay in the shadows, Luke replied, "Seth Taub. I have news of Arielle."

The door swung wide and Luke entered, pulling the door shut behind him.

Inside the lit foyer, the butler could finally see the caller. His eyes widened and he opened his mouth, but the call for help never came.

An enormous paw with the hard claws of a wolf but the ability to retract like a lion—and the combined power of both—slashed his throat from ear to ear so deeply that the man's head sagged to the side. The carotid artery sprayed its contents on the walls and floor. The butler was dead before he hit the ground. Luke stepped over him, transforming back into a man, wiping his now-human hand on

311

the butler's robe and locking the door, putting the heavy bolts in place.

How easy was the becoming now that he had no pangs of conscience or regret. Seth would never defeat him now, even if he allied with the werewoman, should she find a way to get out of that basement.

Soundlessly, his feet seemingly weightless on the old stairs, he slunk down the hall to the servants' quarters. With a strength greater than any he'd ever known before his battle with Shelly Holmes, he lifted a hall armoire almost twice his height and set it in front of the servants' door as easily as if he moved a toy.

Then, knowing his time was still limited because Seth and Arielle would sense his intrusion as soon as they returned, he hurried up another level to the master bedroom quarters. He preferred not to kill the earl, at least not until he'd turned Arielle into the powerful feline goddess she was meant to be. For now, he was still useful.

But he had to find and destroy the book Isis had left Arielle, for only then would the link between mother and daughter be forever torn. Only then could he repair the damage Seth had done in his sexual congress with the chosen one. Hatred burned, acrid and unrelenting, in Luke's stomach, and he broke open the earl's locked heavy oaken door as if it were kindling.

The Earl of Darby awakened to a most unusual sight. He blinked, thinking his nightmares had followed him into daylight.

But a ghastly creature came forward out of the dawn half-light. It was part lion, part wolf, part man, and all lethal. The creature had the long mane of a lion but the neck ruff of a wolf, golden hair mixed with brown, and a face that had a wolf's snout but a lion's eyes and flat ears. From the waist down he had the legs of a man, but they were far more powerful than any normal man's could be.

Most ghastly of all, what remained of Luke Simball was smiling, and cold intelligence and malice gleamed from his glowing green eyes.

"Arielle," whispered the earl, sitting up in bed.

"Precisely," responded a cultured voice all the more horrifying given the visage from which it came. "You will take me to Isis's effects. Now. Or Arielle dies. If she is not mine, she is Seth's minion. Only you can save her."

Trembling, the earl threw back his covers and arose.

As dawn fingered the horizon, Seth and Arielle awoke with a mutual start. Automatically they turned to each other, replete with the wonders of their new bond. But as they began to embrace, the searing vision came to them simultaneously. Seth leaned over the side of the bed, holding his head, as Arielle gasped and sank back against the pillows.

"Luke," Seth groaned.

"Father!" Arielle whispered.

313

They could see Luke blocking the estate's doors. Luke breaking down the earl's bedroom door to force him into his dressing gown and down the stairs.

Most terrifying of all, the brief glimpse showed them how Shelly's bite had changed Luke: the even more lethal way he moved, the glimpse of madness in his green eyes, golden hair mixed with brown, and a face that had a wolf's snout but a lion's eyes and flat ears.

And then they were flying out of the small bed to gather the clothes they'd flung to four corners.

"Why?" Arielle demanded as they dressed. "Why is he after my father?"

"He wants your mother's things. The Book of the Dead is sacred in ancient Egyptian culture. The book she saved for you will have passages marked in it that you must recite, probably wearing her garments, to fully harness the power of your ancestors. She left you such things?"

Arielle nodded. "Just yesterday I heard the servants say she left me books and a costume. My father never told me. After Madame Aurora told me my mother's things could help me, I looked for them briefly, but then Luke came and I . . ."

Seth stomped into his breeches. "If Luke finds them before we do, your mother is doomed, and any power she has to help you will be forever lost. We must get to your estate now, and retrieve them before he does."

"Or?"

314

"Or your mother's spirit will never be at peace. Without her guidance, you are more likely to fall under his thrall." He bent to help her into her shoes, smoothing his hands over her now covered knees as he looked up at her, his face again that of the severe Seth who had so intimidated her in the beginning. "You realize he's doing this partly to draw us there, don't you? He knows we've consecrated our bond and the only way he can fight it now is to force you to protect Isis. He's going to offer you the choice of your own happiness or your mother's. Her eternal doom. Or your own."

Arielle felt a burning in her stomach like a fist. She nodded, unable to speak.

"But if you stay strong, even with his new ability, we can still defeat him with the book's help. The rituals are powerful, and Luke and I have both used them in our transformations. That's why so much of a man's mortal wealth was spent preparing him for the afterlife journey—the Egyptians believed it was the only way into the afterlife."

Dressed, they flew to the carriage. When they were seated and Seth had lashed the horses into movement, Arielle managed, "Why did Luke kill Madame Aurora?"

"For the same reason he wants the book, and for the same reason he sneaked into the séance. He's been systematically severing every link you have with your mother because he knows she's trying to guide you away from her own fate. I had paid the medium to tell you of your mother's

315

things and the power they could give you because I've been trying to keep you grounded in the human compassion Luke lost long ago."

There was something in his face, something so desolate that their new communion made her see what he recalled. A horrific image grew. Luke, barely formed as a lion, slashing an older man with Seth's severe features over and over, blood flying . . . and Seth, fully human as he tried to intervene and pull the man to safety. Luke struck him with vicious claws, ripping Seth's side and thigh open, and Seth fell, bleeding profusely.

Then Luke began to feed . . .

Arielle swallowed back bile.

"I'm sorry, Arielle. I didn't intend for you to see that," Seth apologized over the drumming of the horses' hooves.

"He killed your father, didn't he?"

He nodded grimly. "We were traveling through the Sahara about about two years ago when a pack of wild civets attacked our tent. We were both bitten. The change came in dreams first, as it did to you, but we found the urge to hunt overpowering. First small game, then deer and gazelles, and finally . . ." He trailed off, his eyes closing briefly with pain.

She had to strain to hear him. "We both hated him for fathering us, then doing the proper thing, but not the right thing. He hired expensive tutors, sending us to Eton and Oxford, but rejected us and our mothers in every other way. I saw my father only twice, and both times he looked at me as if I were a heathen. It was Luke who convinced me to come to England. We found our father alone one night at his country estate. I thought to confront him, but Luke, he . . ."

Arielle covered his hand with hers. "You don't have to tell me. I know you couldn't kill your own father, no matter how badly he treated you."

"I tried to stop Luke, but the servants came, and I was wounded. But the sight of my father's death at his own son's hands forever cured me of the bloodlust. From that day forward, I have never killed except to eat, and I will never wound a human being."

Arielle closed her eyes again, trying to block out the image of her own father's similar fate at Luke's hands if she were not very careful. And very strong.

Was she strong enough now that she'd bonded with Seth? Whatever the truth of the legend, it was apparent he and Luke believed it. Luke had chosen the way of the cat because he was obsessed with immortality. Seth had chosen to let his human intellect rule all he did. And it was his utter humanity, the softness beneath the arrogance, that drew her now and made her, for the first time in a long time, hope for a future. But she had no illusions about the horrific choices still remaining for her now that she'd chosen the way of the woman over the way of the cat. Even as she twined her fingers with Seth's, the conundrum she'd faced from the beginning drummed inside her head.

Would good be strong enough to defeat evil?

And where was Shelly while her father was being driven like a lamb to slaughter?

* * *

Shelly was fuming with fury over her own stupidity. She'd tried using her werewolf strength against the door, which was too well reinforced, and the windows, which were too small and too deeply embedded in rock.

She swung back on Ethan with a vicious growl. For the first time in a long time her snout elongated and claws grew at her feet without her conscious will. She was so frustrated at her inability to help her charge when Arielle needed it most that, for an instant, the wolf's urge to punish Ethan almost overcame her cool human intellect.

But then she saw what he'd been doing while she prowled the room.

He held a beaker high, mixing some viscous fluid that was darkening as he stirred. Then he added one tiny bit of another powdered substance. The fluid went colorless. Carrying the beaker very carefully, so as not to slosh the contents, he said coolly, "Get out of the way," and set the beaker down on the ground next to the door, right beneath the latch.

Immediately her werewolf tendencies receded, leaving her fully human—and impressed despite herself at the cool way he'd figured out an egress for them while she'd been needlessly pacing and fuming. "Nitroglycerin," Shelly said. "First made by Ascanio Sobrero in 1846 by treating glycerol with a mixture of nitric and sulfuric acid. Soluble in alcohol but insoluble in water."

As she spoke, Ethan had mixed one last substance in the bowl of a very long spoon, which he'd
lengthened further by tying it to a broom handle.
"Crude, but effective," he said lightly, as if he were
mixing a recipe, not a highly volatile explosive. "As
you are probably aware, the reaction produced is
highly exothermic, so I suggest you take cover under the table."

Shelly obeyed with alacrity, for once not arguing.

He gave her a taunting glance. "So you can
mind. I thought you could."

She glared at him in the shadow of the table, her
eyes taking on that eerie glow.

Smiling, he moved the heavy armchair in front of
himself, knelt in the seat, and lowered the spoon
into the beaker from behind it. "Duck!"

They both ducked, covering their ears as the explosion rocked the flat and sent half the ceiling
down on top of them.

At the entrance to the earl's estate, several bobbies
drew a heavy carriage to a stop. The Scotland Yard
detective got down from his own smaller curricle,
scowling as he yawned, looking around at the
empty road.

"Why do you think Seth Taub will come here?" he
asked the marquess, who dismounted from a fine
stallion, not even looking tired. But then, reflected
the detective sourly, he was accustomed to long,
rough nights sipping brandy and playing cards.

"Because he's obviously been warned not to return to his flat," the marquess answered. "I also know, by all accounts, that he's obsessed with Lady Arielle Blaylock. Where she is, he'll follow."

"And she's being chaperoned by one Shelly Holmes," the detective replied thoughtfully. "If anyone can shed light on what's happening with these murders, it's she. I would not be at all surprised to learn she's also been investigating this Seth Taub." He squinted down at his watch in the brightening dawn. "But it's still confoundedly early. We shall wait to approach the mansion until a decent hour."

He settled back in his curricle, tipped his hat over his face, and gave every evidence of dozing.

The marquess scowled, but he could only compose himself on his far more plush carriage seat and wait for his revenge.

Chapter Eighteen

Meanwhile, in the crypt, Luke stood next to the earl over Isis's casket, staring down at the hieroglyphs. He burned to lift the sarcophagus lid away and tear the earthly remnants of Isis's interfering soul to shreds, but he controlled himself, knowing Arielle would be easier to turn with her mother intact. For now, anyway.

He glanced around, but saw no evidence of a chest or a leather satchel. He scowled at the earl. "Why did you bring me here?"

The earl went to a blank wall and pushed on something. The wall opened outward and Luke saw a cavity. Inside was a chest. He hurried forward, shoving the earl out of the way, and opened the chest. It was packed with female fripperies, a shawl, leaflets from plays, a full dance card from many years ago with the earl's name prominent. But there was no sign of a book or costume of Egyptian origin.

Luke slammed the lid shut and turned back on the earl, his clenched fists sprouting claws. The earl backed away, swallowing, his hands up.

"I . . . didn't know they were gone." But the earl couldn't quite meet Luke's flaming eyes.

Luke knew it for the lie it was. "You're stalling for time," he hissed, sounding remarkably like a cat. "Show me, now, to the book and her garments, or . . ."

The earl backed up one more step, but then he stopped, the legacy of his forebears giving him strength. He stared at the entity that, in the darkness of the crypt, was so much more, and so much less, than a man. Every bit of the earl's breeding showed as he said with sad dignity, "Arielle is my only child, and if I have to die protecting her, so be it. I should have given her her mother's things long ago, and the mere fact that you've killed to get them and done all you could to stop Arielle from communing with her mother's spirit is answer enough for me of the bond between them. I have tried to break that bond in the past. I will not do so now, when she needs it most, even if my life is forfeit."

The earl stayed put as Luke, or what remained of Luke, stalked him. The earl dashed behind a crypt, but Luke bounded over it in one leap. Death gleamed from glowing green eyes now pinpointed with red dots of werewolf madness.

Luke had neither Seth's nor Shelly's moral integrity and intellect, and he had no desire to control the urge to kill. . . .

* * *

Out on the road, Seth drew the horses to a halt before the last turn to the estate.

Arielle started to say, "Why did you . . ." before she peeked around the curve and saw them, too.

The bobbies. The carriage with bars at its windows. And a man she recognized vaguely as a well-known dissolute marquess of the ton, looking bored upon the seat of an expensive phaeton while he glared at a man in a severe coat and hat drowsing in his own plain carriage.

"They're waiting for me," Seth said, turning the horses before they were seen. "We have to go in through the woods." Seth pulled the carriage into the woods just as the sounds of a racing curricle clattered up the road. He helped Arielle down and they started to run into the trees, but they stopped as they recognized Shelly and Ethan.

Shelly was dressed very strangely, in male pants so long they had been turned up at the cuffs and rolled. They were also far too tight across her hips. Her shirt was too long, tucked in and rolled up at the sleeves. She looked as if she'd hastily dressed in Ethan's ill-fitting garments.

Which she had.

Ethan and Shelly saw them at the same time. Shelly hugged Arielle, verifying her charge's well-being. She gave her a searching look, and when Arielle blushed, she glared at Seth.

He said mildly, "I'll do the right thing with all the pomp and circumstance I can contrive once Luke is dead."

Shelly and Ethan nodded, resigned if not satisfied.

"Seth, you must be careful," Shelly warned. "The police are after you for Madame Aurora's murder."

"I know. They're blocking the entrance to the estate, waiting for me. I suspect they were fetched by the dear Marquess of Brackton, who wishes me dead. But that's the least of my worries now. We have to get to the estate and retrieve the book."

"The book?" Shelly and Ethan repeated.

"Isis's version of the Book of the Dead. She must have had it in her things."

Shelly and Ethan exchanged a glance. "The book!" they repeated, this time with excitement.

"You have it?" Shelly asked.

Ethan replied, "I thought you took it."

She glared at him. "No. When I left the study that night, I'm quite sure I left it with you."

"Had you at sixes and sevens, did I? I thought so."

Before Shelly could give voice to the retort trembling on her tongue, Seth broke in. "We must find it before Luke does. Do you have any idea where it might be now?"

"We had no idea it was so important," Shelly said apologetically. "We left it in the upstairs study. The earl gave it to us to review."

"Come, Arielle." Seth turned toward the woods as the sun peeked fully above the horizon.

"Wait, Seth." Shelly caught his arm. "Do you want me to come with you or to meet the inspector and tell him he has the wrong man?"

Seth looked at Arielle. She stared blindly up the

road, fear for her father flickering in her eyes. "He's in danger, Seth. We have to go now."

"My fate as a felon is immaterial if we cannot stop Luke," Seth said, "but I don't want anyone else knowing the power Arielle and I possess. If you can keep them away no matter what they hear, I shall be in your debt, Miss Holmes."

Arielle's mouth had firmed and her spine was ramrod straight as she said grimly, "And Luke Simball has done enough killing. Only we can stop him. United."

Seth gave her a proud smile. He brushed a knuckle against her chin. "I can't wait to see you in your mother's garments. You found them?"

She nodded.

"You must dress in them before we approach Luke. They will not only strengthen your bond with your mother, but they will give him pause."

Seth was walking with Arielle into the woods when Shelly called after them, "Be careful. If Luke has the traits of a werewolf, now you can kill him only with a silver bullet or by ripping out his heart. And if he bites you or scratches your skin, you could also be affected."

Seth smiled. "So it is said. But there are other realms you know nothing of." And then he and Arielle had disappeared into the trees, both of them soundless on the dry leaves.

Ethan sighed enviously. "Dash it, I'm beginning to want you to bite me just so I can walk like a ghost." He gave her a mischievous smile. "But then, I always want you to bite me."

"Believe me, you would not like the emotional coin required to get that particular skill." Shelly got back in the carriage. "As for silver, you have that aplenty."

When he looked at her quizzically, she said flatly, "In your tongue. And you'll need every ounce of it to help me talk our way out of this one."

Before he could make the ribald comment twinkling in his eyes, she said, "Drive."

"Coward." But he drove on up the road as if they'd merely been out for a dawn picnic, waving merrily as their progress was blocked by several bobbies and three carriages, not to mention an angry marquess and very determined detective.

They were in sight of the mansion when Arielle stumbled and fell to her knees, clutching her temples. "Father," she whispered.

Seth closed his eyes and saw it, too. The earl, dodging around crypts as Luke, a ghastly creature, part man, part wolf, part lion chased him.

Seth opened his eyes, the slits already elongating, as he began the change. "Go dress in your mother's raiment and retrieve the book from the study. I'll stop Luke. Come as soon as you can."

Ripping off his clothes as he went, Seth ran toward the crypt.

Arielle had never been so fleet of foot as she ran toward the front of her ancestral home. Her limp was totally gone, and she was so supple that not a leaf or twig rustled at her passage. However, she found the grounds of the mansion swarming with angry, confused servants. They were standing over a bloodied form wrapped in a sheet.

When Arielle appeared, the housekeeper turned, wiping her wet eyes on her apron. "Miss Arielle, what be happening? Who did this? And where be the earl?"

Arielle swallowed as she looked down at the true cost of embracing the way of the cat. This man had dandled her on his knee when she was a child, as much a part of the family as an uncle would have been. Her fury and concern for her father increased tenfold.

"Luke Simball did this," she spit, her own eyes elongating, though she did not know it. "And he has my father cornered in the crypt."

The servants all turned toward the crypt as one, but Arielle blocked them. "No. This is a family matter. My own infatuation with Luke Simball gave him the power to do this, and only I can stop him." And, with God's grace, perhaps her mother could help. "All of you are dismissed for the day. Say nothing to the police outside except that we have given you all the day off. Tell them Luke is threatening my family, and maybe they'll go to his flat and leave us be."

They complained, but at her insistence they finally got into the sturdiest coach and clattered up the street and out the gate. Arielle knew the police would question them, and she hoped that Shelly and Ethan could come up with a likely story to keep the bobbies from intervening. As she virtually flew up the stairs to her room, she also knew that if the police witnessed the battle to come, she and Seth could never set foot in England again . . .

In the crypt, Luke, or what remained of Luke, had the earl cornered against a wall, one paw tearing into his shoulder, the other at his throat. The claws, as black and hard as a wolf's, toyed with the earl by retracting and kneading, as a cat's would. Indeed, Luke purred, so satisfied was he at cornering his prey.

The claws had not bitten into the earl hard enough to draw blood. Yet.

"Do you really prefer to die rather than tell me where the book is?"

The earl slumped, his eyes closing as if he couldn't bear to look at Luke. "I honestly do not know. I gave it to Miss Holmes to read and have not seen it since."

Luke's claws came out, slashing at the earl's clothes. The earl winced at the ripping sound, and with all his might shoved Luke away.

He tried to run as Luke stumbled backward, but Luke's claws latched onto the back of the earl's thick dressing gown. They began to dig in, through layers of velvet and silk lining, penetrating the cotton of his nightgown to his skin. As they were about to draw blood, a roar came from the entrance to the crypt, so loud that it echoed like a death knell in the stone chamber.

Immediately Luke released the earl and turned. His legs were spread; huge arms that were part werewolf, part lion tensed as he crouched to lunge.

Catspell

Seth stood in the opening, majestic against the new day, his black mane rippling in the breeze as he stared at his brother with golden eyes. He was fully a lion, enormous and powerful, as he walked into the crypt, but when Luke lunged at him, he leaped aside. Luke crashed headfirst into the marble wall, falling to his knees.

Seth leaped over him to stand protectively before the earl. "Luke, I do not want to kill you, but you're leaving me little choice," he said in a hissing cat's tone that was still tinged with a hint of human sadness.

"Luke is dead," hissed the cat creature. "Mihos rules."

The earl ignored Seth's jerk of the head toward the door and stayed put. He glanced between the two amazing creatures, his gaze full of fascination and repugnance. Occasionally he glanced at the door, as if expecting Arielle.

"Indeed. He rules you," Seth retorted. "Is that what you wanted when we came here? To be a servant to the bloodlust of a cat and know no joy but in killing? This makes you better than our father?" Seth reared up on his hind legs as this time Luke rushed him so fast, he had no chance to dodge.

The two beings grappled, Luke still standing on a titan's powerful human legs, more stable than Seth could be on his lion's feet. Luke dipped his head, the fangs that were much larger than Seth's dripping saliva, as he snapped at his brother's throat. Seth reared his head back, claws slashing at Luke's back, pulling him away. Luke's teeth snapped air.

But Seth couldn't combat Luke's new strength. With a mighty heave, Luke picked Seth up and tossed him through the air. Seth landed half-on, half-against Isis's sarcophagus lid. With a scrape and groan, it fell to the floor.

Shaking his head, partially stunned; Seth struggled to his feet and turned to face his attacker, but Luke's green eyes were wide, staring past him. Seth turned to follow his gaze into the casket.

The white silk lining, dingy with the passing of the years, was all that met their astonished gazes. It was empty. The mummy was gone.

Outside the gates, Shelly and Ethan were doing their best to persuade the skeptical detective to investigate Luke Simball's flat.

"I tell you, he's the only one with the motive and the opportunity to commit these murders," Ethan argued. "Man thinks he's a lion. I've seen him up to his tricks. Scary, the way he can use knives to make it look like claw marks."

"Send some of your men to his flat," Shelly insisted. "Where's the harm in searching? I cannot yet prove he's the culprit behind these murders, but I've verified that his whereabouts cannot be accounted for on the nights in question. And I do have the documentation to prove he is the estranged son of the diplomat who was the first to die in this strange manner—after Luke Simball arrived in London."

The housekeeper, who had remained behind at her own insistence after the other servants left, nodded vigorously. "Aye, and the earl hisself didn't trust

330

him; that I know. He didn't like him around Miss Arielle, got Mr. Seth's help to protect her, he did."

The detective hesitated, but then he jerked his head at several of his men. They took a carriage and careened off.

None of them noticed that, during the clamor of argument and the departure of several carriages, the marquess had tied his animals to a tree and disappeared. For once Shelly was too preoccupied to note that the marquess had slipped inside the gates.

The Scotland Yard man tilted his hat back to eye Shelly severely. "Now, Miss Holmes, I've done as you asked. Kindly be honest with me and tell me why you're trying to keep me out of this estate. What is going on in there that you don't wish me to know about?"

Shelly opened her mouth, then closed it. For once she was speechless.

Ethan smiled smoothly. "Strange things. You would not approve."

The detective's eyes narrowed. He glanced at the gates and moved toward them.

Ethan blocked him. "You know. Things that go bump in the night. Mummies walk. Ghosts fly. That sort of thing."

The detective looked at him askance. Shelly's eyes had widened with horror. Ethan's tale was all too close to the truth. But the way he spoke made his words sound ludicrous.

"A séance," Ethan finished baldly. "The earl does not want anyone but his immediate family in attendance. Which is why he sent us packing. Do you

331

want to interfere at such a private time for him and his daughter?"

The housekeeper nodded vigorously. "Aye, they had one just the other evening. Strange goings-on, they were."

Glancing at the rising sun, the detective said suspiciously, "I've never heard of a séance in broad daylight."

"Nobility," Ethan said dismissively. "They always do things cart before the horse. Now, old chap, shall we do things the right way, horse before the cart, and go for a spot of tea so we can discuss the most important aspects of this case?" He put a casual arm about the detective's shoulder and led him toward his carriage. The man hesitated, but finally followed, telling the last two bobbies to return to the department.

Looking bemused but impressed, Shelly waved at Ethan. He glanced over his shoulder and winked at her, then ushered the detective into his passenger seat, spreading the carriage blanket over the man's knees before taking the reins and sedately setting off.

"Amazing man," Shelly muttered.

"Aye," agreed the housekeeper.

"Just don't tell him I said that." Shelly swung on her heel toward the gate and noticed the marquess's blooded team chomping at their bits where he'd tied them up.

"Oh, God," she groaned, and broke into a run through the gates. "Go on into town and stay there until we fetch you."

Muttering at the "strange goings-on," the housekeeper tied her apron more securely, settled her cap, and walked toward the main road.

Inside the crypt, for the first time there was a flicker of fear in Luke's eyes. He glanced about, turning this way and that, but there was no sign of the body. He glared at Seth, advancing again. "You did this. You stole her body to make me think she's finally risen."

Seth moved to meet him, answering only with his own aggression.

As they both crouched to spring, a soft voice said from the doorway, "No evil thing of any shape or kind shall spring up against me, and no baleful object, and no harmful thing, and no disastrous thing shall happen unto me. I open the door in heaven. I rule my throne. I open the way for the births that take place on this day." Arielle stood in the door, radiant as never before. She was fully human, yet somehow beyond mortal as she recited the ancient ritual from the book she held.

" 'I am she whose being hath been wrought in his eye. I shall die a peaceful death and walk the afterlife, not the half-life.' " In her mother's magnificent clothes of gold encrusted with jewels, wearing the royal diadem of the serpent and the vulture of her ancestors, she seemed the embodiment of Cleopatra—with the same power to mesmerize.

Seth and Luke both backed off as she spoke. Luke's eyes had darkened with fear, but he began his own recitation, as if his ritual could counteract hers.

" 'The slaughter block is made ready, as thou knowest, and thou hast come to destruction. I am Mihos, who stablisheth those who praise him. I am the Knot of the god in the Aser tree, the twice-beautiful one, who is more splendid today than yesterday.' "

Luke batted the book out of Arielle's hands, knocking it against the stone floor. The fragile volume broke into several pieces. Luke stalked Arielle, intoning, " 'I am the Lord of Eternity: I decree and I judge like Khepera.' "

Arielle seemed to awaken from a dream when the book was taken from her. She blinked, and the glow faded from her eyes.

Luke closed his eyes and took a deep breath. He transformed, once more a golden god of a man clad only in a loincloth. He extended his hands to Arielle. "Join me, lioness of God. Together we can rule eternity. We are gods, if we believe it so."

Seth sat quietly on his haunches, watching.

Arielle looked at the beautiful golden man, then over at the lion who seemed almost bored with the scene that was playing out. He made no attempt to transform, or to help her. As if he knew this final task was hers alone by her birthright.

Then she looked at her father. He gave her an encouraging smile, as if he too knew, finally, that she was strong enough to do the right thing. He bent, gathered together the remnants of the book, and handed them to her, his own brand of apology.

Immediately Luke transformed again, more fearsome than before, swiping at the earl. But Arielle shoved her father behind her and said without looking at the book, "I am the child who traverseth the road of yesterday. I am today for untold nations and peoples."

Looking radiant again, Arielle glanced behind Luke to the back of the crypt. She was the image of her mother at that moment. She repeated softly, "I am the child who traverseth the road of yesterday. I shall die a peaceful death and walk the afterlife, not the half-life."

She peered into the dimness behind Luke, her eyes glowing in the gloom.

Hissing, Luke turned, his arms spread, the ruff of hair on his neck and spine standing straight up.

Isis stood there in her golden costume, looking as she had in her picture, alive, vibrant. She shimmered as she smiled at her daughter.

The earl gasped and reached toward her. He was closest, and when he touched the apparition, his hand passed through her.

Luke growled and sprang, but she was all energy and no substance. He went right through her to the wall.

Looking at him with glowing blue eyes, Isis said, "Repeat the words with me, daughter."

She and Arielle repeated the ritual from the book, both of them staring him down. This time, with every word, Luke seemed to lose strength. He growled and turned on Arielle, but Seth was there to stop him, and this time his swipe of a paw was met by a like swipe that slammed him to the stone floor.

Arielle and Isis repeated the ancient spell again and again, faster in cadence, and Luke roared with agony, falling to his knees. He began to change before their eyes, becoming briefly a wolf, then a lion, and finally a man. A weakening man.

As the ancient words echoed in the chamber, he sank to the floor, eyes closing.

There was a stir at the door, and the marquess stood there, astonished. He blinked, rubbed his eyes, and looked again.

But then a giant wolf's paw pulled him away from the door. There was the sound of a scuffle, a scream, and then running feet.

No one in the chamber noticed, or cared.

Weakly, Luke tried to recite his own spell, but he was now so weak that his voice was merely a croak.

He was no match for the heirs of Cleopatra, for the ancient ways were much stronger in their blood than in his. Arielle and Isis said in cadence, "I am she who protecteth you for millions of years. Whether ye be denizens of heaven, or of the earth, or of the south, or of the north, or of the east, or of the west, the fear of me is in your bodies."

Moaning, Luke began to fade before their eyes. All the beautiful golden color dissipated from his skin; then his hair grew sparse and gray, his skin wrinkling and sagging over bent bones.

Seth looked away as if he couldn't bear to watch. The earl whispered to him, "What's happening? I do not understand."

Seth said, "Each soul carries the burden of the evil and good it does and must pay the price at death before entering the afterlife. Luke did much harm."

"But why are these rituals strong enough to kill him?"

"Because Luke believes they are. And now Arielle has turned against him, he can never be immortal. She is draining the life from him and giving it to her mother so she can enter the afterlife at last."

Luke had reached out a weakened, ancient hand toward Arielle. "Please." He gasped. "I love you."

Tears misted her eyes, but still she chanted along with her mother.

And soon there was nothing left of Luke Simball but a pile of dust and a cotton loincloth.

Seth changed back to his human form, accepting the earl's robe, and knelt over what had once been his brother. He bent his head and whispered a benediction. Then he stood and opened his arms to Arielle.

"See, my darling? You always had the power. Now you have the will."

She buried her face in his chest, sobbing, but she felt a whisper of motion and leaped away to reach out to her mother's fading form.

"Mother, don't go."

The earl took a half step forward, too, but Isis had eyes only for her daughter.

"Shhhh . . . such is the way of life, daughter, since the Nile was born of the sea. It is right that I go to the place you have prepared for me and wait for you to join me. Please send me home. You know what to say."

Her voice trembled with tears at first, but then Arielle said strongly, "I am the child who traverseth the road of yesterday. I shall die a peaceful death and walk the afterlife, not the half-life."

Smiling, Isis began to fade away. For an instant the shadow of Bast the cat goddess lingered, her eyes glowing, and then that, too, was gone. The words Isis spoke, died more slowly, as if she knew they would echo always in her daughter's heart.

"You have learned well, my child. You are strong. Be the woman first, and rule the cat, as I could not. Use your power for good, and we shall meet again in the afterlife."

Then Isis was gone. But she would never be forgotten . . .

Some hours later, at Luke's flat, the searching bobbies found Luke's Egyptian knife, dotted with blood, along with several items from some of the victims, enough to convince them that they'd been searching for the wrong brother. But when they sent their entire force looking for Luke, they found not a trace. . . .

As for the marquess, he had returned to his flat a changed man. He was pale as a ghost, all the arrogance shocked out of him, his jacket in tatters as if a giant paw had ripped it. He never told anyone what he saw that day, but he vowed to his manservant that if he ever came across Seth Taub again, he'd cross the street to avoid him.

When his man asked for details, the marquess said only, "You'd not believe me. I have no wish to land in Bedlam." And he immediately switched clubs.

That night the walls of Hafford Place rang again, for the first time in a long time, with laughter. Shelly and Arielle were dressed in finery, the earl, Ethan, and Seth in black tie and tails.

When Seth flashed an enormous ruby in a sleek setting that showed a snow leopard wrapped around the band and holding the ruby, the earl took a deep breath but nodded his approval.

As Seth knelt to place the ring on Arielle's extended hand, the earl complained quietly, "Damn, I'm not sure I want a lion for a son-in-law. Does this mean I have to serve raw meat at the wedding?"

Shelly smiled and patted his arm. "Perhaps steak tartare." At his glare, she soothed, "No, but it means you must keep an open mind. Some things are meant to be, and sometimes the supernatural can be used for good."

Ethan stared at her intently as she said it, but she avoided his eyes as she'd avoided him all night. As soon as she could decently excuse herself, she retreated upstairs.

She was packing her things when a quiet knock came at the door. She wanted to pretend deafness, but knew Ethan would not be put off. She might as well get this over with. She opened the door.

His welcoming smile faded as he saw her traveling dress and her packed bags. "You were leaving without a word to me?"

"I detest emotional scenes." Shelly returned to her packing. "I'd have left you a note with this."

She tossed an envelope on the bed before him. He riffled through the thick wad of pound notes and tossed the envelope back like a gauntlet. "If you think you can buy me out of your life, think again."

"I merely offer half of my fee. You earned it. I never could have solved this case so effectively without your aid." The admission was difficult, but she forced herself to make it. However, she could not meet his eyes.

"Who would have thought such a powerful creature would be, at heart, an emotional coward?"

Shelly's angry gaze latched onto his face. "Why can you not believe that I do not want your attentions?"

He rounded the bed in two strides and jerked her into his arms. The kiss was full, flaming, and neither asked for nor offered quarter. Shelly tried to resist, she truly did, but he was rare champagne to someone parched for joy and the taste of life on her tongue.

He shoved her away after she'd kissed him back with the same passion. "You see?"

She couldn't. Or wouldn't.

Without another word she picked up her bags and walked out.

He moved to follow, but stopped at the top of the stairs. "I always keep my promises. We shall meet again, Shelly Holmes. And the next time, you will not deny me, or yourself."

At the bottom of the stairs, she turned in to the salon. There was the murmur of voices. Seth, the earl, and Arielle all came out to see her off in a carriage. They waved goodbye, wishing her good fortune.

When they returned to the house, they found Ethan rooted where he was at the top of the stairs, his face burning with a flush of . . . rage? Sorrow?

The three looked at him curiously.

Just then a nondescript man slipped through the half-open door. He looked nervously about as the earl scowled at him, but Ethan's stillness erupted in a blur of motion as he ran down the stairs to snatch at the piece of paper the man held.

"Charleston, South Carolina," Ethan said, reading off the written copy of the passenger list in his hand. "I wonder why she's going there?"

And then he offered his hand to the earl and Seth. "Congratulations." He kissed Arielle's brow. "I heard what happened. I am so glad you helped Isis find rest and found your strength in hers. Be good, Arielle. I'll be gone for a while. Wolf hunting." He turned to the door, the flush fading to a look of deadly determination. Arielle and Seth shared an intimate smile.

"Wolf hunting . . . where? We have very few left here." The bewildered earl followed Ethan down the steps. "You can't leave now, right before the wedding. Where are you going?"

But Ethan was already gone, his steps light as he hurried down to his curricle.

Seth took Arielle in his arms. "I have a feeling Miss Holmes will be the hunted one before long."

The earl watched, not sure whether to dote or

worry, as his daughter exchanged a far too long and far too passionate kiss with her fiancé.

Then, seeking the quiet of his study, he stuffed his pipe, wondering when he could get back to his well-ordered life.

Then he coughed on his own smoke as an even more disturbing thought struck him.

What the deuce would his first grandchild look like? He'd best acquire a taste for steak tartare . . .

Night Bites
NINA BANGS

Cindy Harper has an ice-cream flavor for every emotion. But no sweet treat from her freezer is smooth, creamy, or tempting enough to cool down her dark fantasies about über alpha male Thrain Davis.

This is a man to be enjoyed on a strictly primitive level. Every woman who ever sees him smile wonders about the pleasure his mouth can give her. Too late she realizes the danger of inviting an ancient vampire into her inn. He forces her to examine her past when she is just fine with her present. He does have an upside, though. Who needs ice cream when you have a hot and yummy dark immortal in your bed?
